The Bishop

Goes to

The University

The **Bishop**

Goes to

The **University**

• A BLACKIE RYAN STORY •

ANDREW M. GREELEY

A Tom Doherty Associates Book

NEW YORK

THE BISHOP GOES TO *THE* UNIVERSITY

A Forge Book
Published by Tom Doherty Associates, LLC
175 Fifth Avenue
New York, NY 10010

www.tor.com

Forge® is a registered trademark of Tom Doherty Associates, LLC.

Library of Congress Cataloging-in-Publication Data

Greeley, Andrew M., 1928–
    The bishop goes to the university / Andrew M. Greeley.—1st hardcover ed.
        p. cm.
    "A Forge book"—T.p. verso
    ISBN 0-765-30333-7
    1. Ryan, Blackie (Fictitious character)—Fiction. 2. Monks—Crimes against—Fiction.
3. Russians—Illinois—Fiction. 4. Catholic Church—Fiction. 5. Chicago (Ill.)—Fiction.
6. Bishops—Fiction. I. Title.
PS3557. R358B53 2003
813' .54—dc21

                                                                              2003009215

First Edition: October 2003

Printed in the United States of America

0 9 8 7 6 5 4 3 2 1

Author's Note

The *University in this story is* a creature of mine, not of God. Hence, it shares the physical space of the one in God's world and some of its eccentricities (in both worlds economists do talk at lunch about their golf scores, which I find endearing), but the characters and events are fictional. In God's world I serve on the Visiting Committee at the Divinity School, which Blackie does not in my world. On the other hand, he has become a visiting lecturer in Swift Hall in my world, which I never have in God's world. Any similarities between my creatures and God's result from the fact that the latter is a comedienne.

Or, to put it differently, unlike some far more distinguished writers about *The* University, I am not drawing from life.

However, the incident which happened to Blackie when he applied really did happen in God's world, though not to me.

The Bishop
Goes to
The University

1

—

"One cardinal ought to be enough for Chicago, ought he not, Black-wood?"

His Eminent Lordship Sean, Cardinal Priest of the Roman Church, Cronin towered over me, like a crimson watered silk alien from another planet. Cardinals who are tall (only a few) and handsome (even fewer) and with powerful presence (yet fewer still) can create that illusion. No one of this world would walk around in cardinalatial choir robes in daylight. He might, however, be a character from a Fellini movie or someone playing Richelieu in a theater of the absurd production from North Lincoln Avenue. In any event his hooded blue eyes were wide-open, his forehead furrowed in a deep frown, and his lips pressed together in either serious thought or suppressed anger.

"Arguably," I said, glancing up from my computer, "more than enough."

I had just returned from a bootless trip to Rome. A certain dicastry of the Roman Curia had wanted to consult with me on a problem. By which they meant they wanted to tell me what they thought and could not have cared less about what I thought. They were doing me a favor by talking to me.

"Yet we seem to have another."

"How unfortunate." I sighed in West of Ireland protest.

"He's dead."

Milord Cronin opened my liquor cabinet, removed from the back of it a precious container of Bushmills Single Malt and poured himself considerably more than a splasheen in one of my recently cleaned Waterford tumblers.

"That would solve the problem, would it not?"

I turned away from my workstation. The Cardinal deposited a large stack of output on the floor and reclined on my couch. In full robes with a drink in hand (though it was only early afternoon on a radiant October day), he did look a little like the cinematic version of Armand-Jean de Plessis, duc de Richelieu—if one were to imagine that worthy to have been Irish.

"No, that creates the problem."

Aha, the harmless, indeed almost invisible little auxiliary bishop was about to be dispatched on a mystery-solving expedition.

"There are always a few kooks wandering around this city," he said, sipping cautiously from *uisce beatha* as the Irish were pleased to call the Creature. "This is good stuff, Blackwood," he interrupted his train of thought. "You think they will have it in heaven?"

"Minimally it and sex."

He sighed, not, however, as loudly as I can sigh.

"My own tailor makes crimson robes for them, though he doesn't want me to know about it. They're not really authentic, but parading down Thirty-first Street in what they think is full regalia gives them a kick, I guess."

"As do the several troubled folk who insist on donning papal white. It is, after all, a free city. From the point of view of those who are not of the household of the faith. We're all kooks."

On occasion I have had to persuade some such persons not to enter a ceremony at the Cathedral over which I preside at the Lord Cardinal's pleasure. They depart quietly with sad eyes when I tell them that their presence would greatly trouble Milord Cronin, which may be a touch of an exaggeration.

"This Russian fellow, however, left a full set of choir robes in his closet. They seem to be authentic . . ."

"Russian fellow?"

"That's right, you've been off in Rome, haven't you? This Semyon Ivanivich Popov who was killed in a locked office of the Divinity School at *The* University the other night."

In Chicago there are many universities. However, only one is identified as *The* University, mostly because of frequent repetition of the italicized word by its denizens.

He handed me a sheaf of clippings from Chicago papers.

"Interesting name . . ."

"He was Russian. They all have funny names."

"Simon, son of John, priest? Or if you wish, Simon bar Jona, Pope?"

"The cops tell me that the robes included a pallium. None of the crazies bother with that."

The pallium is a small decoration made of wool, which only archbishops can wear.

I glanced through the clippings.

"No mention of the sacred crimson in the press."

"Cops have kept it secret."

"Aha," I said, "does not his late Eminence look much like Grigori Yefimovich?"

"Who?" He looked up from his tumbler of Bushmills.

"The inestimable and legendary Rasputin."

Cardinal Popov was standing in front of the Divinity School in the flowing robes of Russian monasticism, complete with the hood that was propped up in front and added several inches to his already impressive height and his staff. With dark, flashing eyes, broad shoulders, a long gray beard, and the frown that is required in such pictures, he was a central-casting Russian monk. He must have created quite a stir at *The* University.

"He's dead, isn't he?"

"He was thrown into a freezing river in 1915, but there have been disputes about whether he survived and may still survive."

"This guy was teaching at the Divinity School out there, something about the Mystical Soteriology of the Old Believers. Whoever they might be . . . I suppose you are informed about the subject."

"One could summarize them by saying that they were fundamentalist Orthodox who went into schism over a new translation of the Bible. They were murdered in great numbers by various czars who didn't like dissidents of any sort . . . Have our mutual friends across the pond made any inquiries about Brother Semyon's death?"

Color that beard black and he would look like Rasputin. A man who lived over a hundred and forty years had the right to a white beard, did he not?

"Not a word. Finally, after a couple of days, I called them. Pretty high-level too. All I heard was what a fine scholar Brother Semyon was and what a tragedy his death was and how terrible the American crime rate was."

"They're hiding something?"

"Maybe. That's the way they would talk if they were. But then they may not know anything either . . . How come he's in all those departments? Does he collect salaries from all of them?"

I glanced at the text of the articles. Semyon Popov was a visiting professor in the Divinity School, the Slavic Languages Department, the Committee on Social Thought, the Center for International Studies, and the College.

"Only prestige. The more departments which list you, the more important you are."

"So he was pretty important?"

"More likely as a Russian monk he was pretty fashionable."

"Blackwood, what the hell goes on in that part of the world?"

"The Vatican or the University?"

"I mean out where Russia and Poland come together?"

"It's kind of like the Pecos River in Texas, where there's no law west of . . . Between the Vistula and the Volga there isn't much in the way of natural boundaries. So invaders have swept across those plains for a couple of thousand years—Goths, Huns, Teutons, Slavs, Wends, Magyars, Vikings, Mongols. A few of each group stayed there either on the way in or the way out. Maybe even a few Celts who headed west when the last ice age ended. The borders keep changing so at any given time, half the people are in a country they don't want to be in. There's lots of religions there too, four or five brands of Orthodoxy, a couple of Catholic Byzantine groups, and, of course, the Latin Rite Poles. It's borderland, a region of the world made to order for conspiracy and shenanigans."

As I lectured my eyes drifted briefly to the portraits of three Johns on the wall of my study, childhood heroes—the Pope, the president, and the quarterback. Now all three were dead, John Unitas being the last one to have gone home. *O lente, lente currite noctis equi.*

"We've had underground operations there, I presume?"

"Sure. Probably still do. Some of them as independent of Vatican control as were those Czech bishops who ordained women when the Iron Curtain was still working."

"And the various popes have appointed certain cardinals in petto—secret until they want to reveal it . . . Most of them one kind of Eastern European or another . . ."

"A nice touch," I admitted, "though hardly displaying the transparency that is supposed to be our hallmark these days."

He dismissed this cavil with a wave of his hand, the one with the ring, not the one holding my Bushmills.

"OK, Blackwood, let's say for the sake of the argument that Brother Semyon was in fact a Catholic bishop in the underground over there and that he did such a good job that they gave him the red hat in petto. Why would he travel around with choir robes if it were all a secret?"

"Or even possess them. One suspects that the FSB, née KGB, would find that disturbing . . . It says here that his head was blown off by a shotgun!"

Milord Cronin grimaced.

"Messy, but quick."

He drained his tumbler.

"How, then, did the vigilant Chicago police identify him?"

"It was his office, and his robes. Who else would it have been?"

He searched for a place to put the Waterford and finally set it on the top of my computer output.

"They thereupon sought confirmation from fingerprints or DNA?"

"His apartment was swept clean of all traces. There were plenty of fingerprints in his office, however. The Russians don't know who Brother Semyon is. Or was."

"If it were really him."

He rose from my couch with more alacrity than I could have managed.

"There is also the possibility," I added, "that he identified in some fashion with the Avignon crowd."

That stopped Milord dead in his tracks, just as he reached the door of my office.

"Who!"

I forebore from correcting him by saying "whom."

"It is said that there is a remnant of the Avignon papacy that still survives. Rejecting as they do the solution of the Council of Basle to the Great Western Schism, a few elderly French clerics gather together when their pope dies and elect a new pope, who promptly concedes jurisdiction to the false antipope in Rome for the good of the Church. He then appoints a few more elderly French clerics to choose his successor when that becomes necessary."

"That was five hundred years ago!"

"More like seven hundred!"

"Why would they bother?"

"You know the French . . ."

He turned in the doorway and scowled.

"I don't like any of it at all, Blackwood. One pope is enough. So is one cardinal—unless they make you one as a punishment for your South Side Irish prejudices. I can't have itinerant cardinals wandering around Chicago posing as Russian monks. Or vice versa. Or French popes, or whatever. I want this mess straightened out . . . See to it, Blackwood!"

Thereupon he disappeared down the corridor with much the same éclat as the Superchief when it used to leave Chicago on the rails to storied La La Land.

2

I pondered the problem, which, I must confess was, as Holmes would have said, not without certain interesting aspects.

My first call was to a certain person highly placed in the civil service of the American government who owed me enough favors to last a lifetime.

"I was afraid I'd hear from you, Blackie," he began. "You want to pick up another one of your markers, I assume."

"As a Chicagoan I would hardly be so crass as to begin with that."

"I don't know what happened out there at the University. If I did, I doubt that I could tell you."

"Ah," I said.

"Something pretty weird from what I can tell, but people higher up than I am are reserving it to themselves."

"So they can tell all in their memoirs as soon as they leave the administration."

"Maybe, but I think not. This is something that everyone wants to pretend never happened. So it's pretty heavy."

"Our government might have had something to do with the affair."

After his blunt beginning I thought it better not to mention names.

"I didn't say that."

"Some people are afraid that such may be the case?"

"Some people know there are rogue groups who might do anything."

That was all the hint I would get from him. It confirmed what already seemed patent. This was very heavy stuff.

I asked about the health of his wife and family. Obviously relaxing, he assured me that all was well. I promised to stay in touch, a pledge which did not seem to bring him much joy.

I then phoned the Reilly Gallery over on Oak Street, where Michael Patrick Vincent Casey, the former superintendent of the Chicago Police Department and husband of Annie Reilly, did the impressionistic paintings of Chicago that had kept him busy since his retirement. Mike was known in our clan as Mike the Cop as though there were other Mikes such as Mike the Monsignor, Mike the Politician or Mike the Barber. However, he was the only Mike in the extended family.

I chatted with the good Annie Reilly and promised her I would be over to visit and receive my appropriate ration of apple cinnamon tea and oatmeal raisin cookies. There are those, ignorant of the literature, who claim that he is Flambeau to my Father Brown. Annie argues that in fact I am Watson to his Holmes.

"Blackie! What's happening!"

"From your forced good cheer I judge you already know what's happening."

"I assumed that I would hear from you as soon as you returned from Rome."

"And . . . ?"

"I don't know anything about it, Blackie. Mostly because my friends out there either don't know themselves or they're afraid to talk about it."

"Ah."

"There was another murder out at the Divinity School. A Romanian guy executed in the washroom, presumably by the secret police from his country."

"The Securitate."

"They weren't able to solve that either. We don't have much experience with that kind of assassination around here. They've been told to close it down as soon as they can and get it out of the media."

"Ah."

"You know about the crimson robes?"

"Oh, yes."

"What do you make of it?"

"I don't. And you?"

"Really weird . . . No one wants to involve the Catholic Church in this mess."

"Unless the events have already involved it."

"What does Sean want?"

"He wants me to see to it. What else?"

"So you'll go out there and wander around doing your invisible act and see what you can pick up."

"At the moment I can think of no other strategy."

"Let me make a few calls and get back to you."

He would call some friend of his out there and see if he would talk to me off the record.

Let us suppose, I told myself, that Brother Semyon is indeed a cardinal of the Holy Roman Church, albeit in petto. Let us also suppose that he travels around with his cardinal robes available should it happen that he needs them. Let us also suppose that he is some kind of secret agent, mostly but not entirely for the Holy See, and thus has contacts with some of the various spook shops. Such as and for example the folks down at Langley. Who then would want to see him dead?

Who wouldn't?

Suppose that one or several of his employers wanted to "extract" him as they say in the trade, that is, remove him from a dangerous situation. Might they have disposed of someone else as a cover for this extraction?

Arguably.

But how would one prove that and, more important perhaps, why?

The spooks tend to bungle, an occupational hazard that arises from their inability to let the left hand know what the right hand is doing. Perhaps they had bungled this time, which might give us (whoever "we" might happen to be) a chance to catch them.

An outcome they would not like, as my good friend Nuala Anne would say, at all, at all.

The larger question is why one should bother. The Chicago cops, the government of our Republic, and the Holy See all agreed, perhaps independently of one another, that the whole matter should be forgotten as soon as possible. Could I not simply tell Milord Cronin that his curiosity about an invasion of another, though certainly not an alternative, cardinal was not advisable, perhaps not even prudent.

"Prudent" was not a word he was fond of. It usually had the same impact as the red cape waved at a charging bull. Yet he surely would understand my point.

Such a policy went against the grain. My grain, that is. I didn't like these gumshoe creeps mucking around in my city and my archdiocese. I would explore a little further.

So I placed a call to a certain number in Paris. I will translate the conversation into standard English from the Anglo-French patois in which it occurred.

"Ah, Blackie, what transpires?"

"I'm interested in the Avignon Papacy."

"*Bon!* That ended at the Council of Basle, as you well know."

"Fourteen thirty-nine. Almost six centuries ago, leaving behind only an excellent Rhône wine . . ."

"I quite agree."

"And a schismatic papacy."

"Which soon became marginalized and irrelevant."

"But nonetheless it still exists."

"That is all silliness," Madame insisted.

"A few elderly French clerics, perhaps of dubious orthodoxy, wearing crimson robes, pretending that they still control the throne of the Fisherman."

"Perhaps."

"They normally do not wear their crimson unless they have gathered together for a consistory or for the occasional conclave."

"The French state would not approve of such a display."

"One admits as a basis for discussion the possibility of such a sect."

"It being the south of France, they would continue the custom of liaisons with political groups, most likely far-right-wing political groups, especially since Philip the Fair and that bunch have long since departed."

"Only someone raised in the Auvergne like myself could understand these matters or try to understand them. Perhaps they have a valid argument that the decrees of Basle were illegal. Nonetheless, it is improbable, is it not, that the Holy Spirit would tolerate a false papacy in Rome for six centuries."

"I would not try to budget Her time."

Laughter.

"You may rest assured, Blackie, that they are a harmless little group of, how do you say it, crazies. The Vatican knows about them, of course, and does nothing as it often does when it doesn't know what to do. There was some conversation between them and the Archbishop of Dakar when he and his group went into schism after the Vatican Council. However, they found him far too modern."

"All of their cardinals are, of course, French."

Dead silence.

"One hears it said that the currently popular theories of universalism have had some impact even on them."

"St. Paul would be happy."

"You must understand that it is all very ghostly, no, I mean shadowy. They do not have a press office. They do not seek publicity. They are quite content that their lonely little group clings to its hope that God will eventually correct the mistake he made at the Council of Basle."

"Indeed."

"One must credit them, Blackie, with a certain quality of persistence."

"Oh, yes . . . Any Russian cardinals?"

His answer was prompt.

"One does not hear a whisper of that, but one might not."

We chatted amiably and promised to visit one another soon.

"Merci, madame," I said, ending the conversation. I urged her to give my best to Monsieur and to *l'enfant.*

Perhaps in my misspent life I had accumulated too much useless information. If I had not heard whispers of this persistent Rhône schism, I would not have opened that area for investigation. It was pleasant enough to hear that lilting, bell-like voice that recalled for some odd reason the novels of M. Mauriac and a Catholic France that persisted.

Madame had not closed the door completely. She would sniff around and have more information if I should call her again about the subject at hand. So would *Monsieur,* a most upright lawyer from LaVendee who was not without some contacts among the *flics.* However, the Avignon connection seemed most improbable. Brother Semyon was an Orthodox monk who specialized in the Old Believers.

Who were also a recusant sect that firmly believed that the Spirit was on their side, a dangerous assumption about one who claims to blow whither She will.

Yet the Old Believers and the Avignon papacy shared at least that assumption.

Mike Casey was on the phone almost at once.

"Blackie, there is a captain out there named Phil White who doesn't like what's going on. He'd be happy to talk to you. He's an honest man and will tell you everything he knows or suspects . . . Well, almost everything."

"I assume that like the wide receivers on the Bears and the Secretary of State of Illinois, his ethnic background is African-American."

Mike laughed.

"I don't know any white cops named White, that's for sure . . . He'll meet you at Room 314 in the Windemere Hotel tomorrow at ten. He's a stand-up cop."

From Mike there could be no higher compliment.

I pondered the possibilities. I would be constrained at some point actually to venture into the precincts of *The* University. I might just as well try to make an appointment to talk to someone from the Divinity School.

I was assured by my contact that the University was deeply concerned about the murder of a most distinguished visiting professor. It was not, after all, Cicero, if I knew what he meant.

Cicero was the bailiwick of that distinguished Illinois Republican political leader Alphonse Capone and a long succession of people with whom you would not want to associate. Also of stable middle-class Hispanic families with whom one would want to associate. I did not dispute the point.

He called back in a couple of minutes to tell me that Ms. Dorina Keane, the dean of the Divinity School would be happy to have lunch with me at the Quadrangle Club at noon the next day.

One of ours, perhaps. Times changed even at the University. Probably very smart. Even though the University has had its historic doubts about Catholics, nonetheless because of an almost superstitious regard for our hierarchy, it gives us credit for far more power than we actually possess.

I would have to dress very discreetly so no one would suspect what I was.

Should I bring mitre and crosier, I wondered?

That thought was pure fantasy, especially since it wouldn't do any good. Even equipped with such weapons of office, I would still be the little man who wasn't there again today. I am the kind of person who, when someone gets on the elevator I'm riding, they don't see me. There are those who claim that this is an affectation. My siblings argue that it is rather a matter of adapting the persona to the person.

However, the next morning, I donned my (only) good black suit, one that the aforementioned siblings had imposed upon me. I have always rejected the French cuff shirts and clerical vest most bishops affect (especially those who have any reason to expect promotion). It's difficult enough for me to slide the little Roman collar into the appropriate slot on a standard black clerical shirt. However, in keeping with the occasion, I did wear the St. Brigid pectoral cross that my cousin Catherine Collins Curran had made for me and the matching ruby cuff links and the matching episcopal ring she had also created. (Her son, John Blackwood Curran is now a student at the seminary and is known as Little Blackie, though he's close to a foot taller than I am.)

Thus having prepared myself to look as much like a bishop as I can, I departed the Cathedral Rectory. The only member of the staff who noted the difference was Crystal Lane, our mystical youth minister.

"Something really heavy going down, huh, Bishop?"

Why was everyone using that word?

"For the success of which you must pray, Crystal."

"I always pray for you, Bishop."

It is always useful to have someone praying for you, especially someone like Crystal, who has, I'm convinced, God's ear.

I had hired the services of my personal cab driver, Mr. Woods, for the day. He would at least know how to get to *The* University.

My first stop was the Windemere Hotel, a once luxury hotel, facing Jackson Park, just off Lake Shore Drive. Now that Hyde Park, as *The* University neighborhood is called, was no longer luxury (though you'd not know it from the price of homes) the Windemere had fallen into the hands of *The* University and served as housing for graduate students, junior faculty, and the odd visiting professor. It was no longer splendid but it was still presentable.

I told the doorman who I was—he had some difficulty in noticing me—and that Captain Philip White was expecting me. With the look of profound suspicion that characterizes doormen today, he picked up the phone, turned away from me, and pushed a couple of buttons.

"He don't look like no bishop," he told the captain. "Says he is . . . Uh-huh . . . Okay, I'll send him up."

The last words were spoken in the tone of one telling the captain that the sin was his.

"Sign here, sir."

I signed as I usually do when SO challenged: BLACKIE WAS HERE!

No one has ever noticed, thus confirming my suspicion that signing in is an empty ritual.

The man who waited for me at the open door of Room 314 might well have been a pass receiver for the Bears. He was approximately as tall as Milord Cronin, slim, trim, and handsome, with very dark skin and very bright eyes. Immaculately groomed with a tiny, symbolic mustache, short hair edged in silver, he wore a flawlessly tailored black suit.

Future superintendent, I thought.

"Captain Phil White?" I said, omitting the obvious pseudo witty comment.

"Bishop Blackie Ryan?" He grinned broadly and shook my hand. "What's the matter with that idiot downstairs? Who else would wear a pectoral cross besides a bishop? And a St. Brigid cross at that!"

"What parish?" I asked, accepting his signals.

"St. Thomas the Apostle, right here in the 'hood!"

The two-room suite was spacious enough, though just barely. Outside, the Museum of Science and Industry, only survival relic of the 1893 World's Fair, and the Lake were framed in Technicolor autumn finery. Yellow school buses were disgorging hordes of schoolchildren, supervised by nervous adults, on field trips, and light traffic was wending its way south on the Drive.

"Care to look around, Bishop?"

There was not much to see. The furniture was a little better than shabby, the television set in the parlor/office was small, a table served as a desk on which an old portable typewriter and a stack of paper rested as if wondering why no one was working. The keys were in Roman and not Cyrillic script. A slightly battered filing cabinet contained piles of manuscript in Russian. The bookcases were crammed with volumes, also in Russian. The smell of cigar smoke hung heavy in the air, despite the loudly humming window fan.

The small kitchenette contained a noisy refrigerator, an old-fashioned sink, and a small table. Like the parlor, everything was spotlessly clean, as though no one had ever lived in the room. A half bottle of milk was the only inhabitant of the fridge.

"He ate his meals over at the faculty club," Captain White explained, "or downstairs in the Piccolo Mondo restaurant. However, look at this cabinet!"

He opened a door and revealed a massive collection of vodka bottles, all unopened.

"Two dozen," the captain observed laconically. "They say he drank a bottle every day and ate black bread with it."

"For a Russian, a moderate drinker. Any trace of the black bread?"

"None whatever."

"Everything seems very neat and clean," I said, as we walked into the bedroom. "Good service staff?"

"He was an orderly man, it would seem, with the habits of a monk. The housekeepers said he was always neat."

"Save for the smell of cigar smoke, which along with the vodka does not sound monastic."

"He disposed of the vodka bottle in the garbage chute every morning on the way to the University. He walked, by the way, even during the winter months."

"Russians are used to the cold presumably, especially when prepared for it by their daily ration of vodka."

"His colleagues said that they never thought he drank very much. His disposition was always the same."

"Choleric?"

"Something like that."

"Perhaps the problem was that they never saw him completely sober . . . Fingerprints?"

"Everywhere. They matched those of the deceased."

"Any others?"

"Only of the housekeeper, who, by her own testimony, gave the place a thorough cleaning while he was away recently."

"No one else's?"

"Neither your friend downstairs nor any of the housekeepers saw anyone else enter his rooms."

"Indeed."

The bed was a twin separated from its partner. A large icon of Christos Pantocrator—Christ the Creator—dominated the wall; some of the off-white paint in one corner of the room had begun to peel.

I would not have dared to put an associate pastor nor a temporarily visiting priest in such a suite at the Cathedral Rectory. Yet it was probably superior to accommodations at Zagorsk Monastery outside of Moscow—and indeed to most accommodations in Moscow.

"What do we know about him?"

The captain shrugged.

"His passport has disappeared too . . . He was apparently about fifty-five. Entered the monastery as a young man. Studied Russian mysticism all his life; books published in French translation. When Gorbachev took over he was invited to lecture at the Sorbonne in Paris. Commuted back and forth from Paris to Moscow. Came here as a visiting professor last year. Was on the beginning of the second year of a two-year term. A bit of a colorful character on campus. Shouted a lot. As a matter of fact, shouted all the time. It doesn't seem likely that he would have been offered a reappointment. He sent segments of manuscripts, I am told, off to Paris every week."

"Naturally you examined the manuscript pages in the file cabinet and in his office."

29

"We had someone who knows Russian look at them. He said it was all religious stuff."

"No one had a motive to kill him?"

"No one that we could learn about. We don't know much about his past in Paris or Moscow. Interpol didn't have anything."

"And the locked room?"

"He must have let someone in who killed him. Then the perp slipped out and somehow managed to lock the door from the inside as he left."

That's what they all say in locked-room cases.

"And carried the sawed-off shotgun with him?"

"I never said I liked this case."

"Indeed."

"Anyway"—he opened the door of a narrow closet—"here's the specialty of the house!"

Two worn Russian monastic robes and a frayed business suit hung on old-style wire hangers. And an elaborate case, the like of which I had seen in Milord Cronin's more ample closet.

Captain White unzipped it.

Sure enough. Crimson watered silk of unimpeachable quality.

I sighed loudly.

"This is the thing they call the pallium, isn't it, Bishop?"

It was indeed the woolen collar, marked with crosses, a lapel in front and a lapel in back.

"If feels authentic," I admitted.

"You don't get one of those till you're made an archbishop, do you?"

"I don't get one ever, Captain, but yes, it comes with the office of a metropolitan, an archbishop."

"Do the Russians have such a custom?"

"I don't think so . . . was this not with the rest of the vestments?"

"No."

"Where was it?"

"Hung on one of the vodka bottles in the kitchen cabinet."

"Fascinating!"

There was something very wrong about this whole business. Alas, I had no idea what it was.

"Captain White, how tall are you?"

"About six-three, Bishop. Receiver in college."

"Why does that not surprise me? . . . I think you would look quite striking in these robes. Why don't you try them on?"

He grinned broadly, the kind of impish grin that African-Americans do better than anyone else.

"Promise you won't tell my wife?"

"Scout's honor."

I noted that the robes seemed freshly cleaned and pressed, not an easy task with watered silk.

He fit the cassock, which seemed to be of similar dimensions to those of Milord Cronin, like they had been made for him.

"She-ee-it!"

He made it sound like a three-syllable word,

"I assume the late Brother Semyon, God be good to him, was shorter than you are."

"Hard to tell exactly how tall with his head in little pieces, but maybe five-ten."

"Indeed."

"Right now," he said as he removed the cassock, "I think I'd rather be a cardinal than a captain of the homicide squad."

"What will you do with this information?"

"Note it in my final report. As Superintendent Casey probably told you, the bosses don't want there to be any more bother on this case. Foreign assassins with motives left over from the Cold War."

"The issue is what Brother Semyon was doing with the well-preserved robes of a Catholic cardinal that were several sizes too large."

"Yes . . . My bosses don't want to know. Can't say I blame them."

"Or whether the dead man in Brother Semyon's office," I suggested, "was really Brother Semyon?"

"No way do they want to know."

"Or whether the robes were smuggled in here during the course of the day in which he was killed?"

"That too . . . ," Captain White said. "What are you going to do with this information, Bishop Blackie?"

"That remains to be seen," I replied, though the truth was that I hadn't the slightest idea. "Tell me, Phil, is there any hint that our friends out on the West Side might be involved in this?"

I accompanied this question with the required nod in the direction of Taylor Street though now the hierarchy of the Outfit tended to live farther west, in the suburbs.

"It's not their kind of thing anymore. Single shot in the back of the head with a .22 instead of a sawed-off shotgun. They're usually too clumsy to come up with something as twisted as this. A hit man from out of town comes in and does the job, neat and clean as possible, then returns to wherever he came from. With those guys, though, you can never be sure. I don't think they much like it when people call the Russian guys the Moscow Mafia."

"Understandably."

We rode down the elevator together in silence. We shook hands as I entered Mr. Woods's cab.

"Let's stay in touch."

"Definitely," I agreed.

Don't call me, I'll call you.

I made another call from the cab. To a friend who had friends. I was running out of sources.

"You know that thing that went down the other day out at *The* University?"

"I read the papers."

"I wonder if your friends hear anything from their friends about it."

"I don't hear nothing. Some guys say its wrong to whack a priest, even if he is Russian. That's all."

"No hint that it's one of theirs?"

"Nah . . . A contract that big would have to be approved by the Council. Probably wouldn't have got by them unless there was a really good reason . . . You can't tell what some punks might do on their own, but they'd be taking a real chance if the boys ever found out."

"I assumed as much."

"Call me in a couple of days and I'll let you know if I hear anything. I doubt it though. The boys are all good Catholics, ya know. Like I say, they wouldn't kill a priest unless there was some really good reason."

Yeah.

3

There was a periodical reading room off the lobby of the faculty club. I wandered into it and became invisible. Thus I was able to eavesdrop on two conversations simultaneously. The first involved two men in their middle forties, both wearing ties and radiating confidence in their own intelligence.

"I really don't understand, Theodore, why you think that Ms. Rogers deserves a lifetime appointment at this University. Her output is meager. Given our financial situation we must be sparing in our promotions. Other universities have the leisure of indulging in such dubious choices. We do not."

"I admit that she has only three articles and one manuscript, James, but her work is of the highest caliber. In her case the quality compensates for the lack of quantity."

"Yet I know people who are familiar with her work who have reservations about the quality. She would do well, I'm sure, elsewhere; but she would not quite measure up here. Moreover, she has two children, does she not? That does not auger well for her future productivity."

The other two discussants wore suits too, tweedy garments that suggested the need for pipes clenched between teeth, though in fact smoking was apparently forbidden in the Quadrangle Club.

"I am convinced that the department made a serious mistake, Stefan, in offering an appointment to Mr. Swarz. His salary, staff, and lab demands are prohibitive. He makes trouble wherever he goes. In our present condition this University can hardly afford to invest that much money in a man that Harvard has turned down."

"Our younger colleagues say he will certainly win the Nobel prize in the next couple of years."

"That remains to be seen. You and your allies voted for him to keep our younger colleagues from leaving."

"Only a six-to-five vote. Surely that will send a message."

"To whom? The dean? Come, Stefan, you must be joking!"

"The provost, obviously. He won't turn Mr. Swarz down. He'll stall until it's too late and some other university has snatched him up."

"The provost is very good at that, I admit."

Doubtless conversations like this went on at every major university in the country. Yet I was not edified.

Then, at the ring of twelve on some local bell, perhaps at Laura Spellman Rockefeller Chapel, a woman entered the lobby. Patently she was the dean I was to lunch with. Slender, attractive, about thirty, with luxuriant red hair pulled severely from her pale face, she would have in another era perhaps been a nun, most likely a mistress of novices. Indeed, her plain black suit with a touch of white at the throat might even have been an updated habit.

I reached in my pocket to make sure my Rosary beads were handy.

Now clearly she was an updated version of the true-believing nuns of yesteryear, a true-believing feminist of today, though the match between her suit and the deft curves of her body raised the question of whether she belonged to yet another and newer wave of feminists.

Her eyes swept the lobby of the Quadrangle Club, once, then twice. A prim frown of disapproval on her face. The bishop was obviously late and just as obviously in trouble. How like a man! How like a priest!

At the third sweep of her eyes I finally emerged from my invisibility.

Her face illumined in a bright smile, and she strode across the lobby, hand extended.

"You gotta be Bishop Ryan!"

Pure South Boston accent, the kind that plays games with its "r" sounds, dropping or inserting them, seemingly ad libitum. As in "He drove the cah around the cohner on his way from Atlantar to Savanar."

"I have never had an option in the matter."

"Dorie Keane . . . I use your books all the time in my class!"

Those who have set words on paper for others to read will testify that there is nothing more likely to melt the heart of a crusty bishop than words of appreciation for his writing, especially since they have been invisible on the *New York Times* Best-Seller list, not to say all other such lists.

That the appreciation comes from an attractive woman who seems genuinely enthusiastic at meeting one does not hurt.

How could it be that this charming and tasteful young woman could be a dean at *The* University?

My general feeling of dyspepsia had begun as soon as Mr. Woods had turned down Fifty-ninth Street or Midway Plaisance as the mayor insists it should be called. It was along the Midway, a sunken channel that was part of the World's Columbian Exposition in 1893, that the trustees decided to erect the second attempt at a University of Chicago—complete with the phoenix symbol of a bird rising out of the ashes. The image stood for both Chicago rising out of the ashes of the Chicago Fire and the second University rising out of the ruins of the first. The latter had been built on land owned by Senator William A. Douglas of Lincoln-Douglas debate fame on the lakeshore and Thirty-ninth Street. During the Civil War the notorious Camp Douglas prison camp was so close to the school that guards standing on the roof of the observatory could scan the whole camp. Both the camp and the University disappeared subsequently, the former because of peace, the latter because of lack of money. The new University was organized by a group of Northern Baptists (mostly clergy) in the 1890s who dealt with the money problem by signing John D. Rockefeller on to the board. Characteristic of the "big shoulders" spirit of the city, they created a great university simply by buying a great faculty with Rockefeller money.

Being far too new to look like Oxford or Cambridge or even Harvard, it settled for looking systematically more gothic by lining the Midway with American gothic structures designed by Ralph Adams Cram, also funded by the Rockefeller clan.

Cynically I have always felt that these origins left *The* University with a bit of an inferiority complex. It was a Johnny-Come-Lately school that had made its claim to greatness long after Harvard, Yale, and Princeton and with tainted oil money as its currency. Why else count the number of your Nobel prizewinners and even print them on your tee shirts? Why else distance yourself from the city whose name and symbol you shared? Why else pretend that Hyde Park was a bastion of civilization in a jungle of Chicago barbarism? Why else thoughtlessly offend the two major ethnic groups in Chicago whose support it could have used—Catholics and Blacks?

I reprimanded myself for such unworthy thoughts as Mr. Woods drove down the Midway, the gothic buildings on either side looking stately under the clear blue autumn sky and amid the fall colors on the trees. Still the occasional more modern building which made lip service to *The* University's intermittent need to be up-to-date seemed like a bit of tasteless humor.

I grew up at the opposite end of the South Side, so far away that we rarely had to drive through Hyde Park or down the Midway. So *The* University was a foreign land to us, inhabited by strange-looking folk—that is to say they didn't look like Irish Catholics—whose morals and politics were suspect. It was, we suspected, a hotbed of anti-Catholicism and Communism. Indeed, some of the old-timers (though hardly my father and mother, left-wing New Deal Democrats that they were) called it "Moscow Tech." The label betrayed our ignorance. At the very time they used it, Milton Friedman was launching his revival of classical economics and defense of the free market, which soon dominated economic discourse. "A hotbed of Republicans," my old fella used to mutter under his breath. "Herbert Hoover Tech."

Why go to *The* University when you could go to Notre Dame?

Anti-Catholic? That label was perhaps not altogether inaccurate, as I had reason to know.

Much, however, had changed both in the Church and in *The* University. The students swarming down University Avenue at noon looked normal enough, which is to say they looked Catholic. You let one in . . .

My siblings had lectured there on various occasions, some of my nieces and nephews had attended its graduate schools, the Catholics on the faculty were more than just tokens, Milord Cronin had appeared there to pick up an honorary degree and delivered a stirring and brilliant address (if I do say so myself) afterward. Two of the most powerful institutions in the city—Archdiocese and University—had made their peace (much to the delight of the Organization, which wanted both those constituencies to be happy because they had lots of voters).

I still felt, for reasons of my own, like a stranger in the foreign land.

"What is your field, Ms. Keane?" I asked my babbling host, as we ascended to the dining room.

When William Rainey Harper founded *The* University with all its hijacked talent, he had decreed that it was not necessary to use such terms as "Professor" or "Doctor" since everyone already had doctorates. "Mister" would suffice or in the rare case "Miss" or even rarer case "Missus." *The* University began to use "Ms." only after the *New York Times* had dutifully accepted it.

"American Religion. That's why your books are so important in my courses. They demonstrate the impact on American religious culture of the emergence of Roman Catholicism as a culturally significant religion. They're almost as much sociology and history as philosophy."

Indeed. I would not have thought it, but it was welcome news. Also highly improbable.

"You, of course, are a graduate of the Golden Dome," I countered.

She did not ask how I knew it.

"Half of the Div School students are Catholic and almost half the faculty."

"There goes the neighborhood."

She thought that was very funny.

"Actually we train more doctoral candidates than all the Catholic seminaries in the Chicago area put together."

"I will warn Milord Cronin that he should keep this news from the Holy See."

We had arrived at the hallowed door of the dining room of the Quadrangle Club, characteristically more elegant than the faculty dining rooms at either Harvard or Yale. In the old days it was de rigueur (though not obligatory) that everyone wear jackets, ties, and white shirts. Only when President Edward Levi (sometime Attorney General of our resilient Republic) once appeared in blue shirt with white collar had the norms begun to slip. Yet the men and women in the dining room were at least as well-groomed as a group at lunch in, let us say, the dining room of the IBM building. Out of deference to the Northern Baptists (who had long since become invisible) liquor was not served till after four, though I believe it was now available at lunchtime down in the billiard room.

The dean pointed at a circular table near the door on our right as we entered.

"That's where the Economics Department sits," she whispered with some awe. "Nobel prizewinners."

"What are they talking about?"

"Often it's their golf scores."

Somehow I found that endearing.

It had always seemed to me that the atmosphere in this room of gothic windows and oak panels radiated self-satisfied complacency.

There may be many things wrong in the world, but here were men and now women who are the very best in all the world at what they do. Taken together, they knew almost everything that was worth knowing. That atmosphere tends to follow academics wherever they might be, but it was especially strong here. And not unjustified. Except that some of them were not as good as they thought they were.

Much like a meeting of American Catholic bishops.

"I see that the Nobel prizewinners no longer wear distinguishing caps," I remarked.

"That's because there are so many of them here we'd have to make those that don't have the prize wear distinguishing caps."

"A prudent decision."

"I know the kind of priest you are, Bishop Blackie," she chortled. "We have your kind back in Southie: troublemakers!"

Oh, yes.

"Right this way, Bishop," the maître d' grinned. "We're happy to have you with us. We've given you the president's table over in the corner, because he is out of town today."

I almost blew the line, but I managed to say, "How generous of him."

I trailed after Ms. Keane as she strode to the far end of the dining room.

At several tables along the way, people looked up, smiled, and greeted her.

"Hi, Dorie!"

She responded with a handshake, a smile, a word of greeting, and with one woman a kiss on the forehead.

Political family, I decided. Queen Maeve greeting her troops. Did they realize that in a few more years she would own the University?

No one noticed me, despite my pectoral cross, episcopal ring, and ruby cuff links. I should have brought at least the crosier. Even then, however, in the wake of Dorina Keane, I would still have been invisible.

"I'll say it before you do, Bishop Blackie," she said, as we were seated at the table, "I'm from a political family."

"Aren't we all . . . Did Brother Semyon, God be good to him, often eat here?"

Her face returned to its original somewhat nunnish primness.

"Every day. He created quite a stir when he strode in wearing his monastic robes. He would shout 'A table!' at the top of his voice and shake up all the discreet and quiet conversations in the room. He scared people, a visitor from another world."

"I knew I should have brought my crosier."

Feminist, dean, professor of American religion, and graduate of the Golden Dome that she was, she nonetheless giggled.

Points for Blackie Ryan.

"No way you could shout as loudly as he did."

We ordered lunch, one lasagna Bolognese for me, a fruit salad for her, iced tea for me, a decaf for her.

"Did he eat alone?"

"Usually he came with colleagues. When he was alone, others joined him. Poor dear man, he was really rather sweet when you got to know him. Very holy in his own way and generous to students even though he scared the living daylights out of them. I think a lot of the time he was putting on an act. You know what kind of people the Russians are."

I think I did. Like the Irish, they love a show.

"Yet you were not going to bring him back for a second two-year term."

She shrugged.

"This University is not quite ready for that kind of color. I voted for it. So did most of the Catholics. Sometimes you win, sometimes you lose."

Then, before I could find out more about the human side of Brother Semyon Ivanivich, she launched into an intense and, to be truthful, very flattering discussion of my work. She cited frequently someone called "David," apparently a professor of church history.

"This person is also a Domer?" I interrupted once.

"From Evergreen Park," she said, her face turning red. "He thinks we're engaged. I'm not sure yet."

A dangerous mixing of the races.

"He would know perhaps about la famiglia Ryan."

"All about them. Maybe you'll meet him later."

"Doubtless."

Then the subject turned to whether I would lecture in one of her classes.

For reasons of my own I wanted no part of it.

"Not before we solve the problem of the death of Semyon Ivanivich Popov."

"Fair enough," she said sadly, "but we'll never solve it, Bishop Blackie. It's too horrible."

I thought I saw a tear appear in each of her blue eyes.

"My record is not all that bad," I said.

She did not answer that.

It was, in fact, perfect. Thus far I had never failed to solve a problem to which Milord Cronin had assigned me. However, I would not boast because pride goes before the fall and the Lord, impatient with my arrogance, might throw a banana peel in my path. I know He does not do such things, but my mother had warned me often enough of that risk that I could not drive it out of my memory.

"Bishop, may I ask a personal question?"

"Priests ask such questions, they don't answer them. However, since you have such good taste in philosophy books, go right ahead."

"Why did you go to Seabury for graduate school?"

"Because it was deemed necessary that I acquire a doctorate."

"Why not here?"

Dangerous ground.

"I would still be a student."

She laughed.

"It's really not that bad . . . Did you apply."

Now we were on thin ice. Blackie Ryan must contain his resentment.

"Actually I did."

"And you were accepted, of course?"

"As it happens, I was not."

"No! Why?"

"I met with some sort of admissions officer who pointed out to me that resources of the Divinity School were strictly limited, that it had to turn down most applicants, and felt a moral obligation to be sternly—his word—selective in those that it did admit. I had attended an unaccredited college seminary at which I had managed to collect a couple of Bs and hence did not have a straight-A average. The school felt I would not be happy in its rigorous academic environment."

"How awful!"

"It was a long time ago," I said meekly.

"You must have been heartbroken!"

"More relieved than anything else," I said honestly enough.

We left the dining room and the club. Dorie's ritual of greetings as we left were less enthusiastic than before.

"Do you think it was anti-Catholicism?"

"Arguably. I was later told that only three or four members of the faculty were convinced there was a God."

"That's changed. Everything has changed, Bishop, though not quite. There are still some people in this university that don't like us."

Outside the Indian Summer day continued in all of its lush, lazy perfection. The students—Asians, Muslim women in scarves, Catholics, Protestants, Jews, every color under heaven, truly a catholic bunch—ambled down the leaf-strewn streets with notable lack of vigor.

"It has been argued," I replied to Dorie, "that I was way behind my time."

"You mean ahead of your time?"

"The implication was that I would have fit in the Sorbonne of the 1200s, but not *The* University of the 1900s. However, I learned long ago that there is no point in resisting the plans of the Spirit because She patently has a mind of Her own."

"You think that everything happens for the best?"

"In my case it usually does."

We turned into the main quadrangle, which extends from University Avenue to Woodlawn and from Fifty-seventh Street to Fifty-ninth Street. It would be an example of gothic perfection (or perhaps only bastard gothic perfection) if only the Administration Building at its far end were not a solid New Deal block. On its left-hand side, standing in judgment of its ugliness I thought, was Swift Hall, the home of the Divinity School and the center during the contretemps of the late 1960s of student unrest. Some of the Establishment at that time (Economics and Business and Law School) were alleged to have advocated its expulsion.

"Shall we stop in Bond Chapel to say a prayer?" Dorie asked somewhat shyly.

"Even if Jesus isn't there?" I asked, since Bond was a "non-denominational" chapel in which the Blessed Sacrament was not, as we used to say, "reserved." For what it might be reserved I never quite understood.

"We have the Eucharist there every Sunday," she said, "as if you didn't know that your cardinal presided over it not so long ago."

"Like I say, the neighborhood is finished."

Bond is a tiny gothic gem with splendid stained-glass windows, on which not a single graven image appeared. Probably when we took it over we would not change the windows.

I asked the Deity to bless and protect the University and all who lived and worked within its boundaries, to grant peace and joy to whoever had died within the walls of Swift Hall, and to protect everyone among its faculty and students. I also suggested that it might be useful if Her mostly useless servant John Blackwood Ryan found the grace to work a little bit more effectively on forgiving and forgetting. Finally, I mentioned that this might not be the time to punish said useless servant by breaking his record for solving puzzles.

There was no immediate response to my requests. I had the impression, however, that they were being taken under advisement.

Andrew M. Greeley

"Also," I added, "please bless and protect the dean, even if she is from South Boston, and her young man, even if he is from Evergreen Park."

We left Bond Chapel without the genuflections that its gothic interior seemed to demand and entered the back door of Swift Hall.

"Better to bring the bishop in the back door," I observed, "lest you scandalize the faithful."

She giggled for the second time.

"Did you pray for me in there?"

"I figured it would do no harm."

"And for David?"

"I figured he might need the prayers."

Third giggle.

4

"Dean Keane," said a black-bearded giant, who was leaning against a staircase, correcting a batch of papers. He was tall and slender, with dangerous blue eyes and hair as dark as his beard. He wore the mandatory khaki slacks, a blue pin-striped jacket, and a white shirt unadorned by a tie. He might have been a Russian pirate, save for his patently Irish grin. More likely that he was an agent of the Irish Republican Army. His grin was, however, not for me but for the dean, whom his eyes devoured with the amused hunger that love permits. I was even more invisible than I usually am.

"Professor Dolan," the target of his affection replied coolly. "May I present the Most Reverend John Blackwood Ryan."

"Ph.D.," I added, as we shook hands.

His grip was firm but not overpowering. A strong young man, well aware of the power of his personal charisma.

"The legendary Blackie," he said, transferring his smile from Dorie to me and changing its content. "The unobtrusive and practically invisible little auxiliary bishop who isn't there again today."

"All the more so when in the company of the valiant Dean Keane."

"My fiancée does dazzle, doesn't she?"

"Not quite fiancée, David."

The electrical current between them was intense, but fortunately for their work and peace of mind mostly humorous. The dean, I thought, hesitated about the current because she feared that if he accepted his emotional need for her, she would simply disappear in its power.

How clever of God to create humans in such a way that they generated these energies for one another and thus revealed the energy that unites Him with His creatures.

"I used to caddy at Beverly for your sister and brother-in-law," he informed me.

"The doctors Ryan and Murphy."

"What nice people and what great characters."

"Actually, I'm the only truly sane one in the family."

He laughed at that. Obviously my sib and her husband had defamed me.

"I hope you can help us learn what happened to Brother Semyon Ivanivich." He became grim. "It was a brutal murder of a nice and harmless man."

"David and Brother Semyon were great friends. They used to drink a glass of vodka every afternoon, rather in violation of the University ban on such behavior."

She led us around the corner to a row of offices.

" 'Just one small drink vodka,' he would say and laugh. 'Good for health.' "

"He drank a bottle every day," Dean Keane said disapprovingly. "That's why Russian male life expectancy is so short."

"At least one bottle," David added. "He always kept a bottle in the drawer of his desk here which would be pretty well worn-out when I'd leave and there was a big supply in his apartment, I'm told . . . This is my office, Bishop Blackie. Brother Semyon was next to me and the dean's is right around the corner."

"How convenient," I murmured.

"They used to invite me to join them for their small glass vodka. I am feminist, he would say, women can drink vodka too."

"Naturally you refused."

"Naturally."

"Your friend the dean"—David laughed—"is a bit of a straight arrow. I think all the Protestants around here have had a bad effect on her."

Dorie sniffed.

"This is the key to Brother Semyon's office, Bishop. We are very careful about keys around here as you might imagine. There is no master key for the offices, only the key the occupant has and another one kept in a safe in my office. This lower lock is a dead bolt that Brother Semyon asked us to install. 'Thieves take precious stuff,' he'd say, 'all time.' However, it could be locked only on the inside. So I think it was for keeping people out when he was working or drinking vodka with Irish Catholic males."

"He used to lock it whenever I came in for my one glass," David Dolan admitted ruefully. " 'What Protestants don't know won't hurt them.' "

Dorie opened the door. Inside, the dead bolt was not in place; otherwise, we would not have been able to enter.

We went into the office. Dorie closed the door and slipped the dead bolt into place.

"Now there are two locks that can be opened only from the inside, unless you had this key or Brother Semyon's to open the upper lock from the outside. His was in his pocket and mine was in my safe. When faculty were in their offices, they often left the regular lock unlatched. David's door is always unlocked, especially for the women students who flutter around him."

"Whenever a woman is in my office," David said piously, "I always leave the door open! Even if it's the dean."

The inside of the office was as meticulous as the monk's apartment. It also smelled of disinfectant, doubtless from cleaning up the mess made by his exploding head.

Dave Dolan opened a bottom drawer of the desk.

"No vodka. Someone must have stolen it."

"Did you have a drink with him that afternoon?" I asked.

"No, for some reason he had suspended our custom the last week or two before he died."

I walked over to the windows.

"Was it a particularly warm day?"

"No, it was cold and raining. He didn't open the windows much. 'Fresh air bad for you. Chase away cigar smoke.'"

"Anyway," Dorie added, "the windows were locked too. That was the first thing the police looked at when they came."

"So someone came into this office, presumably admitted by Professor Popov. He carried a sawed-off shotgun, shot the professor, God be good to him, put the lock back on for the faculty door, and departed. Whereupon, Professor Popov, despite the loss of his head, rose from the chair, flipped the dead bolt into place, came back to the chair, and succumbed."

"It would seem so," Dorie admitted. "It is all so ugly and terrible. He was such a nice man."

"You were in your office, David Dolan?"

"Working late because I'm up for a tenure review. Fantasizing occasionally about my bride to be."

"David!"

"A man in love is entitled to his fantasies, isn't he, Bishop?"

"Without them the species would not survive."

"Anyway"—Ms. Keane ignored my comment—"Mr. Dolan is scheduled for your first appointment, Bishop. I'll try to set up the second for two hours from now. That would be about three-fifteen?"

"Make it three-thirty, Dorie. You know how talkative I am!"

Mr. Dolan was pushing his luck with his true love, doubtless deliberately. He was South Side Irish all right.

"You should finish your work on those two articles. If they are actually in press at the time of the final review, the tenure committee will be impressed."

"Aw," Dave already dismissed her concern, "no committee in this school would dare turn down the dean's sweetheart."

He had pushed his envelope of luck, again deliberately.

Dorie's face flushed, her lips tightened, her eyes flamed.

"I apologize for David's remark, Bishop, though you probably realize that some South Side Irish males are crude. Actually, I have spoken to no one about his case and will not do so. Nor has anyone spoken to me. This school is not run like the Cook County Democratic Organization."

"Pity," her self-proclaimed sweetheart murmured as she strode away. Utterly unrebuked, he consumed her with his eyes as she departed. He sighed loudly and opened the door of his office.

It looked like the police had searched through his papers, books, and computer output all around the room. Much like Milord Cronin when he came to my quarters, David Dolan dumped a stack of output on the floor and gestured towards a chair.

"Tea? Bewley's Afternoon?" he said, removing his seersucker jacket.

"Capital."

He picked up an electric teakettle, glanced into it to see if there was any water, shrugged, and went out into the corridor. In a couple of moments he returned, plugged in the kettle, and pushed a half-open window to let in more air.

"The place is a mess, Bishop Blackie. I'd like to blame it on my tenure struggle, but it would be a mess if I were already an associate professor."

"I believe that the illustrious professor Milton Friedman once remarked that the marginal value of tenure was no more than twenty-five cents."

"When I marry her, I'll have to return to the neat habits of my youth. Small price to pay, wouldn't you think?"

He smiled contentedly, not quite suggesting the joys of having the dean in bed with him, but not precluding a consideration of those delights either. As I had suggested earlier, in the absence of such fantasies, the species would not long endure.

"How serious is the tenure crisis?" I asked

He shrugged again.

"I'll get it, nary a doubt. Poor Dorie knows I will, and she knows that the committee would never reject her suitor. The whole school adores her. She's a pet, a mascot, a favorite little sister, a bright light for this very dark institution. Break her heart? Never. I don't mean that she has or will intrigue. She will give all appearances of being absolutely impartial. She'll even excuse herself when the tenured faculty votes. That's the way we universalistic academics function. However, the Southie inside her knows what will happen and why, even if she won't quite admit it to herself."

"Ah."

It seemed perfectly reasonable to me. That's the way humans operate, even when they pretend not to. We are all of us premodern.

"Actually my two books are more than enough. Even these two articles would do the trick. All the journals want is minor changes and they'll be accepted. My credentials are impeccable. Alas, I am a bit of a wild man, not to say on occasion a smart-ass. There are some creeps around here who would like never to see me again. So the relationship between me and Dorie—a lot less physical than some of them would like to think, by the way—cancels that out. I'd probably win anyway, but it's nice to have some reserves."

"Your two books?"

"Both in press. The first is a revision of my dissertation. It's called *The Theotokos Women and the Papacy: Proto Feminists*. The second addresses itself to the question of why there have been no bad Popes since 1700. It's called, *Good-bye to Bad Men: The Virtuous Papacy of the Last Three Centuries*. You can tell from the titles why some of the creeps around here are less than enthusiastic about me."

He grinned beatifically.

"Great titles, huh?"

"Grabbers."

"Yeah, well, you see, I went to Harvard, so I'm not as much impressed with the seriousness of this place as is the fair lady, er woman!"

Another beatific grin.

"Well, we better get to work. I was sitting here that night about seven-thirty. Outside a noisy autumn thunderstorm was assaulting *The* University indeed without permission of the Committee of the Council. I was touching up this article on whether Mary as Theotokos was really imprisoned in the Castel San Angelo for fifty years by her son. The point is that historians of the papacy have to be prepared to discount those who were writing the history of the times, often from the point of view of a moralizing revisionist. Turns out that there were a couple of other accounts of her life that the writers of the standard histories didn't find . . . Personally I always have had a soft spot in my heart for those women who tried to run the papacy. Not that I would want to be close to any of them if they were around."

"Indeed."

He loved to talk, to shape words, to revel in the sound of what he said, to delight in irony and contradiction. The culture of the South Side and through that to the culture of Ireland ran true.

"Anyway, I was daydreaming about the fair Dorina, maybe even nodding off to pleasant dreams, when I heard this terrible explosion, like someone had set off a bomb beneath my desk. I thought I saw a flash of something. My first guess was that the Div School had been hit by a thunderbolt. Was God trying to punish me for lusting after my young woman! Then I jumped up and looked around. No sign of an explosion in my office. Just a bad dream. Then I smelled the rancid smell of cordite. Someone had shot off a gun.

"I stumbled out into the corridor. There was a light in only one other office on the floor—Brother Semyon's. I pounded on the door and shouted for him. No answer. I shouted again and again. Still no answer. The cordite smell was coming from his office. I know cordite because my father was a cop. He had taken me to pistol ranges a couple of times and wisely decided that I ought not be a cop as I would be a threat to all the other cops.

"I tried to think, not very successfully. We academics are not very good in crises because we have to analyze what's happening before we respond. Finally, I got around to trying to turn the door handle. It was locked. Perhaps Brother Semyon was inside, wounded, bleeding to death. I couldn't get in without a key to the door. Who had the keys? My true love of course! How could I reach her?

"By the telephone, stupid. So I staggered back into my office and tried to call her. My fingers were shaking so badly that I misdialed the first three times.

"Finally, as cool as a night in Chicago winter, she answered.

"Dorie, it's Dave . . . Yes I know I sound terrible. There's been an explosion in Brother Semyon's office. He's locked the door. I need the key to get in . . . Yes I know it's in your office, but I don't have the key to get in there either. . . . Okay. I guess you have to come over . . . Take a cab please . . ."

"Not exactly one of the Bengal Lancers, huh?"

He had acted out the whole incident dramatically as he described it, complete with his inability to punch in the numbers on his phone and his stumbling conversation with Dean Keane. The man was a seanache, an Irish storyteller. He was doubtless a great teacher.

"So I came out of my office and found three of my colleagues congregated around Brother Semyon's door; Doug Strong, Patrice Comerford, and Israel Golden. All three of them, by the way, think I'm off the wall, but they dote on Dorie. They're all badly shook, just like I had been a few moments before. So I decided I'd play take-charge guy, just like my old man does or used to do at a crime scene.

"Patrice is sobbing . . . Something terrible has happened. We can't afford another terrible crime at this University. Israel was tugging bravely at the door. Of course it wouldn't open . . . What is a door if you can't open it if you need it . . . Doug is frozen like he's just come in from the North Pole, white-faced like he might have even frozen to death.

"So I say the keys are in Dorie's office. I phoned her. She said she'd run over. Then we can open the door.

"They all relax. Thank God, you're here, Doug says, though I don't think he really believes in God. We each describe what we were doing when we heard the explosion. We don't think anyone else is in the building. Doug, who did time in Vietnam, says it sounded like a hand grenade.

"Then there's a terrible pounding on the front door. You see, if you're in the building, you just push the bar and go out. But after six they lock these entrance doors, so you can't get though but you can still go out . . ."

"So the presumed cause of the explosion could have hidden in the men's room and when you rushed out and then when you returned to your office to phone the ineffable Dorina and before your colleagues appeared, this perpetrator could have ducked out of either the front door or the back door of the school."

He thought a moment, rubbed his face, and nodded.

"It would have been risky, but yeah . . . Anyway I'm wondering where Dorie is and I glance at my watch. It's been less than five minutes since I called her. Then I wonder who's pounding on the door. Finally, I put two and two together and realize she's probably the one who's knocking.

"So I rush down to the main entrance and push it open. There she is in running shorts and a sweatshirt, soaking wet from the rain, shivering and breathing heavily. She pushes me aside and rushes to the door of her office. I follow. She's trembling so much, she can't unlock the door. I take the key from her and open it . . ."

"You gotta realize, Bishop Blackie, she's totally gorgeous, absolutely delectable. I'm so shook-up, I don't even notice. She can't open the safe where the keys are stored. What's the combination I ask. She tells me and I open it. She grabs the key and runs down the hall to Brother Semyon's office. She's not trembling so badly that she can't put the key into the lock this time. She turns it and we hear the click. She turns the handle, but the door doesn't open."

"His dead-bolt lock," I say.

"We can break the window down here. I point to the pane which should be closest to the dead bolt. The windows as you can see are an intricate gothic frame with lots of little panes of glass.

55

She is still breathing so heavily and shivering so hard that she can't talk. She just nods. I rush in my office, pick up a big paperweight, and dash back and smash the windowpane. There's still a lot of shreds of glass in the pane, I knock each one out and put my hand through the opening. Careful, she says like a mother with a reckless little kid. I slide back the dead bolt, the door pops open, and we all look inside.

"Patrice screams, my stomach turns, dear God, says Doug, beside me, Israel sways, Dori sobs in horror, I put my arm around her, and she leans against me.

"Call the police, Dave, she says. Campus and CPD.

"I call my dad first, tell him what's happened, and ask that he call out his troops. He tells me later that I sounded like I was fully in charge. Anyway. He calls them. Then I mess around with the campus directory and finally find the listing for the University police. I punch it in.

"Dave Dolan in the Div School, I say. Terrible murder here. Send someone over. Since they're University police, they want to play the University game. They want to know who I am, what floor, who the victim is, the whole story, all the details. I tell them to come over now and see for themselves."

He drew a deep breath.

"Sorry, if I got caught up in it, Bishop. Talking about it brings the whole thing back."

"Understandably."

I conclude that this young son of a cop with a Ph.D. in papal history from Mother Harvard has his head screwed on properly and that Dean Keane would be well advised to join forces with him ASAP.

"My four colleagues are still standing at the door of Brother Semyon's office, shocked, silent, horrified. None of them has vomited yet, though they look like they want to. I sure do. The love of my life is leaning against the doorjamb and battling tears with an inadequate tissue. She's shivering too. I take off my jacket—this one—

and wrap it around her shoulders. She leans against me, so I put an arm around her too.

"The cops are coming, I tell her. She nods and says thank you. Is he really dead? Patrice asks. Have they really killed him?

"I wonder how she can ask when she sees all the blood and bones and brain pieces scattered around the office. The force of the blast has driven the poor man over the desk, so he dangles near the floor. I'd say headfirst except he doesn't have a head anymore.

"They blew his head off, Patrice, I reply to her. Double-barreled shotgun blast, Doug Strong tells us. Probably sawed-off.

"I don't see any gun, Dorie says in a little schoolgirl voice. Where is it? The killer took it with him, I say. How did he get out with the door locked? Israel wants to know. It dawns on me that this will be what the cops will want to know. Even if Brother Semyon had killed himself after he had locked the door to his office, what had he done with the gun. No one has figured that out yet, Bishop Blackie. Anyway, I think we finally persuaded the cops that we weren't making the story up."

"Indeed . . . Did you open the door to your office immediately after the blast next door?"

"In time to see if someone was trying to escape down the corridor? Cops kept asking me that. The honest answer is that I don't know. I was half-asleep, as I told you, enjoying respectfully lascivious dreams about herself . . . I think my reactions were slow. I was temporarily deafened by the explosion. I might not have heard anyone rushing out of the building. I wasn't looking either. Just trying to get into Semyon's office. Or like you say, perhaps someone was hiding in one of the washrooms. I don't know . . ."

"You said you observed a flash of light?"

"I thought I did. I don't know how I could have seen a light through the wall. Maybe it was lightning from outside."

"It might have been a long time then before you suspected that it wasn't the storm but something else that had rocked Swift Hall."

"No more than a minute or two. I wasn't worried about anyone except Dorie, though I knew she'd gone back to her apartment on Fifty-fifth Street. Maybe she'd returned."

"I see . . ."

"Then the cops arrived. Dorie had gone back to her office to call the president of the University. Typically they shouted that someone should open the fucking door. I did. The first cop in, a red-faced, obnoxious Irishman began with their stereotypical first line. What the fuck is going on here? There were eight of them, four Chicago cops and four University cops, the former, of course, shoving the latter out of their way, almost like they were sheriff's police or some other kind of lowlife. For the next several minutes they didn't utter a single sentence without at least one word of obscenity. You know how cops are, Bishop, they don't mean anything by it."

"Neither do the Irish."

"Yeah, we probably infected the rest of the police forces. Anyway, Dorie tries to take charge. She introduces herself as the dean of the Divinity School, which cuts no ice with Chicago's finest, especially since she's wearing wet running clothes, which are pasted against her skin and an oversize seersucker jacket. Her attempts to respond to the question of what the fuck was going on around here somehow didn't make much of an impression, especially since they keep asking her whether she's a student."

"So you took charge?"

"Well, what else? I shout, listen up you fucking assholes. This woman is Dr. Dorina Keane. She's the dean of the Divinity School, which occupies this building. She was not here when the killing occurred. She ran over in the rain to get a key to open the door where the crime occurred. Now show a little respect or, cop or not, I'll bust a few front teeth. I went on for a while, just the way I'm sure my old man would talk. The cops shut up for a few seconds. Then a big, good-looking black guy who came in while I was shouting elbowed his way up to me. I'm Captain Flip White, he says. You've gotta be Davy Dolan, Pete's son. You cuss just like him. When in Rome, I says."

This tale would be told over and over again for the benefit

eventually of children and grandchildren. Nothing would be lost in the telling.

"I introduce him to Dean Keane. They are perfectly polite to one another, herself acting like she was at least a grand duchess. He tells her that she was very brave to run through the thunderstorm and asks whether Professor Dolan uses such language all the time around the Divinity School. She tells him that I certainly do, which is a lie, but Flip knows it's a joke. She introduces him to the three other faculty members. He is courteous to them. They say that they heard the explosion and came running down from their offices on the third floor. He asks them if they'd mind talking to Sergeant Gonzalez for a few minutes, then they can go home if they want. He adds that he assumes none of them is planning a long trip for the next couple of days and assures them that they are witnesses not suspects.

"Then we take him to the actual crime scene. Already a cop has tied one of those yellow ribbons around the doorway. Flip looks in and gasps. Who is the poor man? We tell him that is Brother Semyon Ivanivich Popov, a Russian Orthodox monk who is a visiting professor. He whistles softly. Then he wants to know about the broken window on the door. I explain that I broke it because it was the only way we could open the dead-bolt lock. He says he thought that Dean Keane had found the key to open the door. The regular lock, she says, not the special dead bolt that Brother Semyon requested. He thinks about it carefully. So the perpetrator would have to lock the dead bolt after he left the office? But how could he do that? And bring the gun with him, I add."

"He saw the point early," I said.

"Yeah, he got the idea, but he couldn't believe it. He lifted the yellow ribbon and went over to the windows. Locked, he says, this is impossible. It is impossible, isn't it, Bishop Blackie?"

I was pretty sure I knew how the trick had been worked, though I didn't know why or by whom. However, this was not the time to advance a solution.

"Arguably."

Andrew M. Greeley

"So the cops are deputed to do what they do at homicide scenes. Various technicians are called in. All the regular crime scene investigation. We walk by this office with its door open. Whose office is this, he demands sternly. I admit that it's mine and tell him my story. I don't mention that I'm imagining various advanced marital amusements with the dean when the explosion occurs.

"Hmm . . . Pretty messy office, Davy. Your mother wouldn't approve. When I marry, I tell him, I'll have to return to the habits Mom taught me. I don't look at Dorie. He ponders and says, you won't mind if we poke around your office, will you? The dean tells him that they will find lots of my fingerprints in Brother Semyon's office and his in mine, because we had the habit of violating University regulations in the late afternoon by drinking vodka in one another's office. He wonders why that information doesn't surprise him. I remind her that for the last couple of weeks, the beginning of the quarter, the custom had kind of lapsed. Why, he asks me. I tell him that Brother Semyon was working on some important documents and I was putting the finishing touches on a couple of articles for tenure review, so we were both busy. We drift down towards her office, which is in the northeast corner of the first floor.

"Will he get tenure? he asks the dean. He deserves it, she says candidly, more than I did, more than most of us did. Some people are put off by his South Side Irish personality, but they'll probably vote for him.

"That's as close to an endorsement as I've yet heard.

"Just then the phone rings. It's President Reed Alan, obviously upset and worried. Dorie succinctly summarizes what happened. From the expression on her face, it is clear that he is not reassured. Will we be able to open tomorrow morning? She asks Flip. Right now I don't see any reason why not. We'll have to close off this corridor. We'll also want to fingerprint the washrooms, not that we'll find anything there.

"She relays this to the president. He asks a lot more questions to which she gives straight answers. Professor Dolan was in his office and heard the explosion. He called me and I ran over. Professor Dolan a suspect? She laughs. He doesn't kill flies. To the last one she says, I have no idea who the perpetrator is. Finally, she says, thank you, Reed, and hangs up. Then she says, I didn't tell him, Captain White, but I think we're at a dead end, like in the last case. He says he hopes not

"Then he reviews all we know about Brother Semyon. Yes, he was a little strange. No, he seemed to have no real enemies, though some people disliked him because of his robes and his monk's staff and his somewhat noisy style. Academics don't kill one another for those reasons. He was tough on students but also generous to them. We probably would not have renewed the appointment and would certainly not have offered him a permanent appointment because there were not enough students interested in his field. But we might have. Then we go over my story again about the explosion. In other words, Captain White says at the end of it, there was no time when one or the other of you were not at the door of the crime scene? Right? And no one went into the room? Correct. So then he tells us we can go home. It's still raining, so I say I'll go over to the Midway, where I'm parked, and come back and pick her up. She hesitates and then agrees. She's got this thing about not wanting any special favors because she's a woman. So I drive her around the corner to Ellis and suggest maybe I should take her home to my parents' house and put her up in my married sister's bedroom. This is not a come-on because she's stayed there before for one reason or another. She and my mother have bonded already, which bodes ill for me after we're married. It doesn't increase my fantasies any that she's in the house. But she says, no, it was nice of me to make the offer, but she'd better return to the apartment and prepare her clothes for the next day. A good thing she does because when I sneak in through the back door—the Bond Chapel one—the next morning, every reporter in Chicago is gathered in front of Swift. Also, the president, the P.R. vice president, most of our faculty, scores of other faculty, a mob of students, and the light of my life in the same black dress she's wearing today. Naturally she's the bright spot on television. It develops that she was officer of the deck last night. Some idiot reporter asks her if she has any idea who might have killed Brother Semyon Ivanivich Popov. She answers that he was a dear sweet man and that we would all miss him. Classy answer, I thought. But then I'm prejudiced."

"And she offered you no personal thanks for your stalwart help the night before?"

"Yeah, she did. After the press conference broke up, she put her head in the door and thanked me. She didn't use the word 'stalwart' though. I do recall she might have said wonderful."

"Generous," I commented.

His account had been clear and detailed. There had been only one patent lacuna in it, one of which he was probably not aware because it had seemed so small. Nonetheless it was critical.

"Dorina's real problem," he continued, "is whether she can reconcile the mask of a proper woman academic and her exuberant South Boston personality. Hell, when she relaxes and sings and dances with my family, she fits in better than I do. If I lose her, they'll never forgive me."

"Ah," I said. There was also the problem that, despite his attractiveness, David Dolan was a commanding masculine presence, made all the more frightening for a woman because the presence was combined with sensitivity and respect. Yet a woman, particularly a thoughtful and perceptive woman, could be terrified at the prospect of living with and sleeping with a man like that for the rest of her life. He was an appealing and scary fellow, perhaps just a little too irresistible. The valiant Dorina would have to decide for herself.

"Also," he added, "I think the Boston Irish feel inferior, a majority with the attitude of a minority. So this place intimidates her. We South Side Irish don't feel inferior to anyone. We're a minority with the attitude of a majority. So neither Harvard nor this place intimidates us. Know what I mean?"

"I presume you have not shared this insight with the subject of your affection."

"Not yet . . . ," he admitted.

The subject of his desire at that moment appeared at the door of his office. His eyes lighted up with joy.

"Keen Dean," he said. "You've come to make me go back to work just when the good bishop and I are resolving the mystery of Southies from Boston and the South Siders from Chicago."

She made a wry face. "That's not a mystery at all. We have an inferiority complex and you have a superiority complex . . . Whenever you're ready, Bishop Blackie, Israel Golden would like to take a walk with you. He thinks an Indian Summer day in Chicago is too good to waste sitting in a dusty office."

"This tragic event will not, I trust, have a negative impact on David's quest for academic immortality?" I asked her as we climbed up the stairs to Rabbi Golden's office.

"On the contrary, the story of how he dealt with the police last night has already become a legend, even a myth. It has finally dawned on some of them, that David has certain impressive leadership qualities."

"Patently."

5

"I did not like the man," Rabbi Golden said, as we began to circum-
navigate the central quadrangle. "The Orthodox Church has always
been the enemy of my people, unlike your church, which for a thousand years did us no harm, though most of my fellow Jews don't know
this. The Orthodox have always hated us."

"Though Catherine the Great found room for both you and the
Jesuits in her empire."

He laughed, suspecting perhaps that he would be able to indulge
in a good talmudic-like argument with me.

"Whatever her moral problems, the woman was not a fool."

"Our Teresa of Avila once said she would rather have a learned
confessor than a holy one."

"Same insight . . . Anyway, I voted against the man. I argued that
we ought not to let our passion for multiculturalism lead us to make
appointments of scholars whose field provided little appeal to our
potential students. So this good Protestant school brings in Catholics
and Jews, and Moslems and Hindus, so fine. But now are we to have
animists and those who believe in human sacrifice and a student of
the Old Believers?"

"Who were, as we know, virulently anti-Semitic?"

He shrugged his shoulders, a gesture he repeated far more often than David Dolan. David's signified "What the hell!" Israel Golden's meant "What can I tell you?"

"They were Russian peasants, what else would they be? This man was not a peasant, though I have often suspected he might be a Cossack, which would be even worse because they had horses and sabers. However, I would like to think that it was not worth raising that issue because his scholarship, while doubtless of high quality, was not the sort in which there was a notable reason for this Divinity School to display interest. I still think so. I suspect that many of my colleagues now would be more likely to have voted the same way and would have done so if the question of reappointment or even a lifetime appointment had come up. A university has just so many lifetime appoints that it can make and it must be cautious in the way it uses them. This University, because it lacks the resources of other universities of comparable quality, must be even more careful. We must be sure that our appointments are sound."

It sounded like the argument that had been used against admitting me as a student. Essentially it was a very conservative argument. We must not waste our precious lifetime appointments (a rarely heard description of tenure) on fads and fashions and on risks and enthusiasm. Sounded like a strategy for desiccation and eventual death. Yet it suited the atmosphere of the Quadrangle Club dining room perfectly.

Moreover, who was to say what a sound appointment is? Paul Tillich? Mircea Eliade? Ives Simon? Jacques Maritan? Saul Bellow?

Nonsense!

"We take no risks, for example, when we offer such an appointment to a young man like David Dolan. He is obviously brilliant, exuberant perhaps and often outrageous, but he is, after all, Irish, is he not?"

"So I am told."

"That young woman must come to her senses and marry him. That way we will have two first-rate and young people indefinitely. They are also pleasant colleagues."

"You let a couple of Irish in," I said, unable to resist the temptation, "and pretty soon the whole neighborhood goes."

He laughed so loudly that it must have been the first time he heard the dictum.

"You see my point, however, Bishop Ryan. In this city young men and women will flock to their courses. They will establish a whole new Chicago school of religious historiography and their students will also bring us much distinction. I failed to see and still fail to see how Brother Semyon would have accomplished such things."

"Ah."

We turned north on University Avenue, walking by the Reynolds Club, where students ate, and across Fifty-seventh Street and the Regenstein Library, which did not fit into the gothic character of the environment but was nonetheless a striking place.

"I must also confess that I personally did not like the man. He had picked up a considerable amount of Yiddish, which as you know is essentially a Germanic language with Hebrew letters, just like Ladino which is a romance language with Arabic letters. So he would talk to me in Yiddish, gratuitously assuming that I could understand it, which of course I can. Nonetheless, I asked him to speak to me in English, which he did but without much grace."

"Indeed."

"Then I found his bumptious disposition annoying. He was, I thought, playing to a stereotypical Russian image. I know many distinguished Russian scholars who find that unnecessary. Admittedly they are loud people, like the Irish, but they should when they come to other cultures, adjust to those cultures. The monastic robes, the crucifix around his neck, the staff which he pounded often on the floor, mostly I believe, for effect, his stentorian tones—all of this was intended to say to us that he was Russian and would we please notice that fact. I found it tasteless and unpleasant."

It was perhaps wise of me not to have brought along my own crosier, which the good Catherine Collins Curran had carved to resemble an Irish high cross.

Andrew M. Greeley

"All of this is a rather long prologue to my saying that I mourn his death. No one of us deserves to die. No one deserves a violent death. May the Most High One protect us all."

"Amen," I agreed.

"I know our tradition well enough to know that we should believe in a World to Come. I believe that's where your tradition learned it and has chosen to use it more widely than we do. It is my hope that we will meet Brother Semyon in that World whenever and whatever it may be."

"Amen," I agreed again.

We were now walking down Ellis, where the monument to the beginning of the atomic age was in the squash court of the old Stagg Field. It is a somber and indeed frightening work.

"As for me, I was working in my office on a newly discovered manuscript of the Babylonian Talmud when the poor man was killed. There was, as you've doubtless heard, a terrible thunderstorm. At first I thought the explosion was the result of a flash of light hitting Swift Hall. I suppose I wasn't the only one to think it might be an act of divine vengeance. Then I thought that I had better go downstairs and see. I saw no one in the building. I heard nothing. My office is on the third floor. I encountered Mr. Sharp and Ms. Comerford on the second floor. Like me, they wondered what had happened. By then the smell of gunpowder was very strong. We came upon David and Dorina in front of Brother Semyon's office. As I have said, some of us did not like him, but no one in the Divinity School disliked him that much."

"Indeed."

"And what is your interest, Bishop Ryan, if I may ask?"

"Cardinal Cronin thinks I have some slight skills at solving mysteries, particularly of the locked-room variety. He thought I might be of some help."

"I don't think you will be able to solve it." He sighed and shrugged his shoulders. "Like the last murder in the school, there is no natural explanation for it."

"Supernatural?"

68

"We both believe in demons do we not?"

"In principle."

"I fear for the future of this institution to which I owe so much. We will be fortunate to survive this incident. I wish you good fortune in your search, but rites of exorcism might be more appropriate."

Inside Swift Hall, I noted that the door to David's office was open and the office empty. I thereupon walked around the corner to herself's door, which was also open. Neither looked too happy, but they had not, I thought, been quarreling.

"The funeral liturgy for Brother Semyon is tomorrow," Dorie began, "at the Holy Virgin Protection Cathedral on Lee Street in Des Plaines. The Russian Archbishop of North America will be there. We think we should go even if there will be an eventual memorial service here."

"It's dezplanes in Chicago, my love, not that phony French stuff. Trouble is I don't know where it is. Do you, Bishop?"

"You merely drive up the Kennedy expressway onto the Northwest Tollway and get off at Lee Street, which is the first stop after the toll booth. For a denizen of the South Side like you, Dave, it will be a liberating experience."

"What did you learn from Israel?" Dorie asked.

"He thinks we should turn an exorcist loose on Swift Hall!"

"Couldn't hurt." David agreed. "Solemn high? With the Cardinal here in his full crimson?"

"Before we take that step we should ask about the curious incident of Brother Semyon's staff, should we not?"

"There has been no incident about his staff!"

"That's what is curious."

6

―

"I suppose you've solved the locked-room puzzle." Milord Cronin leaned against the doorjamb, as was his wont when he was checking up on me. He was wearing perfectly pressed black trousers and a snow-white shirt, without a collar but with French cuffs, his usual fatigue uniform.

"Arguably." I sighed, clicking off my e-mail. "I know how it was done, but not why or by whom. Also I find persuasive the thesis that it is only a minor and perhaps accidental part of the larger mystery."

"That does not sound good," he said disapprovingly. "We need a solution!"

"Indeed."

"I'm going up to the funeral liturgy tomorrow in Des Plaines."

"Ah."

"The Russian Archbishop of North America is coming in for it, so I should show up even if our late friend was not a brother cardinal . . . Do you think he was?"

I pondered that possibility. Brother Semyon Ivanivich Popov may or may not have been a Cardinal Prince of the Roman Church. However, it seemed likely that the one to whom the crimson watered silk in the Windemere belonged was not the one killed in Swift Hall.

"Perhaps. However, even if he were not, your presence would do no great harm."

With most people that sort of endorsement would have gone unnoticed. Milord Cronin noted it, like he noted almost everything anyone said. No premature Alzheimer's in that brain.

"Well, I called them out there and asked if it would be appropriate for me to come. They seemed delighted."

"What choice would they have? This is Chicago."

"Their funeral services are long, aren't they?"

"All Russian liturgy is long. Our people would not tolerate it. They will sing many hymns, all sounding to our untrained ears like choruses from *Boris Gudonov*. Moreover, the Chicago Cardinal must not be seen napping by the Orthodox faithful."

"Yeah, but I'm pretty good at napping while I seem to be wide awake."

"I have noticed that on occasion."

"By the way," he said, turning to leave, "your friend from the Outfit called. The Megan thought him sufficiently mysterious to refer him to me."

We have four teenage porter persons, all named Megan, who act as gatekeepers at the Cathedral Rectory after school, Asian American, African-American, Latina, and, of course, Irish. During their hours of duty they run the parish for all practical and many impractical purposes.

I had never told Milord Cronin that I had a contact out on the West Side (actually in River Forest, but "West Side" in that context referred not to geography but to "connections") but he had guessed the first time he heard the man's slimy voice on his phone what his role was.

"He said what you would expect. Tell the bishop that a friend of some friends of his called."

"Ah."

When the Cardinal Prince had swept away from my office, I punched in the number of my friend.

"Blackie," I said.

"Oh, yeah . . . Hey, those kids shouldn't have bothered the cardinal, he's a busy man."

"Arguably."

"So I'm calling about that incident out at *The* University."

"Indeed."

"Yeah, it turns out that the friends of my friends, the big guys, if you get what I mean, are very upset about it. You don't whack a priest in Chicago without asking them for permission, know what I mean?"

"They are, after all, good Catholics."

"Yeah, well they find out that it was a Russian contract."

"That does not surprise me."

"Well, you know what they think of the Russians?"

"I can well imagine."

"I mean these friends tell me that their friends don't like these foreigners muscling their way into our territory, know what I mean?"

I admitted that they did. I wondered, however, whether the aging dons had the stamina and the decisiveness to repel the invasion of the Russian outfit. They had not contested the drug turf with the Latino outfit, perhaps because they extracted their take at a higher level.

"Well, they're going to put down the party responsible. Use the same method, know what I mean?"

"Blow off his head with a shotgun?"

I sat up straight in my chair.

"That would not be a good thing to do," I said.

"The contract is out."

"Is it a local guy?"

"Yeah, them foreigners don't have enough sense to call in a hit from out of town . . . I thought you'd want to know."

I did not want to know. The dons, for reason of their own, had decided to tip off the Church that they were about to put down the Russian mobster who had killed Brother Semyon. Not living in medieval Sicily (which still exists) I could not tolerate such a crime. I rushed down to the lobby of the rectory and on the public phone (installed by one of my predecessors) called the Reilly Gallery. Mike answered the phone.

"Mike, call me from the public phone outside the gallery. Urgent."

Fortunately for me, he remembered the number of the lobby phone from previous use of it as an inexpensive safe line.

"What's up?"

"Would you call our good friend Flip White. Tell him I've heard on the street that the big boys have put out a contract on the Russian thug who killed Brother Semyon."

"I don't think we can prevent it. Is he local?"

"I assume so."

"Maybe some of our guys have a line on him. Tied up with the Russkie outfit?"

"The boys think so."

"I'll see what we can do. We're all afraid of a gang war between the boys and the Russkies. St. Valentine's massacre only a lot worse . . . I better call Flip now."

The porter person's room was filled with a couple of Megans, Crystal Lane in sweats, and a couple of similarly clad male louts. Teen club smelling of sweat in the Cathedral Rectory. Worse places for them to hang out.

"Are we making too much noise, Bishop?" a lout named Justin asked politely.

"Did not the Lord say that we should suffer the little children?"

Derisive laughter.

Crystal would not permit the noise to go beyond what she deemed acceptable limits. Fastidious parishioners who didn't like it could complain, as they often did about many things, to Milord Cronin, who would listen sympathetically as he always did, then ignore them, especially when the complaints were aimed at Crystal, under whose spell he had also fallen.

On the way up the elevator to my rooms I wondered how the Boys had figured out who the hit man was. Less and less did I like this puzzle.

I returned to my e-mail. More had piled up since I had left the

machine. I immediately eliminated half of it—downloads from people
I did not know, pornography, get-rich-quick schemes, promised solu-
tions to my financial problems, and calls for repentance from well-
meaning evangelicals. Some of the others were idiot questions about
whether it was still permitted to call an archbishop "Your Grace" as
well as "Your Excellency," about problems with divorce and remarriage
(many caused by ignorant and insensitive priests). There were also complaints, doubtless true, about what their pastor (RCIA director, director
of religious education, parish secretary) had done or said. Finally, there
were issues of acute human suffering that needed priestly compassion.

This daily avalanche served me right for printing my e-mail address in the weekly Cathedral bulletin (frblackie @aol.com).

I turned off the computer firmly, poured myself a touch of
Bushmills Green, and settled back to reflect on the events of the day.

The puzzle was a twisted and kinky one. It seemed certain to me
that someone within the faculty of the Divinity School had cooper-
ated in the shotgun attack on the putative Brother Semyon and thus
made possible the locked-room conundrum. However, I had no explanation for the difference in the height of the victim and the man to
whom the crimson watered silk might have belonged. How difficult
might it have been to substitute another monk or would-be monk in
the divinity school? Did all bearded Russians in monkish gowns look
alike? The semester at Chicago began in October, this very week indeed. Had the presumed Brother Semyon met with any students? Or
was this a quarter during which he wasn't scheduled to teach?

I made a note to ask that question discreetly.

Moreover, he had apparently given up his afternoon "glass
vodka" with the peerless David Dolan. Had he curtailed his interaction with other faculty colleagues?

Even if such behavior suggested he was a secret replacement for
Brother Semyon, who had staged the replacement? Why? Did those
responsible for the killing know they had the wrong man, if indeed
he was a wrong man? If the man killed were not Brother Semyon,
was the latter still alive? Where?

There were no available answers to any of these questions. Nor was there any reason to think that I might be able to find answers. The forces at work behind the scenes were hiding behind many cloaks of invisibility.

Nonetheless, one could substitute a man who looked like Brother Semyon—or who was made up to look like him—under certain circumstances. One would have needed an actor or a person who had some acting skills. One would have needed a chance to observe up close for some period of time. One would need a helper on the faculty with whom the bogus Brother Semyon could consult. It was possible to meet all of these requirements in Paris during the summer or so I thought. But why bother?

Most likely the late and lamented surrogate for Brother Semyon was to be present for a brief period of time while he searched the real Semyon's files for some document or documents that were of great value. Had someone shot him to protect the documents? Or perhaps someone else, assuming that the surrogate was the real Brother Semyon, had shot him to prevent the release of this document?

What could a Russian monk, specialist in the Mysticism of the Old Believers, possess that would stir up such furies?

Then there was the mystery of his staff, which I had dumped into the laps of the slightly star-crossed lovers before Mr. Woods bore me away from the crime scene. Had the real Brother Semyon, assuming that it was not his body at the funeral liturgy on the morrow, taken the staff with him as a sign that he was still alive?

And, finally, what about the lacuna in the testimony of David Dolan? Was he protecting someone? Or, more likely, had he forgotten the small detail that was so important?

Finally, had the friends on the West Side put out a contract on the one they thought had killed Brother Semyon for the reasons implied—to teach the Russian outfit some respect? Or were they involved in a deeper way? And why had they wanted to assure me that they were good Catholics? That seemed gratuitous. Perhaps it was the proverbial red, white, and green herring. I was innocent of answers.

Moreover, it was not true, as in so many other cases, that the answers lurked behind the closed door in my memory and when the door opened I would have an explanation.

Nor were there any more deep sources I could phone. I would perhaps try on the morrow to contact again my friend inside the Beltway.

Then there was a call from Northwestern Hospital. The Megan wouldn't have sent it up to me on that day unless the other two priests on the staff were not available, arguably at the hospital themselves.

So I collected the materials for the various sacraments, dashed over to the hospital—in what for me passes as a dash—and received back into the Church on his deathbed a man who had "fallen away" for forty years because a priest told him he was living in sin with his wife. In fact, there had not been then and there was not now any obstacle to a Catholic marriage. So I aided them in administering that sacrament to one another also. As to the priest who had given them misinformation, I charitably said, "I'm afraid Father was mistaken."

I did not say, lest I offend pious ears, that Father was an asshole.

I promised that someone would stop by in the morning with the Eucharist, for the second time in forty years.

I didn't think he'd last that long, but I would come myself, so reassuring was the joy in the room. Priests need to experience that joy occasionally. Nor did I suggest that the Lord give the guilty priest a good kick in the appropriate place. I contented myself with piously asking for his illumination.

At supper that night, Milord Cronin reported that he had received complaints from two elderly parishioners about the noise teenagers were making in the rectory offices. They also objected to the sweaty smell of teenage bodies.

"Naturally I sympathized with them and expressed my dismay. Then I personally went down to the offices and detected no trace of the smell of teenage sweat."

"Crystal sprays disinfectant after they're gone," one of the young priests remarked.

"I should hope so," Milord remarked.

As I say, Crystal could do no wrong in the Archdiocese of Chicago.

After supper I called the priest who teaches mystical theology at the seminary.

"Fritz," I said, "what do you know about this late and lamented Brother Semyon?"

"I know that I'm going to the liturgy tomorrow."

"There will be one more priest there tomorrow, one in crimson watered silk."

"Sean's coming? Hey, that's cool! He'll steal the show!"

"That thought may not have escaped him . . . Anyway, tell me about Brother Semyon."

"He kind of emerged from nowhere when Gorby took over. Apparently he had been teaching in a seminary out in the Ural Mountains. As soon as it was safe to be Orthodox, they transferred him to Zagorsk. He began to publish his previous work in French, then set about doing more work, which most of the reviewers think is pretty good. We had him out here for a lecture. No one knew what he was talking about, but he charmed the faculty."

"And what is he talking about?"

"He's something of a disciple of his namesake St. Semyon the New Theologian, a man with whose work I am sure you are familiar."

This was a deliberate ploy to trip up the poor little auxiliary.

"Apophactic stuff, kind of like Eckhart, huh?"

I am very rarely tripped up in the game. Fortunately, I had heard the word earlier in the day from Dean Keane.

"Yeah. All you can say about God is that there's nothing you can say, so you say what He's not."

"Which is saying something, isn't it?"

"Those guys usually go beyond that. Eckhart's void, as Father Tracy says, is a benign void. And St. Semyon back in the tenth century described the light about which you could say nothing in glowing terms, which emphasized its sweetness. But that wouldn't mean much to an empiricist like you, would it, Blackie?"

You lose again, Fritz.

"Yet in my book on Willy James, did not I assert that you could not say anything about the ineffable and yet you had to say everything. Witness your very good friend John of the Cross!"

"You win again," he acknowledged with a laugh.

"So he's authentic . . . In his pictures he reminds me a bit of Grigori Yefimovich Rasputin."

"Rasputin has been dead since 1916!"

"So it is said."

"He was no Raputin, Blackie. He was a big, tall, teddy bear with a white beard and a great laugh. A Russian Santa Claus."

"As tall as Sean Cronin?"

"At least."

After we had exchanged recent clerical gossip, I pondered what I had learned. The answer was nothing, except what the word "Apophactic" meant.

The man whose head was blown off was patently not as tall as Brother Semyon. Yet perhaps the Russian monkish hood created the impress of greater height. However, the crimson robes at the Windemere would have fit Milord Cronin quite well.

I needed more information about what Brother Semyon had done before he showed up at Zagorsk. Where would I get that?

Still, somehow, I suspected that part of the answer could still be found at Swift Hall. There was no logical reason to expect that. Just gut instinct.

I returned to the computer to deal with the late e-mail traffic and to update my program for the Cathedral schedule, a user-friendly, totally transparent bit of software which all other members of the staff claimed they could not understand. Even Crystal.

The next morning, after breakfast, I returned to Northwestern to find that my penitent of the night before was now out of danger and that they gave me full credit for it.

I then returned to place a call to my contact inside the Beltway.

"What are you guys trying to pull on us?" I demanded. "Why didn't you tell me that the guy whose head was blown off was not Brother Semyon?"

Dead silence on the other end of the line.

A gotcha!

"Who told you that?" he whispered, his cultivated East Coast Protestant voice unsteady.

"Anyone could see that he was three, maybe four inches shorter than Semyon Ivanivich Popov. And you should have made him leave his staff behind."

More silence.

Second gotcha.

"I can't make any comment, Blackie. You shouldn't mess with this kind of stuff. It could be dangerous."

"Look, we're burying the replacement up at the Holy Virgin Protection Cathedral this morning. Sean Cardinal Cronin is on his way up there. The Outfit has put out a contract on the killer. I presume it's one of yours . . ."

"No, it's not!"

Third gotcha. Maybe.

"Well, it's probably gone down by now. The Boys were very upset, as you might imagine. You may have started a gang war here between the Italian Mafia and the Russian Mafia by these comic tricks."

"I won't discuss it anymore," he said, and hung up.

I felt a certain satisfaction. I had made my normally ice-cold contact panic. I had almost certainly created a nest of hornets that would buzz through the so-called American intelligence community all morning. There would be hell to pay. I had confirmed my suspicions: the crime victim was not Brother Semyon. Who he was and why he was there remained unclear, but my friends in Washington were involved in his replacement of Brother Semyon. Whether he was one of them and had died a hero or someone they were trying to set up or someone who had been inserted without their knowledge remained mysterious.

If the Feds had terminated him with extreme prejudice, I would probably never learn unless one of them came in from the cold and went public. It might well be I ought not go any further. The actual killer was already dead or soon would be. Brother Semyon might well still be alive but imprisoned at a "safe house" as they would argue for his own good. The Chicago police would retire the folder to the file cabinet of unsolved but still technically active cases. The University would try to spin the second Divinity School murder out of donors' memories. The Div School itself would struggle on, hoping that the event would be forgotten, save perhaps for those of its staff who had seen the actual body.

If the dead man were actually a federal agent, then the Feds would try to eliminate those who killed him. Perhaps they had put out the contract to the friends on the West Side to take care of the hit on the hit man. These arcane and subterranean affairs would be protected by layers and layers of what they like to call deniability.

What could a virtually invisible auxiliary bishop do to penetrate through the murk? And what if he found out the truth? What then?

What then indeed?

The first thing to do was to contact Mike the Cop on our "safe" line.

"I don't know whether you had a chance to look at the morning papers, but there's a small item about the body of an illegal Russian immigrant found by the Des Plaines police in a bunch of weeds up on Lee Street, a couple of blocks from the Holy Virgin Protection Cathedral, with his head blown off. Same OP as out at Swift Hall. Your good friend Flip White is pretty sure it's the same shotgun."

"They know he's Russian because of an ID in his pocket?"

"Right. They're trying to find out more about him. Want to bet that they don't?"

"Not hardly . . . Can the admirable Captain White confirm his suspicions about the shotgun?"

"No."

"Nor link him certainly to the Russian outfit?"

"No . . . But it's a tidy solution for him."

"Except for the crimson robes down at the Windemere."

"He didn't mention them."

"I see . . . This is for your ears only. Our Feds are involved in it. I don't know how or why, but they are."

"Sounds bad."

"Moreover, certain threats were made."

"Against you?"

"Arguably."

"I'll put a double guard on you, twenty-four/seven. No guarantees. Better that you back off."

"I just might," I said.

"Bishop Blackie," Crystal Lake, murmured reassuringly. "Don't look so grim. There's nothing to worry about."

She had walked in the door while I was talking on the phone. As usual she radiated goodness, joy, and peace.

"In general or in reference to my present grim expression?"

She paused to consider.

"Both, I'm sure."

"The Cardinal thinks it's prudent of you to fumigate the office after you get rid of the teens."

She smiled happily.

"I thought it was a good idea too."

It was absurd on the face of it that the Almighty, obviously busy in keeping the Big Bang going in our Cosmos and He alone knew in how many others, would bother communicating directly with me through our local mystic in residence.

On the other hand, there is no accounting for God's oddities.

Back in my office, I decided that I would at least probe a little further. I wrote up an account of the case so far, sealed it in an envelope, and addressed it to Sean Cardinal Cronin. I named some names.

It was another typical day at our understaffed rectory—hospitals,

counseling, marriage preparation, phone calls, anonymous mail complaints and denunciations, salvaging of marriages, arranging annul-
ments, listening to people with doubts, welcoming back in returners,
sympathizing with those who thought they had lost their faith, apol-
ogizing to those who had suffered from the idiocy of a priest or nun
a long time ago, reassuring parents who were worried about their
obstreperous teens or fallen-away young adults. Nothing very new or
exciting, just the agonies of the human condition.

I was catching up on the e-mail when Milord Cronin returned,
dressed now in a flawlessly fitting suit with the slightest edge of
crimson where his Roman collar met his clerical vest. He collapsed
on the same vacant space on my couch that he had cleared a few days
before.

"Even though they permit a married clergy," he informed me
with a monumental yawn, "I do not have a vocation to the Orthodox
priesthood."

"Only celibate monks, however, are admitted to the episcopacy."

"Despite your perennial argument that bishops should be com-
pelled to marry . . ."

"It would teach them humility and sensitivity."

"Arguably." He yawned again. "Three and a half hours, Blackwood. All the hymns sound the same . . ."

"I sometimes think that of the Mexican hymns."

"They're all singable after you hear the first stanza. The Russians
seem to be shouting at God. Over and over again, as if to remind
him of something."

"Or perhaps to wake Him up."

"I hope heaven isn't like that."

"You've been at Orthodox liturgy before."

"I forgot . . . Then this business of hiding behind that
screen . . ."

"Properly called the iconastisis."

"Well, what we do must seem equally silly to them—fast-food
liturgy."

83

"And deplorably lacking in mystery . . . You spoke with their archbishop?"

"Yeah, he speaks with a New Jersey accent. He told me what a wonderful scholar the deceased was. True?"

"If it really were Brother Semyon."

"It might not have been?"

I shrugged, "Arguably not."

"Now he tells me . . . Oh I met your friend up there."

I knew whom he meant, but I was not about to play his game. "Ah."

"I don't know what your secret is, Blackwood, but beautiful women seem to dote on you."

"Virtue."

"This dean of yours told me that you were sweet."

"Patently."

"She's from Boston, I gather."

"South Boston."

"And that great big Irish gorilla who follows her around like a sheepdog, is he some kind of professor?"

"In addition to being an agent of the Irish Republican Army."

He dismissed that absurdity with a faint grin.

"They'll let anyone into the faculty these days, won't they? Where's he from?"

"Most Holy Redeemer," I said, identifying David Dolan's origins by his parish as we Chicagoans must.

"*Our* Most Holy Redeemer?"

"Indeed. He lives there with his mother and father, the latter of whom is a retired cop."

"I didn't know we produced any intellectuals out there."

"The world is changing."

"Yeah." He yawned again and rose from the couch. "I think I need to rest my eyes."

For a moment I thought of giving him the sealed envelope.

"Praiseworthy behavior."

If I had given him the envelope then, it would have interfered with the necessary rest for his eyes. Later in the day, I would have reason to wonder about that decision.

A Megan buzzed me.

"This real nice woman named Dorie called to say that you're supposed to have lunch with the president of the university tomorrow at noon and that she has set up appointments for you after lunch."

The Megan had relayed this information in a tone of voice that implied that the matter was settled and I'd better conform to the wishes of this "real nice woman named Dorie."

"You think I'd better go out there, Megan?"

"Like totally," she replied, incensed that I would even think of not following the instructions of the dean.

"OK," I said. "Then I'd better."

"Hey, Bishop Blackie, Crystal wants to talk to you."

"As I said this morning, Bishop Blackie, don't worry."

I discovered that I was very worried. I had not the time during the day to worry.

"I'm glad to hear that, Crystal."

"Come on," I said to the Deity. "She's really not delivering messages for you, is she? With all the stupidity, arrogance, incompetence, malice, idiocy, and madness in the world, how can one not worry?"

There was more office work after supper, including with a couple, both Catholic with sixteen years of Catholic education, who had been living together for two years and thought that maybe it was now time to marry, but unsure what the point was in a church wedding unless to please their respective parents. They were both Catholics, of course, but they didn't like the institutional Church because of its dishonesty.

"Tell me about it," I said and went into a long discussion of all that was wrong with the Church in which I attributed the fault to Jesus himself, who had turned it over to humans instead of the seraphim.

They found themselves defending the Church against an attack by one of its bishops. Only after several minutes of this dialogue did they realize what I had done and begun to laugh. However, we kept on arguing. Finally, they insisted that I pencil in a wedding date and promised to come back for more "dialogue."

It had been a fun discussion. They were both smart young people, unaware that I had perfected my technique for responding to them by scores of previous similar conversations. They want you to argue them back in and you respond by creating the illusion that you want to persuade them to stay out. You lose, of course.

I returned to my rooms, said some prayers, checked the late-night e-mail, and decided that it was time for bed. I eschewed my late-evening splasheen of the Creature on the grounds that I was already sleepy enough.

I glanced out of the window on Wabash Avenue, quiet and almost empty at this time of the night since the "action" had moved north to Division and Rush and the environs.

I hesitated. Were Mike's people outside? I couldn't see them, but that was the general idea. An idea flitted across my mind, then slipped away. It was a silly idea, but what was it? I reached back into the sub-basements of my memory and found it again.

Maybe I should not sleep in my usual bed tonight. Maybe I should leave the lights on in both my rooms and withdraw to one of the empty rooms down the corridor.

Why?

Why not?

That is not the issue.

I gathered the materials necessary for sleep, slipped down the corridor, and into an empty suite (used in the days before the priest shortage when the Cathedral Rectory was a hotel) and prepared for my well-earned rest in darkness.

What if someone in the staff should seek me out and find I was not in either of my rooms, then discover me, cowering as it were, in an unused suite.

That's their problem, I thought as I phased out of reality and into the blessed land of Nod.

7

Sometime later I woke up to gunfire and shattering glass. We were under attack. It was a dream, of course, so there was nothing to worry about. I crept over to the window, lifted the shade slightly, and peered out.

Folly of course, but I knew it was all a dream, you see.

An old car of indeterminate make had stopped in the middle of the street. A darkened figure stood at the opened door of the vehicle. He was casually spraying the windows of the Cathedral Rectory with automatic weapon fire. I had no doubt which rooms were the target.

Lying on the floor I reached for the house phone and buzzed the Cardinal's suite.

"Don't get up, don't turn on the lights, roll out of bed and hide behind the wall, and don't argue."

I hung up and punched the buttons for the Reilly apartment and love nest in the John Hancock Building.

Mike answered at the first ring.

"We got it, Blackie. We've notified Chicago Avenue. They're on their way. Don't go outside."

"Not hardly."

I then buzzed everyone in the house with the same instructions I had given the Cardinal, even Crystal downstairs in what had once been the assistant housekeeper's suite.

Then, in the height of folly, I crept back to the window and peered out.

Two black cars, new models this time, had pulled into Wabash, one from Chicago Avenue and the other from Superior Street. They blocked the exit for the gunman's car. He turned and fired some desultory blasts at the car on Superior. He was answered by a volley of exploding firecrackers—revolver shots. He jumped into his car and drove towards the barrier. A bevy of Chicago cop cars, blue lights flashing angrily and sirens wailing in protest, appeared at either end of Wabash. The "perp's" car ground to a halt. A male voice on a public address system warned him to come out with his hands in the air or they would open fire again. There was a moment of silence. Then the door opened and the "perp" appeared, hands in the air, blood streaming down one arm. A dozen Chicago police persons swarmed all over him.

"Mike Casey's guys act quickly," Cardinal Cronin said behind me.

Patently he had ignored my instructions.

"It would seem so."

"Are they protecting you or me?"

"Arguably you."

"Then why are you hiding here?"

"A seraph warned me."

I thereupon whispered a prayer of gratitude to the local seraph.

"This is Mary Jane Mulhern in front of Holy Name Cathedral Rectory. With me is the pastor of the Cathedral, Bishop John Blackwood Ryan. Bishop Ryan, were you frightened last night when the shooting started?"

"Not at all. I was convinced it was a dream. Alas, in the dreams I have an automatic weapon of my own to fight back."

"The windows were shot out only in your suite. How do you account for that?"

"I think the shooter confused my windows with those of Cardinal Cronin, who would be the obvious target of an assassination attempt. Why waste your ammunition on an innocuous little auxiliary bishop when you have a cardinal as a potential target."

"You were not injured in the attack?"

"I don't think so. The seraph who has charge of me is entitled to a bonus."

"Was there any serious damage in your rooms?"

"Alas, the gunfire did not destroy either my computer or my television set."

"Will the Church take any steps to heighten the security around the Cathedral?"

"We are planning to park an M1-A1 tank at the front door. Other than that, a platoon of Marines might be helpful."

"The Chicago Police Department responded rapidly, did they not?"

"They did, for which we are very grateful."

"The police say that the shooter is a member of a South Chicago drug gang."

"Moonlighting perhaps."

"To your knowledge was Sean Cardinal Cronin frightened?"

"The last time the Eminence was frightened was when he was thirteen years old."

"So you see, Belinda, Bishop Ryan continues to be his usual unflappable self. This is Mary Jane Mulhern, Channel Six News on Wabash Avenue in front of Holy Name Cathedral Rectory."

Around the Cathedral breakfast table one heard laughter, then cheer.

"Mary Jane knows you're having her on, doesn't she, Bishop?" asked a young Vietnamese priest who was with us on his first assignment.

"Oh yes."

"You certainly seemed unflappable," he added.

"I was last night," I replied, honestly enough. "Like I say, I thought it was a dream. Now I am quite flapped."

Later Milord Cronin joined me in my office.

"No damage to the liquor cabinet, I hope?"

"It would seem not."

"The statue is undamaged?"

He examined the medieval ivory carving which, it was said, looked like my mother Kate Collins Ryan (God be good to her, and He better or He'll hear about it).

"Everything else can be replaced?"

"We have excellent insurance coverage, though whether it includes terrorist attack I'm not sure."

"Your friends in Washington?"

"Oh, I think so. They warned me yesterday."

"So you alerted Mike Casey."

"Patently."

"Blackwood, I want you off this case."

"No," I said firmly. "These assholes attacked my house, I'm going to get them."

He considered issuing an order and thought better of it.

"Unless they get you first."

"They won't dare."

I handed him the envelope I had prepared the evening before.

"Put this in a safe. Should anything happen to me, summon the charming Ms. Mulhern and read her the whole story."

"But, you'll be dead!"

"I will call them shortly and tell them that if there are any more attempts, a sealed envelope deposited in a secure place with all the details of the Brother Semyon case will be opened and made public."

"Who's behind it?"

"John Ashcroft perhaps."

"You're joking!"

"Patently. However, someone at or close to his level and who has his disregard for the Constitution."

"Call them now while I'm here."

He couldn't sit on the couch, which had been riddled with bullets. So he sat on my computer chair.

I turned on the speakerphone and punched in the number. The familiar voice answered.

"What the fuck are you assholes trying to do?" I said, abandoning my languages rules for the moment.

"I don't know what you're talking about," he said nervously.

"You ought to be ashamed of yourself. That bush-league caper last night is a disgrace to the federal government. Someone at your store should be fired."

"I didn't even know about it till this morning."

Sean Cronin grinned at me. I had smoked him out.

"Yeah? Look pass the word up that I'm profoundly angry and intend to get even. I know you folks have Brother Semyon . . ."

"We don't!"

"At least you know who does have him. I want him back."

"I don't know."

"This place is my home, in my neighborhood, in my city. You bastards don't know anything about Chicago if you think you can get away with this shit."

Milord Cronin grinned appropriately each time I used inappropriate language.

"Blackie, drop it all."

"I also warn you that I have written a complete account of the entire case of Brother Semyon, which is now in a secure place. If any more attempts are made on me, it will be released to the media. Is that clear?"

"Yes," he said meekly.

"So tell your idiot bosses, no more attacks."

"There won't be any."

"And tell them that nothing had better happen to Brother Semyon."

"He was buried yesterday, Blackie. The services were at the Holy Virgin Protection Cathedral in Des Plaines."

"And chickens have lips," I said. "Also you endangered the life of a second cardinal who happens to be my boss. Can you imagine the headlines, 'Fed Hit Men Endanger Cronin'?"

I thereupon hung up.

"Very impressive," Milord Cronin said, with a nod. "I think your friend is talking to his bosses right now and warning them off. Don't mess around with Blackie Ryan, he's saying, he's a mean little son of a bitch."

"He's the kind that knows how to get even."

"So we know that Brother Semyon is still alive and that the Feds at least know who has him? That was very neatly done, Blackwood. As I have said before on occasion, I'm glad you're on my side."

I was attempting to calm down after my outburst. I don't get that angry very often. On the other hand when I do it is useful for prying out information.

My phone rang. The parish secretary who takes the calls until the Megans arrive told me that it was a man who would not identify himself but who had called before.

My West Side contact.

"Ryan," I barked into the phone.

"Hey, glad you're all right."

"I survive."

"I hear from my friends that their friends are greatly embarrassed by what went down last night and they hope their apologies will get to you. They're good Catholics. They wouldn't let something like this happen. It's those Hispanic drug gangs. They show no respect."

One of the negative effects of *The Sopranos* is that now everyone who is in any fashion "connected" has to talk like they're a television character.

"I know they weren't involved. I suspect they know who was."

"Out-of-town people."

"Beltway people," I said, not asking a question but stating a fact.

"Those guys are a disgrace to our society. Someone ought to do something about them."

"I quite agree."

After I hung up, the Cardinal shook his head.

"Blackwood, I hope that when you succeed me, you destroy that list of yours. No archbishop should have those kinds of contacts."

"If our mutual friend were still president," I said, "a call to him would do it."

"Someday"—he stood up—"some of those guys will realize that you are anything but harmless . . . Crystal tell you move to another room?"

"No, she just assured me that everything would be all right."

"Figures."

8

Since Dean Keane had provided me with a pass permitting me to park in the president's lot (right behind his house at Fifty-ninth and University), I excused Mr. Woods from service and drove out myself. It was not so complicated to drive down Lake Shore Drive to the turn in front of the Museum of Science and Industry and turn off on Midway Plaisance.

My siblings and their offspring are all car freaks. Periodically, they impose on me their idea of an appropriate car for an inept auxiliary bishop.

As in, "Punk, this was made for you."

"Punk" is a lifelong nickname which is mostly affectionate, save when they are displeased with me.

So they had taken away my turquoise 1955 Ford Thunderbird convertible and replaced it with an almost new Mercedes G500 SUV. What a bishop would do with such a vehicle escaped me completely but they seemed to think it was "perfect."

Yeah.

I think the G500 is evidence of the deleterious effect on Daimler Benz of their merger with Chrysler. It is a square, boxy car—always black—which looks like a World War II jeep with sides on it. Or perhaps a tank from World War I. It rode, however, like something from the Benzenwerk should ride.

I sighed in loud protest if any of the local seraphs were still on my case and happened to be around listening. I assume that they were being assisted by Mike Casey's people though I could see none of them trailing me.

However, the critical question was why the said inept and innocuous auxiliary bishop should be a target for the Feds' hit people. One might argue that he was messing in a matter they thought to be of critical national importance.

All right, *datum non concessum* the issue still remained as to why the apparent murder of a Russian monk specializing in the mysticism of a heretic sect should impinge on the national interest. One might also wonder why the monk had been replaced just before the beginning of the quarter at *The* University. Also at issue was why the elaborate locked-room puzzle had been enacted. I knew how it had been, but I had not the slightest idea why.

It was material for an acute headache.

I turned off the drive, cut through Jackson Park, avoiding scores of school buses, and managed with only minor difficulty to find the Midway. A number of drivers behind me, more familiar with the intricacies of the route than I, leaned on their horns. Apparently they were unafraid of the robust strength of the G500.

I maneuvered around several one-way streets and finally found University Avenue at Fifty-eighth Street and refuge in the parking lot between the president's house and the Oriental Institute. The seraphs had brought me there only by much skill and patience.

I was able to appear in the lobby of the Quadrangle Club just before twelve and thus anticipate the advent of the president, who appeared at precisely twelve.

"In my experience," Reed Alan said with a broad smile, "clergy are not so punctual."

"It's the result of my family's total lack of concern for time. I am, you see, the white sheep in the family."

The remark always gets a laugh. However, the president merely observed, "I don't know much about psychology, but I think the literature takes those dynamics into account."

Oh my.

On the other hand, he praised Dean Keane for her work and had a kind word for "her, uh, is 'partner' the right word?"

" 'Swain' would be better."

"Yes, I suppose it would . . . They are both excellent additions to the faculty. When they offered Dorie the job as dean she promptly asked for an early tenure review. She deserved it, of course, but some were taken aback by her, uh . . ."

"Pushiness."

"Well, perhaps."

"You let a few Irish persons in," I said, "and there goes the neighborhood."

He merely laughed loud and long without any reference to a literature.

"The literature on the Irish political style," I offered, "would lead one to be unsurprised by Dean Keane's behavior. We, of course, always count the votes."

"Well, I for one, would like more Irish on the faculty. They add zest and surprise, as they have done to whatever far corners of the world they seek out . . . That's why I'm delighted that there is a possibility you might be joining us in some sort of visiting lecturer capacity."

For once the harmless little bishop was reduced to silence.

"It would not be a tenure track appointment, though your published work would merit that. As I understand it you already have a tenure on your own."

"That's one word for it," I said, reaching for my iced-tea glass.

"Nor would we require anything special in the way of teaching. A lecture or two a year about your work would be more than enough. We want to establish in a concrete way a link between the University and the Archdiocese. Something we should have done long ago."

"I'm afraid I'd have to discuss such an arrangement with Cardinal Cronin . . ."

"He led me to believe yesterday at the funeral that he would be delighted with such an arrangement. He even suggested that he might, on the odd occasion, audit one of your lectures."

Trapped. The Keen Dean had done her work well.

I must not appear too eager.

"It's an interesting idea. I'll talk about it with the Cardinal and be back to you on it."

Not that I had any chance in the world of saying no.

I glanced at a table near ours over in the far corner of the dining room. The dean, surrounded by colleagues who did not include her swain, smiled at me.

Little witch.

The president and I wandered over a wide variety of topics. Only at the end of the meal did he, Irish-like, raise the question that was most important, "I hope we can clear up this regrettable affair in Swift Hall. It's the second killing we've had there you know."

"The unfortunate Romanian."

"Indeed and under equally mysterious circumstances."

"The locked-room puzzle is not difficult," I said. "However, there are deeper forces at work."

"You think the assault on your Rectory last night is linked to it?"

First time he had mentioned it.

"Arguably."

"Who would have wanted to kill Brother Semyon, then shoot up a priest's house?"

"What did the government tell you when you agreed to accept Brother Semyon?"

He put down his fork and stared at me.

"Dorie was right."

"I suspect she usually is."

"I was the only one who knew about that call."

"Except the person who made it and his superiors."

"Obviously. And you."

I said nothing. The truth was that I had merely guessed.

"The call was a little confusing," he went on. "The man told me that Brother Semyon was a distinguished scholar and an important human being. I knew both of these facts. Then he added that we must treat him with care and caution because he had lived a traumatic life. I said that I had some awareness of that. Then he said that there might be some people who would wish him dead."

"Now they tell you."

"Precisely. My blood, as you might imagine, Bishop Blackie, ran cold. What are we supposed to do about that? I asked. 'Just keep a close eye on him. But don't tell anyone else about this call.' "

"Make bricks without straw."

He smiled faintly.

"Precisely. I had our security people keep a close eye on him and asked the people at the Windemere to do the same thing. Nothing happened. I don't know if we could have prevented what happened last week . . ."

"You could not have prevented it. Has your friend called you again?"

"Not yet."

So the Feds had taken their own precaution and were not worried about security at the University. I decided that I would tell him a confidence so that he might spill more to me.

"What I'm about to tell you, sir, is in strict confidence. Yet I think you ought to know it. In a closet over at the Windemere, there is a complete and authentic set of the crimson robes of a cardinal of the Holy Roman Church."

"Brother Semyon was a cardinal!"

"Arguably. So you can understand why we are interested in the affair."

"Did the Vatican give you any warning?"

"None. They view us locals as errand boys. They tell us things on a need-to-know basis, only there never is any need to know."

"And you have approached them since his death?"

"They pretended not to understand the question, which tells me that they were hiding someone, just like the Feds."

"We already had our link with the Church and we didn't know it," he said with a wry smile. "I'm afraid our friend Brother Semyon was a spook of some sort. Or more likely had been at one time. Yet I would not consider Swift Hall exactly a safe house."

"Your caller hinted as much?"

"His precise words were—and I remember them perfectly—Brother Semyon has done much good work for the cause of freedom. There are some intelligence services around the world who don't like that and they have long memories." He shook his head in dismay.

"In all my years as an academic administrator I have never received a call like that. I had almost forgotten it until Dorie called me at home that night and told me what happened."

So she had really called him. That was an important piece of a minor puzzle.

"Does the Vatican have its own spy service?"

"Not really. It picks up things and sometimes even understands what they mean. No spook bureau is really very good, but if we had one it would be worse than all the others."

"Not even the Jesuits?"

I rolled my eyes. "Good men and true. But, whatever may be true of the past, they aren't very good these days even at spying on one another."

"After the phone call, as you might imagine, I gave the matter considerable thought. Brother Semyon was arriving in a couple of days a year ago. I could not send him back. It would be inadmissible for me to question him. I called some of my counterparts in Europe. One of them, as a matter of fact in Cracow, said that the brother was a very good man, but not always what he seemed. Another, in Budapest, told me that he did brilliant work but sometimes appeared and disappeared, then appeared again, without any explanation. I said

I thought he was in Zagorsk most of the time. He laughed and said that was after the 'social transformation.'"

"The implication being that he was about many things before 1991."

"Precisely. No one at the Western universities had much to say except one man who said he had the impression that Brother Semyon was in Berlin at the time the wall fell."

"Indeed."

"All of this is in confidence."

"Naturally."

"I wonder if it is of any help to you."

"A few more pieces fit in place," I admitted. "There's still a lot missing."

"Well, I see that Dean Keane's colleagues have left and she is undoubtedly waiting for us. May I tell her you will consider our offer?"

"What good would it do me to try to refuse?"

We both laughed and rose to join the Keen Dean at her empty table. She was wearing a beige blouse, beige slacks, and a beige ribbon, which again severely restrained her red hair. Any other arrangement might lead to her arrest as an Irish Gypsy.

"Do you foresee an eventual union between her and her, ah, swain?"

"Perhaps sooner rather than later. The posture now is that he wants to marry and she's reluctant. Yet when the scenario comes to the denouement and she calls for closure, he will be the one who hesitates."

The president chuckled. "A wise man would."

"Patently."

"Bishop Blackie and I have had a fascinating talk," he told her. "I think it safe to say that he is willing to become a part of the University."

"*The* University," I agreed.

If she had not been in the dining room of the Quadrangle Club, she might have kissed one or the other of us. Arguably both.

"I'm delighted to hear that," she said with a bright smile. "It will be most interesting to have you with us."

"Don't bet too much on that. You would have been better advised to hire the valiant Tyrone Willingham."

"I was really scared to hear about the shooting at your Rectory last night, Bishop Blackie." She sighed. "Nothing to do with this mess here is it?"

"Absolutely nothing," I said, not lying but hiding the truth as the good Jesuits at the seminary had taught us was valid in some circumstances. "Some doped-up guy having fun. The seraphs protected us."

"Why didn't they protect poor Brother Semyon?"

"Perhaps they did," I said enigmatically.

My conversation with the president had been most useful. Brother Semyon had been a spook and probably a Catholic spook. Perhaps he had gone around Eastern Europe and ordained priests and consecrated bishops, a risky operation. Yet why didn't he come in out of the cold when the walls came tumbling down? Maybe he just liked being at Zagorsk.

Was he out of danger now? Was it possible that my messing around would endanger him?

My DC contact had not warned me of that possibility. He must have known that I would suspend operations if it were true.

"I suppose," she said, "there's no point in arguing with God."

She was deeply troubled, as well she might be by the horrific scene of death in an office just around the corner from her own.

"Ah, but there is, so long as one does not expect to win, at least in the short run. God is pleased with argument as any lover."

"How do you deal with the problem of evil, Bishop?"

"Mostly by referencing the opposite problem of good."

"Which is?"

I fell back on my standard argument on the subject.

"How come there is good in the world too? How come there is anything at all? The complaint against God comes down to the basic issue of how a presumably loving God can permit His allegedly beloved creatures to die at all. The time, the place, the manner, the reason for death may add to the problem. But it is death itself at the core of the challenge. How can God create a being that wants to live and yet condemn it ultimately to death? Does not that fact prove either that there is no God or that God is a monster?

"So, in this line of reasoning, a loving God should have created us immortal. Anything less than immortality and they win the argument. The argument is utterly convincing to those who make it. So easy is it to dispose of God. Only the argument, as tight as it is and as logical, misunderstands the deal with God that faith makes. The believer does not demand of God protection in the short run. The believer knows that bad things happen inevitably, sometimes very bad things. And they happen to good people. All the believer can do is cling to the faith that finally, when all the bad has happened, God does not abandon His people. This argument is as plausible as the other and at least it does not beg the question of why there is anything at all, why the world fits a mathematical order, why humans expect justice, why they hope.

"A very wise man[1] has said, 'Just as believers in a beneficent deity should be haunted by the problem of natural evil, so agnostics, atheists, pessimists and nihilists should be haunted by the problem of friendship, love, beauty, truth, humor, compassion, fun. Never forget the problem of fun.'

"The atheist is satisfied with his toughness, his hardheadedness, his realism, his immunity to sentimentality, and finds in these characteristics reinforcement for his belief in unbelief. The only possible answer to him is that there are phenomena he cannot explain—life itself, for instance, beauty, and love."

"I'm sure you'll be asked that question this afternoon."

"Oh?"

"When you're meeting with my class. They've read your books

---

[1] *John Horgan in his* Rational Mysticism.

and are dying, you should excuse the expression, to meet you."

"Ah."

I had no recollection of having committed myself to such an enterprise.

"You don't have to, if you don't want to."

She had made sure that she knew how I would answer the problem of evil question before she informed. Suspicious child!

"It will be interesting to see if I can cope with bright young people," I said, feigning humility.

"You'll do just fine."

"Perhaps."

I noted that the Indian Summer day was fading. A line of dark clouds had appeared on the western horizon and was heading right at us. The forecast of heavy rain apparently was accurate.

"About love?" she asked, as we neared the door of Swift Hall.

"Odd of God to use that word to describe Herself, is it not?"

"Very . . . I mean I think I love David, even though he is a scary person. But I might be wrong. A lot of people who think they're deeply in love end up hating the other person. How does one know beforehand?"

"One doesn't. One considers the issue, consults with one's family and friends, and jumps off the bridge into the river."

"My family and friends think he's wonderful, but he's such a smooth-talking blarney artist, that doesn't prove a thing."

"You can't stand him when he's playing the blarney game?"

"No, I love it because he's so good at it. But I might get tired of it."

"You might well."

"Anyway, you'll talk to Ms. Comerford at 1:15. My class is at 2:20. And we have scheduled Mr. Strong at 3:30."

We entered the building. She paused just inside the door.

"They're both stories of unhappy love. Patrice is a radical from the 1960s. Demonstrated in front of the Conrad Hilton. Still angry. An ardent feminist. Does her work on feminist theological theory.

Can sometimes be very abrasive on the subject. No known religious affiliation. Doug is an Anglican, very high church, though I don't think he practices it much. He's an expert on the New Testament. Spends most of his effort ridiculing the Jesus seminar people. Both of them have lost spouses, then lost partners. They are currently unattached and display little interest in the opposite sex. Patrice voted against me, I'm sure, and is just barely civil. She thinks I've sold out feminism for academic power. Doug seems to like me in a platonic sort of way. He may take a little bit too much of the drink. He'll vote for David for sure. Patrice probably won't, but people will discount her. Neither will be an easy interview."

"I may not survive the afternoon."

"I doubt that." She laughed.

We walked down the corridor towards her office. I noted that one door was wide-open. Professor Dolan's, of course. Keeping an eye on the corridor to note the safe return of the fairy princess and his ladylove.

"Hey!" he yelled. "Look what I got!"

She winced at his bellow.

"Good afternoon, David. What have you got?"

He leaped from his chair and waved a piece of paper at her.

"A letter from the *Cambridge Historical Review* accepting my final revisions of the article on Reginald Poe. They'll publish it in three months."

"Congratulations," she said, a touch too formally.

He ignored her lack of enthusiasm and hugged her.

"And I called the *Journal of Church History.* They said they'd have the letter of acceptance in the mail first of next week! That should ice it!"

"Wonderful," she said, again formally.

Then quite to everyone's surprise, perhaps including her own. She stood on her tiptoes and brushed her lips against his. With, if I may say so, not a little passion.

"That'll show 'em," she whispered.

David Dolan blushed.

"Gosh, maybe I'd better finish a couple more articles!"

"These two will do for the moment," she said, formal again, but grinning.

Turnabout is fair play. What's sauce for the goose is sauce for the gander. And all other pertinent clichés.

"I hate to be a spoilsport," I said, "but I'd like to talk to you two for a minute."

I closed the door of the office, sat down in the chair from which I had previously cleared the output, and adopted the "let's get down to business" persona I sometimes manage. If they wanted to go into a more amorous clench, they would have to do it on their own time.

They struggled with some success to become unflustered. The thought crossed my mind that I wouldn't bet against a wedding by Christmas.

"There is, first of all, the matter of Brother Semyon's staff. I cannot imagine an Orthodox monk losing it. Yet it is not in his apartment nor in his office. Where might it be?"

They looked at one another, and Dorie was the first to talk.

"We talked about it on our way up to the funeral yesterday—by the way, your Cardinal is a very sweet person."

She used the word freely, didn't she?

"Many women use that adjective to describe him."

"He told us that we could make our own decision about receiving the Eucharist but he didn't think they offered it at funeral liturgies."

She was still flustered. If a woman kisses an Irish clan chieftain that way she runs the risk of being carried off to his bedroom. Somewhere in David Dolan's genes there was a clan chieftain, but we had civilized that type. Over a couple thousand years. Somewhat.

"The thing is," Professor Dolan smoothly took up the narrative, "we can't remember when we last saw him with the staff. We wondered whether he might have left it in Paris."

"Paris?"

"He went to Paris this summer to lecture at the Sorbonne as he does every summer," Professor Dolan continued. "He returned two weeks ago, just in time for the start of the autumn quarter."

So now I learn for the first time that Brother Semyon had spent the summer in Paris. That puts a very interesting light on the situation.

"He did seem a little different after he came back. He said he was working hard on finishing a manuscript. We didn't have our late-afternoon vodka anymore, much to Dorie's relief. He was more quiet, more reticent. I don't think we would have noticed it if you had not asked about the staff."

"There were carvings all over the wood," the dean explained. "He told me once that a wood-carver made it from a very sacred oak tree that had lived in the mountains for a thousand years."

"Not something that one might leave behind in Paris," I observed. "Nor something that a thief might steal on the metro."

"No," Dorie whispered softly. "What does it mean, Bishop Blackie?"

I contented myself with a restrained answer.

"It's one more puzzle within a puzzle."

"He was still Brother Semyon," David Dolan said. "Yet he was a little bit different, like something had happened to him while he was away."

"You were here when he left?"

"No," Dorie said. "We took two weeks off in early July, one week with my family on the Cape and another with David's at Sheridan Beach in the Dunes."

"I was on my good behavior," her swain admitted, "so we didn't have too many fights."

Dorie giggled.

"It's around here that he's not always on his good behavior."

"My other question," I interjected to interrupt any more banter, "is about a lacuna I observed in David's report of the events of that evening. He stated that one or the other of you were always present after you opened the door."

"That's right," Dorie agreed.

107

"And that no one entered the room."

"We kind of felt we shouldn't," Dave said, rubbing his bearded jaw.

"Yet someone did."

"I don't see how . . . Wait a minute, Dorie, you remember you went to phone the president just as I left to open the doors to let the cops in . . ."

"I do remember . . . It was only a few moments, Bishop."

"Yet someone could have slipped into the room, then slipped out."

"They would have to have done it quickly," David pointed out, "especially if they knew the cops were entering at the other end of the corridor."

"What needed to be done," I said, "could have been done very quickly."

Israel Golden had assured me that no one had entered the room. Yet patently someone had.

There was also the possibility that everyone had walked into the death scene, including David and Dorina, and that there was a conspiracy of silence to cover it up. But why? I thought it more likely that the entry had occurred during the few moments when the dean and her young man were absent. The question remained as to why. Except I knew the answer to that question.

We sat silently for a moment.

"Just a moment," Dave said, and searched in one of the drawers of his desk.

He came up with an unwashed Waterford tumbler, which he held gingerly with two fingers.

"I kept this glass for our one-glass-vodka parties. Brother Semyon always used it. Probably it has his fingerprints and DNA. Maybe I'll take it home and ask my dad to check it out."

"You never used it after he returned from Paris?"

"No . . . if it's different from the prints and the DNA of the dead man . . ."

"Then the man who was killed might have looked like Brother Semyon, but it wasn't he," the dean finished for him.

"Your father's friends on the police force won't be happy with the new evidence," I suggested.

"Dad will love sticking it to them."

"And he might think," Dean Dorina added, "that you would have made a good cop after all. Even if you couldn't shoot straight."

David carefully brought his prize back to his desk.

"I'd better bring you up to Patrice's office." Dorie broke the silence. "She's a stickler for punctuality . . . David, I don't suppose you put your final draft of the articles in your tenure folder in my office. Why don't you put both of them on my desk along with that letter of acceptance? I'll see that we make the appropriate modification in your CV. When will the second article be published?"

"Spring issue. Like I said, the letter will probably come next week."

"You will try to remember to give it to me?"

His wild Irish grin returned.

"Do my best!"

"I hope I didn't shock you, Bishop Blackie," she said, as we climbed the stairs to the third floor—no elevators for the young in heart.

"Not as much as you seemed to have shocked poor Dave."

"He's very sweet," she murmured.

That's three of us I thought, though I suspect the word was used analogously for Milord Cronin, his invisible little auxiliary, and a man you had just made up your mind you were going to marry, sooner rather than later. Poor Dave Dolan didn't stand a chance.

I had unearthed much interesting information. Alas, I had no time to reflect on it.

9

Ms. Comerford was something less than delighted to see me. She was a handsome woman, very handsome indeed—tall, Junoesque, with long hair, thick glasses, behind which lurked dangerously flashing lights, and thin compressed lips. She wore a long, gray dress which managed to look plain and still deftly emphasize the luxuriant shape of her body. There was not the slightest hint of makeup, but a faint smell of Chanel. Her presentation of self said in effect, I am not proud that I am attractive, even sexy. What are you going to do about that?

Yet the virtuous Dean Dorina said that there was a sad love story somewhere in her past and probably an even greater beauty, whose elegant survival she now pretended to hate but in which she secretly reveled.

Her office was like that of Crystal Lane at the Cathedral, impeccably neat. There were no papers, no books, no computer monitor. Only a clean desk, two chairs, and empty bookcases. Ms. Comerford did not permit even a speck of dust to mar the perfection of its neatness.

Not what one might expect from a specialist in feminist theory.

"I am reluctant to spend this hour with you, Mr. Ryan," she began.

"Dr. Ryan," I corrected her.

"I only use that term of someone who has earned a valid academic degree.

"Seabury Western," I said. "On William James."

"Very well, *Doctor* Ryan. In any case I do not respect organized religion. Much of the abuse of women in human history has been supported, if not caused directly, by organized religion. I despise it and its practitioners."

"Yet you teach at a school which in part is concerned about the education of practitioners."

"It gives me an opportunity to tell such men what I think of them. In particular, I abominate the Catholic Church."

"Tell me about it," I said with a loud sigh. "But we are not here to talk about my tattered church, but about the late and lamented Brother Semyon Ivanivich Popov."

"I do not lament him in the slightest. He was a rude, crude man, even worse than most men. I found his very presence in this building to be a personal affront."

"Yet he seems to have been an important scholar."

"Only if one takes seriously Orthodox fundamentalist gibberish. I do not believe in mystical experiences. They are the product of disordered brains. Science has been able to replicate such interludes merely by inducing changes in the brain chemistry."

"I am not prepared to argue that the ability of science to produce an altered state of consciousness does not impugn the authenticity of those altered states which were not caused by exogenous intrusions."

I liked those last two words. They sound so dreadfully academic.

"Rather, I am interested in trying to explain why someone saw fit to blow off the head of Brother Semyon."

"I'm sure I don't know and don't care," she said. "I happened to be in the building when the shot was fired. I heard the explosion. His office, after all, is exactly two floors below mine. I went down to the first floor to see if we were under attack. I joined the others around the door. I know nothing more."

"You did not see a flash?"

She hesitated a fraction of a second too long.

"I certainly did not."

"Did you think it might have been thunder from the storm?"

"That thought never occurred to me. It was clearly an explosion, perhaps the beginning of revolutionary action."

Why deny it?

"Some of the others saw a flash."

"I refuse to work for the pigs in the Chicago Police Department!"

I did not point out that she could be charged with cooperating in a felony if she did not tell the truth to the police department. She doubtless knew that and craved the same martyrdom that arrest after the peace demonstrations had occasioned thirty and more years before.

"And the colleagues who were with you?"

"I would rather not use that word. They are hardly colleagues. Rather they are people who happen to teach in this building."

"Indeed."

"That miserable old Jew Golden who expects a discount on his own professional incompetence because of the holocaust. Douglas Strong continues a hegemonic all-male interpretation of the Bible, drinks too much, and harasses women. The little simp Keane has sold herself to acquire power, and Dolan, a preening macho rapist who is her pimp."

That was a lot of hatred in one outburst. Still it was an impressive redo of the rhetoric of thirty years ago. I wondered what the students thought of her, those who bothered to sit in her classes. They would be radicals seeking a mentor and not finding one because she hated them too. The young men might ogle her, but would be very careful, lest she catch their hungry eyes undressing her.

I have a bad habit of dealing with such people by scoring verbal points against them, playing the "gotcha" game. It is an amusing waste of time because they never realize that you've scored points. Moreover, with women like Patrice Comerford it ignores the terrible pain in their lives. Playing "gotcha" is not a substitute for compassion. Yet it would be impossible for compassion to break through the thick armor of anger she had built around herself.

"All of you went into the office where the crime was committed?"

"Who said that?" she exploded

"No one said it. I'm asking."

"I didn't enter the office," she said flatly.

"Others did."

"Let the pigs do their own work."

"I imagine the stench was terrible."

"Death always smells terrible."

"No air coming through the window either."

"That little whore Keane did not realize that the wind was blowing his papers all over the floor. She had no more respect for the dead than she does for the living."

"So."

"You'll have to explain to me how your God permits something as ugly as a death like that."

"Or any death," I said, giving into my "gotcha" propensity.

"If one of those who were at the door with you might have been in some way responsible for the death of Brother Semyon, which one might it be?"

"Strong, of course. He is a criminal type. Macho male. Would rape any woman he could get his hands on. He enjoys violence of every kind. He would delight in murder."

"In these cases of sexual harassment charges, he'd not be likely to get away with attempted rape, would he?"

"You'd be surprised what a man like him can get away with. He should be barred from the school and from academic scholarship! Yet he has powerful friends who protect him. If you ask me, he is the one who should have been murdered."

"I've been told that Brother Semyon was in Paris this summer."

"I have much better things to occupy my time, Dr. Ryan, than attending to the comings and goings of the other members of this faculty. I don't know and I don't care what they do."

"I see . . . Has he seemed different in any way in the last couple of weeks?"

"He was as offensive as ever, loud, boisterous, obnoxious. As usual he bowed deeply whenever he saw me and called me 'madam' in phony respect."

"Is that not the way with Eastern European intellectuals?"

"In case you have not noticed it, this is not Eastern Europe."

"Not yet," I admitted.

"At least he did not carry that ugly stick of his around. I was disgusted every time he pounded it on the floor. Clearly it was a phallic symbol and he was engaging in transgressive behavior with it."

"Ah?"

"Simulating rape, of course. He was signifying the thrusting of his phallus into the body of a defenseless woman. I'm surprised that the women in the faculty did not cry out in rage."

"Did you suggest it to some of them?"

"They merely laughed at me. One said that sometimes a monk's staff is nothing more than a monk's staff. Everything that men do signifies something degrading for women. If one looked into his eyes and saw the glow in them, you knew that he was reveling in the debasing of some victim."

"Do you know whether he made any attempts on faculty or students during his term here?"

"Of course he did. Men cannot resist their sexual impulses. Monks are no different from others . . . You carry one of those staffs too, don't you?"

Blackie on the defensive.

"The crosier," I replied, "represents the shepherd's staff with which one guides the sheep and fights off the wolves."

"You mean to tell me that you never imagine thrusting it into the vagina of a young woman in your congregation."

"As a matter of fact, no."

"Don't you want to beat the ewes in your congregation with it?"

"On occasion I have gestured with it at misbehaving teenage males. They laugh at me."

"So you would rather shove it up the rectum of a boy than the vagina of a woman?"

"I don't think so."

"Then you are either out of touch with your fantasies or dishonest about them. All men are predetermined by their testosterone to do violence to the weak."

"Perhaps." I tried to take control of the conversation again. "Did Brother Semyon ever make any sexual advances to you?"

"His whole being was a sexual advance. I would not throw myself at him, as I'm sure some of the students did. His glowing mysterious eyes had no impact on me at all. I knew what he was and what he wanted and I dismissed him."

"I see . . . Did you notice that glow in his eyes in the weeks immediately before he died?"

She actually paused to think about the question.

"As a matter of fact, I did not. However, I had no reason to look for it."

I thanked her for her cooperation and candor and beat a retreat. Dean Keane was waiting for me at the head of the staircase.

"Rough time, Bishop Blackie?"

"Not particularly . . . She is, however, a very angry woman."

"Angry and sexually frustrated."

"I believe I noticed that."

"She tell you that Brother Semyon was looking at her with lust in his heart?"

"She made some sort of allusion to that fact."

"He made no moves on anyone, Bishop. His eyes glowed often, but that was part of his mystical nature. He was a good monk."

And a lot of others things besides, not the least of which was a Cardinal of the Holy Roman Church.

"When you opened the door to the murder room," I changed the subject, "did you notice a mess of Brother Semyon's papers on the floor?"

"As a matter of fact, I did . . . He fell across his desk and the impact must have sent the papers flying. I suppose the blast of the gun did too. I thought there was a breeze blowing through the windows but the police later said that they were all locked."

"Ah."

"Patrice would have noticed something like that. She is obsessive about men and about neatness."

"She would be pleased with your swain?"

"Is that what he is? . . . Not a bad word."

"Or knight protector?"

A faint tinge of color spread across her pale face.

"Perhaps that too . . . You know what he's doing now? He's threatening to bring sexual harassment charges against me and calling you as a witness, unless I agree to set a date for the marriage."

"I will testify that he initiated the embrace."

"That's not true."

"Neither is it true that your chaste affection was harassment."

She giggled.

"Maybe it was a little . . . He won't do it, of course. David is a cupcake. He'd never hurt anyone."

"Yet you fear him, Dorina?"

"Cupcakes are a lot scarier than predators." The tinge on her cheeks was more intense this time.

"Patently."

"You would not believe it but Patrice was once a beautiful woman. Pictures of her twenty years ago, she was a real knockout."

"I would have no trouble believing it."

"Folklore has it that she and Doug had a thing going. It didn't work out. Doug married someone else and his wife died a few years later of an aneurysm. He tried again with Patrice. She brushed him off and then, they say, deliberately let herself go to seed . . . No man is worth that, is he, Bishop?"

"Decidedly not."

She ushered me into her classroom. The usual hum of student talk stopped instantly. Everyone straightened up to attention. Mother Superior had entered the room.

Patently, Dorina ruled with an iron hand. A lovely young woman with flaming red hair did not have much choice. The women students would want to identify with her and the men students would want to ogle her. If she gave an inch to frail humanity, especially in a midafternoon class, the proverbial Katie would have to bar the door.

"Since Bishop John Blackwood Ryan is visiting us here for a few days and since you have read his book in preparation for this class, I have asked him to talk to you for a few minutes and to answer your questions. I insist that you be correct and respectful in the style of your questions. Bishop Ryan may join us next quarter as a professorial lecturer. I do not want him to leave here today with a bad impression of the students in this school."

It would have been impossible for me to play the role of the serious academic even if I had wanted to. Doubtless I would offend the Keen Dean's sense of propriety. That, however, was her problem. She had shanghaied me into the situation.

"Mother Superior," I began, "told me about this assignment only at noon, so I have prepared no lecture notes. Thus you will have to ask questions."

"What should we call you, Bishop?" a young Latina asked me.

I couldn't have asked for a better set up question.

"How does *Moby-Dick* begin?"

" 'Call me Ishmael,' " she said hesitantly.

"Call me Blackie," I said, "as in Black Bart, the Black Prince, the Black Knight, in Mother Superior's hometown Boston Blackie, black as midnight on a moonless night, a black hole in space, Black Friday, and the Black Horse Troop."

All appearances of order and discipline in the class broke down. Even Mother Superior was laughing.

"*Bishop* Blackie," she said.

"I stand corrected."

"Bishop Blackie, is celibacy a difficult burden?"

"Only on Sunday afternoons. I think celibacy should be an option for a few hours on Sunday."

After the laughter I explained how celibacy was a burden perhaps but so was marriage and parenthood—ask your own parents—and that men who were happy in their priestly work rarely left that work to marry. Sunday afternoon after Mass was the time when the parish slowed down and there actually might not be any work to do for a few hours.

Then I got the question of the problem of evil.

"Mother Superior asked me that on the way over, I think to vet my response. As best as I can remember this is what I said."

Applause. Oh my.

"Why do Catholics eat their God?"

"That's not what the Eucharist metaphor discloses. We incorporate God into our organism because we are incorporated into Him. It is a union of love, just like that between a man and a woman on their marriage bed. When they incorporate themselves into one another they are representing both the Eucharist and the love of God and His people."

"I never heard that before," one kid informed me.

"Perhaps because we who teach are afraid to teach it."

"Why would you be afraid?"

"Might give you dirty thoughts at Mass, especially if you were there with your spouse."

"Would that be bad?"

"Not as far as I'm concerned, so long as you listen to my homily."

"What is God like?"

"On the record He claims to be love, which is rather odd of God once one ponders how messy love can be—a passionate drive towards union."

"Does that mean God needs us?"

"How could the one who ignited the Big Bang possibly need us? Yet I am reminded of the words of the Irish Dominican poet Paul

Murray, 'he who gives us all the gifts we give, who has no need of anything we have, nonetheless, if one of us should cease to exist, would die of sadness.'"

Silence while they pondered that.

"Yet He sends some of us to hell."

"I kind of doubt that, though it's an option we should not lightly dismiss. However, God is very clever. Because He is implacably forgiving love, He's not likely to let any of us get away."

"Have there been many bad popes?"

"An Oxford don, not of our church, says that there haven't been any since 1700, but that virtue doesn't mean either wisdom or administrative ability."

Then someone asked why the Church did so many stupid things. As is my wont I blamed Jesus for turning it over to humans instead of seraphs.

Towards the end of the forty-five minutes, an African-American woman asked if my name meant I was black Irish and I said no it did not. She then asked what were the black Irish.

"They are denizens of the West of Ireland with pale skin, thick black hair, low foreheads, heavy beards, and deep blue eyes. You know Nuala Anne, the singer? She's black Irish."

"Where did they come from?"

"I believe they represent the remnants of the Neanderthal genes that were absorbed when *homo sapiens* took over, though whether the behavior of our species deserves that redundancy is perhaps open to question. The Neanderthals fled to the edge of the world, the West of Ireland surely being that. If you look at their menfolk, you realize that they are big, apelike, shuffling fellows with dreamy eyes and sweet dispositions which belie their appearance, not unlike the silverback gorillas of the Congo rain forests. They write poetry, often drink prodigiously (two pints of Guinness a night), and sometimes sing all night long and into the morning. They have been known to shout and on occasion to pound their chests, but they are in fact very gentle, vulnerable creatures. I think they merit historical preservation."

Everyone was giggling, including the dean, who was also blushing furiously.

"Have you met Professor Dolan, Bishop Blackie?" an Asian child with a beatifically innocent face asked me.

"Is he that skinny silverback ape down on the first floor?"

The bell rang.

"Saved by the bell!" Dorina announced.

"I'm sure none of you will tell this story to Professor Dolan," I admonished the class, as they dismissed themselves.

"All right, Bishop Blackie," the still-blushing Dean Dorie admitted as we trudged down the stairs to the first floor. "You win. I won't try to trick you into a class again . . . I bet you made that up as you went along."

That was true of course.

"I had planned it for years, just in case I should need it."

Professor Dolan waited for us on the first floor. He pounded his chest and bellowed. In truth he didn't sound much like a silverback.

"Bishop Blackie," he thundered, "you're corrupting the youth of the land with those stories about the black Irish."

"And embarrassing the dean too," I said. "I can't imagine why."

To change the subject, Dorie suggested a cup of tea. In Dave's office, lest it seem that the dean wasn't working. She poured the tea, however, as is the woman's right.

"Everyone goes away in the summer here at the University?" I asked.

"Just about everyone," Dorie replied. "Some even leave after the last day of class before the traditional study week and the week of exams."

"You've worked for eleven weeks," Dave agreed sarcastically, "so you're entitled to head for the mountains or the shore or the coast or even the Dunes, where you can start thinking again. That's the business we're in, Bishop Blackie, we're thinkers. Some of us go to meetings in odd parts of the world like Trieste or Bilbao or Umeya or Strasburg or similar centers of wisdom. We poor untenured assistant professors have to be content with a week at Sheridan Beach, where we do our best to create the illusion we're thinking instead of just worrying."

"It's hard to think, Bishop," Dorina added, "when you're out on a boat sailing every day."

I sighed loudly. "I am told that is so. However, I wonder where your colleagues who were standing at the door of the murder scene might have gone."

Silence for the moment while they pondered that odd question.

"Doug Strong goes to Oxford . . . ," Dorie began.

"He'd rather say 'back to Oxford,'" her swain continued. "He brushes up on his English accent there.

"Israel Golden goes to Israel, where else? He teaches at the University of Tel Aviv and argues with the other rabbis."

"Which is what rabbis do," I observed. "And Ms. Comerford?"

They looked at one another.

"She never says exactly," Dorie said. "Doesn't leave any forwarding address. I have the impression she goes to Paris, or used to go to Paris. Do you know, Dave?"

"I'd be the last one she'd tell. She does speak French fluently."

So La Patrice would have been in Paris the same time as Brother Semyon. Perhaps. But what did that prove?

"Is it important, Bishop Blackie?"

"Just an idle question."

"You worry me, Bishop Ryan," Dave Dolan said with an attempt at sounding serious, which your silverbacks do occasionally.

"Indeed?"

"The students told me that you had them laughing all through the class this afternoon."

"There may be partial truth in that report."

"I'm not sure that we can tolerate such behavior at this University. I think the dean will support me in this. We have only limited resources here and we must make the most of every classroom hour we have with the students so that they will be able to compete with the graduates of other universities."

"I think I've heard something like that before."

"University education, particularly at the elite graduate level, is a serious activity, both for the instructor and the students. We can't afford to waste time and money in frivolity."

"David!" the dean, who should have known better, protested.

"I take your point," I said. "What would John D. Rockefeller think if he knew that there was frivolous Irish Catholic laughter in this, of all buildings."

"We simply can't tolerate it," David continued. "I concede that the Irish are a comedic people . . ."

"They cry when they're happy, and laugh when they're sad," I finished for him. "That may be admirable, but in a Baptist institution? What would William Rainey Harper say?"

"Precisely! So I call on the dean to reconsider this offer of an appointment, even if it is untenured, to someone who reduces serious students to laughter!"

"Will you two stop it!" Dean Keane shouted in protest. "You're both crazy."

"Oh, yes," I agreed.

"I've at least learned how to talk like a tenured faculty member," David said.

"You didn't mention lifetime appointments," I pointed out to Professor Dolan. "Though in my case that point is not relevant."

"Bishop, you're worse than this silverback oaf!"

"I'm flattered."

"We better get you up to Doug Strong," Dorie rose from her station on the edge of Dave Dolan's desk. "I'll clean up the tea things when I come back."

"Woman, you will not," Dave insisted. "I want to make my feminist statement."

"Be sure you dry them," she said as she led me down the corridor to the elevator.

Then in a whisper, "Isn't he sweet when he's in his courting mood?"

"If I know his mother," I replied, "and I assume that I do, he's learned to clean up even when he's not in a courting mood."

"I suppose you're right . . . Do you think I ought to marry him?"

"What do I know?"

Douglas Armitage Strong was a tall, vigorous WASP with a deep voice and lively brown eyes, handsome despite the lack of hair on the top of his head, and given to driving home a point by pounding his desk. He would have made a fine drill sergeant in the Royal Army or a splendid archdeacon in an Anglican diocese. He exhausted me almost before our conversation began.

"A drop of something at the end of the day, Your Grace?" he asked, removing a bottle of (ugh) Scotch from his desk. "The rules of *The* University forbid it, of course, but neither of us are Northern Baptists, are we?"

"I must drive back to the Cathedral during the rush hour," I pleaded, waving off his offer, which was kindly intended, though I abhor all imitation whiskeys. "I note, however, that the Northern Baptists are on the run around here. There seems to be something of a papist invasion going on."

He threw back his head and laughed loudly, something he would repeat often during our conversation.

"I don't think there are any Northern Baptists left. Thank God the Irish have arrived. We need more young people like Dorie and David. They breathe fresh air into this stuffy old place."

"You let a couple of them in"—I sighed loudly—"and first thing you know there goes the neighborhood."

He laughed till the tears ran down his cheeks. One more victim for my silly joke.

Reluctantly he put the bottle of Glenlivet back into his desk.

"Your field is philosophical theology, like Father Tracy's."

"My field is being an auxiliary bishop, something like your suffragans."

"What precisely does an auxiliary bishop do among Roman Catholics?"

"Perhaps you saw the film *Pulp Fiction*?"

"I saw it, yes, though it was a bit too bloody for my taste."

"You will remember the role that the excellent Harvey Keitel played."

"He cleaned up messes for the criminals."

"My precise role vis-à-vis the Cardinal."

Another burst of laughter.

Then, more seriously, "I assume you are aware of the Jesus Seminar."

"It does strike me as unusual that one would want to decide by majority vote where Jesus actually said something attributed to him."

"Exactly," he said, leaning forward and pounding his desk. "And what do you have when you have finally decided by majority vote that you have the rock-bottom Jesus, pure and undefiled?"

"A collection of interesting incidents and sayings of a man so unusual that he might very well have been who and what he claimed to be."

"Perhaps," he agreed. "But to get there you have violated the whole intent and purpose of the authors of the books, who, it is assumed, are irrelevant witnesses to the tradition of the early Church."

"*Reader's Digest* Jesus."

More laughter.

"Yet they are skilled in public relations and get for themselves a lot of public attention, which troubles some of the faithful."

"In my experience," I said cautiously, "only those who want to be troubled."

"In a way." He sighed, and leaned back in his deeply cushioned chair. "I'm glad they came along. Another windmill for me to joust against . . . But you want to talk about our poor friend Brother Semyon Ivanivich."

"I take it that you liked him."

"He was a delight. You must understand, Your Grace, that most of my colleagues are rather dry sticks. They live for their work and very little else. They are devoid of humor and even the ordinary social graces. Indeed they are less graceful even than the terrible men and women over in the humanities."

"Indeed."

"Semyon Ivanivich saw that immediately. He was very perceptive and a sophisticated man of the world. He loved to come up here early in the afternoon and have a sip or two of Glenlivet with me."

And later on a jar of vodka with David Dolan. A strong man indeed.

"He would tell me funny stories about how silly some of our colleagues are . . . He liked our young Irish friends, of course. Who wouldn't? He did think their courtship had gone on too long."

"It is my observation that they both think that too, though alas at different times."

That rated another laugh.

"He tried hard to be friends with everyone, an impossible task around here. Israel Golden blamed him for the holocaust, Patti Comerford thought he was a rapist, but then she thinks every man is a rapist. Patti blamed him for the Russian rape of two million German women at the end of the war."

Patti, huh?

"Patti is a strange one. We were in love once, twice actually."

"Indeed!"

"Yes." He sighed. "She was a very beautiful woman then. Still could be if she hadn't deliberately let herself go to seed."

I let him talk.

He slipped deeper into the cushions of his chair as if dreaming about the time before the Big Chill.

"We were graduate students at Harvard thirty years ago. Exciting times. Protests, sex, drugs, rock 'n' roll, Woodstock. We were the hinge of history sort of thing. Make love not war. Change the whole world. Looking back on it we were fools, more than most young people. Illusions. Reelected Nixon. I wanted to marry her. She seemed ready, even eager, though the ideology those days said that our generation didn't need a civil contract to ratify our love.

Then one day she told me I was a rapist like all men and she never wanted to see me again. I tried to argue, but she would not speak to me. For a while I was brokenhearted—she would be the perfect wife for my generation. Then I fell in love with my first wife. We went to Vanderbilt and had a child. Lad I'm still proud of. She died of an aneurysm. I had been happy at Vanderbilt. After Sue left me, I hated everything about it. So I accepted an offer from here."

He shrugged his shoulders.

"Not a very nice university if you ask me. Filled with people whose insecurities are bigger than their vast egos. Anyway, I get my work done. Sam has grown up to be a fine young man. Marine captain. I knew Patti was here, but I figured we could avoid each other. Maybe I wanted another chance with her. I found that she was even more beautiful. We paired up right away and had good times. Then the same thing happened. I still can't figure it out. She never left the hard-line ideology behind, like the rest of us did. A Marxist feminist she calls herself, whatever that is. Like I say, she deliberately let herself go to seed. Ignores me. And ignores everyone else. She's quite a problem at tenure meetings. Can't deliver any votes but vicious not only to the candidate but to the rest of us. If we could get rid of her, I'm sure we would."

"Not angry enough to kill Brother Semyon, I presume?"

"Patti would never kill anyone, Your Grace. She won't even step on ants. It's all talk. Mind you, she believes the talk. We all did once. Most of us have grown up. She hasn't."

"Who would have?"

"You think it was an inside job? I doubt that. There's a lot of nasty people with offices in this building. But they're the kind that kill with words, not with swords. It was probably an outside job, like the poor Romanian chap who was killed in the toilet several years ago."

I ignored the allusion to Oscar Wilde's poem.

"With inside help perhaps?"

"A long time ago, Your Grace, we prated about mounting the

barricades. All that remains now is organic food and jeans. We were revolutionaries! There may be some people around this building who hate Russians, but they wouldn't even conspire in murder for fear the police would find out and they'd be sent to a prison where they would be roadkill for homosexuals. Even Patti wouldn't want to be pawed over by Black butches."

The last comment seemed gratuitous. Doug Strong was still angry because of his double rejection.

"You and Israel Golden and Ms. Comerford were in the building the night of the murder."

"And Dolan too, right next door. We all ran downstairs and found him pounding on the door. 'Get the key and open it, you fool,' Patti says to him. He went back to his office and called the dean, who has the keys locked up in her office. We're nervous around here about someone stealing our scholarship. She runs over, quite literally, and dashes into her office to get the key. Patti says something nasty about a stupid little whore. No one pays any attention to her when she says those kinds of things. Dorina opens the door. It was gruesome, brain tissue all over. Terrible smell. We turn away from it. Dorina returns to her office to call the president. The cops show up finally and rattle the door. Dolan goes to let them in. The three of us—Patti, Israel, and I—stand there and stare."

"And one or more of you go into the office."

He sat up straight in his chair and stared at me.

"Who told you that?" he said sharply. "It was a place no sane human being could possibly want to enter. I would have vomited on the spot if I had walked into that room."

Overreaction, I thought to myself. I'd push a little harder.

"Someone went in."

"It wasn't me!"

But it was someone. No point in pushing any further.

"Did Brother Semyon seem especially concerned about anything when he returned from his vacation?"

Doug Strong relaxed, slipping back into the comforts of his chair.

"I hardly had a chance to talk to him. I came back from Harvard only two days before class began. No point in hanging around this place unless you have to. I saw him once or twice in the corridor and mentioned that I had several bottles of Glenlivet. He never came up here, however. I gather he was very busy on some project or the other. He wasn't teaching this quarter."

"Indeed."

"So I'm afraid, Your Grace, I can't be of much help. I think it's a damn shame. The administration of this University seems quite incapable of protecting its faculty from kooks and criminals. I'm going to raise the issue at the next meeting of the Committee of the Council and ask for an investigation."

"Kooks," I said, "or agents of the secret police."

He waved his hand, dismissing the idea.

"That story belongs in an Alan Furst novel, Your Grace."

10

"Bishop Blackie," a *Megan told me,* "there's a very polite man down here to see you. He's well dressed and looks like a wrestler and speaks with a funny foreign accent. I think he's Russian."

The Megan must have been Megan Kim. She's succinct in her description and has an ear for accents.

I looked at my watch, the one my old fella had worn on the deck of his DE during the battle of Lingayin Gulf.

"It's nine-thirty, Megan. Isn't it about time for you to go home?"

"My dad was delayed at the hospital with an emergency. He'll pick me up in about fifteen or twenty minutes."

Naturally Megan Kim's father was an MD. So too her mother.

I did not want to deal with a Russian. Or anyone else. Particularly on a day when I had more than enough Russians.

"Okay, Megan, tell him I'll be right down."

I slipped on my Roman collar, perhaps as a superstitious totem against Russians carrying sawed-off shotguns under their coats.

By some miracle of grace, I had managed to navigate Lake Shore Drive during the rush hour, though my brain was whirling as it tried to sort out the wheat from the chaff of the day's events. I knew a lot more than I did when I had driven down to *The* University in the morning. I did not, however, know what I knew.

In the Rectory there were notes for hospital calls, telephone messages to return, checks to sign, and an inordinate array of e-mail. I went to the hospital first and managed to get lost several times in the new Northwestern maze. I was late for supper, which fact induced Milord Cronin to inquire of the staff as to whether they thought Bishop Ryan needed a long vacation. They all fervently agreed that he did.

The meek little auxiliary replied that he would cheerfully leave tomorrow for Bora-Bora if the Lord Cardinal would take his proper place as pastor of the Cathedral. Said auxiliary bishop even volunteered to help him learn the computer program on which all events in the Cathedral depended for their very existence.

That was the end of that discussion.

"Hard day at *The* University?" the Cardinal asked, as we rode up in the elevator.

"Overload and no time to sort it out."

"Any closer to a solution?"

I considered.

"I am reasonably confident that I have deciphered the locked-room puzzle. I have a pretty good idea who created it, though I do not understand why. I also know with some degree of certainty that His Eminence Semyon Cardinal Popov was not the man who was shot. I do not know, however, where he is or was or whether he might still be alive or who was responsible for the replacement and why."

"Oh," the Cardinal said, somewhat meekly. For him.

"It grows more serious and, I believe, more dangerous."

"Were the Feds responsible for the firefight last night?" He assumed his favorite place against the doorframe of my study.

"Arguably. Foreign spooks would have been more efficient."

"Was that man they found up in the woods near the Holy Virgin Protection Cathedral the real killer?"

I had forgotten about him, as I had almost forgotten about the gunfire the night before.

"Perhaps. The Chicago cops will certainly say so because it closes

the investigation of Brother Semyon's killing. I cannot believe, however, that the Outfit really put him down, though they seem to be
claiming they did."

"Because they're good Catholics?"

"What else?"

Milord thereupon had left for a confirmation in a Wrigleyville
parish and I to my phone messages. There seemed to be more than the
usual number of crazies who wanted to complain than on an ordinary
day. Then I had finally turned on the computer to catch up on my
e-mail when Megan announced the advent of this nice-looking wrestler person who sounded like a Russian.

She had put him in the "living room"—an office which had been
redone to look warm and comfortable—couches, subdued lighting,
wallpaper, even an unused TV.

Her wrestler metaphor was accurate. The man had the build, the
frown, and the bald head of the retiring governor of Minnesota.
However, his face was square and solid, very Eastern European. He
wore a carefully fitted dark blue, three-piece suit, a sparkling white
shirt, and a red-and-blue tie.

"Ivanoff," he said crisply, bowed respectfully and handed me a
business card.

It announced him as Rodion Petrovich Ivanoff, president of
Ivanoff and Company, Importers and Exporters.

That's what the Russian mob claimed to be. It was never quite
clear, however, what they imported and exported.

"I am very happy you could find time to see me, Your Lordship,"
he said in a rich, bass voice that could easily have been heard in
Leningrad.

Pardon me. St. Petersburg.

"You are most welcome, Rodion Petrovich," I said, bowing back.

I would have been Ivan Ivanivich if I were Russian. Not very exciting.

"I am not of your faith," he went on. "I do not want to impose
on Your Lordship's time."

Andrew M. Greeley

The Russians, I had learned somewhere, reveled in long and complex apologies.

"In this Rectory," I replied, "everyone is welcome, regardless of religion, race, gender, sexual orientation, or previous condition of servitude. Won't you sit down."

He did, not trying to figure out my last statement. I felt that it would be appropriate to offer him "glass vodka," if I had any in the house.

"I wish to discuss with you," he said stiffly, "the unfortunate matter of the death of Brother Semyon Ivanivich Popov."

"It is a matter of serious interest for us," I agreed.

"He was a wise and holy man, Your Lordship. It has been said that my associates and I were responsible for his death. I want to assure you that the charge is not true."

So the Russian outfit seemed to think that it had to protest its innocence to Sean Cronin's innocuous little auxiliary. Wery, Wery interesting.

"I'm delighted to hear that."

"We're all good Russian Orthodox. We would never kill a priest or a monk."

"Certainly not, unless of course there were a good reason."

"Exactly. I do not know why some business rivals would want to spread a story like that."

"Envy of your success, perhaps."

Megan Kim knocked on the door.

"My honored father is here, Bishop Blackie. I'm going home now."

"Good night, Megan. Thank you. Give my best greetings to your honored father."

"Korean, Your Lordship?"

"Yes."

He sighed loudly.

"A very gifted people. We have many of them in Eastern Russia."

He said it sadly, perhaps because if you're Russian, you have to be sad much of the time. Or perhaps he lamented that Korean Russians were not working for him. Doubtless attending medical school.

"This man who they say killed the monk, this Sergei Borisevich Smirnoff, worked for us at one time. He was not, ah, satisfactory so we unfortunately had to discharge him. We have not heard of him for several months. Then we see his name in the paper and read that his body was found near the Holy Virgin Protection Cathedral on the day of the funeral liturgy. This was most troubling."

My friend Ivanoff was patently a *capo*, or whatever the Russkies called their principle henchman. Indeed he may have been the functional equivalent of the *capo di tutti capi*, the godfather himself. If he wanted to deliver a message to the Catholic Church, he would face the relevant bureaucrat directly and not relay a message through layers of "friends of friends." Different style. In any conflict between the two outfits, the Sicilian style would probably be more effective.

"I can understand that."

"We believe that our business rivals hired this Sergei Borisevich Smirnoff to kill the monk, then killed him to implicate us."

"Your rivals," I said, "are quite capable of such tricks."

"They read their own Machiavelli, no?"

A literate mob boss.

"I doubt it, Rodion Petrovich. They don't have to. He made what they know from birth explicit."

He laughed heartily at that.

"Very good, Your Lordship, very good!"

My instincts said I should throw a bomb. What was there to lose? So I threw it!

"We are greatly troubled by the whole affair, my friend. We believe that the man who was killed was in fact an imposter!"

"An imposter! How can this be!"

"We have reason to believe that the real Brother Semyon was lifted in Paris sometime this summer and the imposter was sent to Chicago in his place. To many Americans, a Russian with a white beard, a monk's robe, and a staff looks like any other such man. The

135

ruse would have been discovered eventually, but apparently his work required only a little time."

I had never thought of that before.

"It could easily be true," Rodion Petrovich agreed, his eyes glowing with the paranoia that is part of Russian character. "The FSB, the Sûreté, the FBI, the CIA, MI6—any of them might do it. They would not even need a reason."

"Possibly they were searching for something they thought Brother Semyon had in his possession."

"Yes, that seems very reasonable."

Even if I had only thought of it now myself. But what would they be looking for? Someone had told me in the last couple of days that Brother Semyon's papers were spread all over the floor of his office. Who was it?

I needed time to think. Tomorrow morning perhaps.

"One must not," Rodion Petrovich mused, "exclude the men from Trans-Dniester."

That was a new one on me.

"Who are they?"

"You know about Moldova, naturally?"

"Also called Bessarabia. You and the Romanians have stolen it back and forth from each other for a couple of centuries."

"Remarkable! After the Great Patriotic War, Comrade Stalin established it as the Moldavia Soviet Socialist Republic with Russian as its official language though most of its people are Romanian. He also forbade the Latin alphabet and replaced it with the Cyrillic. So naturally when the USSR collapsed, the Moldavians reestablished the Romanian language and the Latin alphabet, much to the displeasure of the Russians and the Ukrainians who lived along the east bank of the Dniester. Those who lived on the east bank of the river established their own republic with the help of the Fourteenth Red Army, which was stationed there. There was some threat that the army would march on Moscow and restore the Soviet Union. Vodka talk."

He shrugged expressively.

"However they soon realized that their future was in business rather than in military exploits. They have become very successful businessmen."

Export-import business, no doubt.

"Sometimes, alas"—he rose to leave, his task accomplished—"because of their military background, their tactics are a little rough. They also have a very active security group. I believe that this Sergei Borisevich Smirnoff was associated with them in the past."

I assured Rodion Petrovich that I would relay his message to Cardinal Cronin, thanked him for his consideration in keeping us informed, and urged him to feel free to contact me either in person or on the phone whenever he wished. He beamed happily. His mission a success.

Why, I wondered, did he think we were so important?

I ushered him to the door. Outside there was a black Rolls limo, one man inside, two outside. As soon as I had opened the door to the Rectory, the two outside men—burly types who surely were veterans of the Black Berets—rushed up to escort Rodion Petrovich to his car. He waved to me just before he turned to climb in—a large and sweeping wave.

I wondered whether the American military had not made a serious mistake. I should have hired these folks, the cream of the Red Army, before they turned to organized crime, initially to keep themselves and their families alive.

"Who were those guys?" Milord Cronin, who had been watching from the lobby of our offices, asked.

"Russkies," I said. "The boss of their outfit, I think. He wanted to assure us that they had no part in the killing of Brother Semyon."

"Why us?"

"Beats me."

"This is really weird stuff, Blackwood. I don't want Russian gangsters hanging around my Cathedral. Clean it all up."

"It won't be that easy. Think of someone over there who will tell me the whole truth if I confront him in his office."

"You're planning a trip to Rome?"

He knew my aversion to travel.

"Arguably."

I should have gone to bed. However, the e-mail never answers itself. So I turned on the computer and began to work through sixty or so missives, most of which I could delete without the slightest tinge of conscience.

The phone rang. Was I on call tonight?

"Father Ryan."

"Flip White here, Bishop."

"Ah."

"What should we do with these crimson robes? Do you want them?"

"We will assume protection of them until the real Brother Semyon returns."

"You still think the man who was killed was not Brother Semyon?"

"I take it to be patent."

"Yeah, but my bosses want the whole thing out of the way. It's moving from the active to the pending file. Right now we don't know who was killed or who the killer was . . ."

"I thought it was the hapless Sergei Borisevich Smirnoff, whose body the Des Plaines police found the day of the funeral."

"That's his name? How did you learn that?"

"The Russkie mob denies that he was working for them."

Flip thought for a moment.

"Well, they would, wouldn't they? However, the bosses here are content with that explanation. They'll be happy I can pass on the name of the corpse to Des Plaines. Our case goes into the pending files to sit there until something else turns up, if it ever does. Their case will be active for a while too, then slip off the desk."

"Indeed."

"What should we do with all his papers?"

"Call Dean Keane and tell her that you assume the University will want them . . ."

That reminded me of a question that had fled to the lower sub basements of my mind.

"By the way, in what state were the papers in his office when you came upon them?"

"The whole office was littered with them. Others were stuffed into the file cabinet, like someone had ransacked them and maybe the wind from the storm had blown a pile off the desk."

"I had assumed that the windows were closed?"

"They were when we got there."

"Your man who read through them found nothing?"

"He learned more than he ever wanted to know about Russian mysticism. Nothing else. Some things might have been taken before the shooting of course."

"And sent to whoever might have been curious?"

"Yeah . . . You gotta understand, Bishop, we're not set up to deal with this kind of crime."

"The Feds?"

"Too busy and not interested."

"Naturally."

Too busy planning an inept raid on my Rectory.

"By the way, young Dave Dolan found a Waterford tumbler which he thinks might have the prints and the DNA of the real Brother Semyon. I think he's handing it over to his father."

Flip White groaned.

"That's all I need."

I was too tired even to pour my tiny splash of Bushmills before I collapsed into bed, mentioning to the Deity that I was sorry I couldn't say any appropriate night prayers, but He had sent all these tasks and it was His responsibility.

There was no response, though I imagined tolerant laughter.

As I was crashing into the land of Nod, the elevator door opened suddenly. I had plunged into the deepest recesses of consciousness.

Andrew M. Greeley

Inside the door, all glowing and resplendent was the solution to the whole puzzle. I rejoiced. So that was it. Of course. What else? I had to sleep now, but when I awoke in the morning I would have it all, right?

140

11

Wrong!

By morning my resplendent solution was as the little kids say, "aw gone!" In fact I remembered my hypnagogic insight only at Northwestern Hospital on my morning calls. While we have a veritable army of lay ministers to bring Communion to the hospital, most of the sick still want to see a priest, which is their right, even if the leaders of our institution are not willing to make the changes necessary to resupply the current priesthood. Just as I was bidding farewell to a lovely lady of ninety years and promising her that we would meet again, the elevator door opened again, light burst forth. Then I lost it.

Would it come back? Sometimes it did and sometimes it didn't.

Before I could read the melancholy news in the *Sun-Times* about the latest problems of the Chicago Bears, Dorie Keane was on the phone.

"The police want to turn Brother Semyon's papers over to us, Bishop. I'm sure we'll take them provisionally until someone else claims them. Then we'll catalog them for the University archives."

"Apparently they were in some disorder, like someone had been searching his files."

"I can't imagine what secrets they might find."

"Unless he had a secret, secret file."

"That's why I'm calling, Bishop Blackie. He did have such a file. He gave it to me when he came here last year and I put it in our secret safe."

There were enough secrets already. Who needed any more?

"It's still there?"

"Yes. We can't give the file to you, but I talked to President Alan and he said that, if you come out here, you could read it."

"I don't do very well in Russian."

"You could glance at it . . ."

Arguably the file contained information for which the real Brother Semyon had been lifted and the phony Brother Semyon was searching. Those who wanted it would obviously stop at nothing to get it. Someone in their organization would figure out that there might be interesting material in the Divinity School. They could stage a daylight raid, ride in like the James Brothers and shoot the place up. More likely it would be a night raid. They would blow off the doors of whatever safes they found, scoop up the loot, and ride out of town, guns blazing.

I did not like it.

"I don't like it, Dorina. Someone wanted that file badly enough to kill. They will doubtless try again. Would you ask your good friend the president of the University to call me."

"Right away, Bishop."

Within five minutes Reed Alan was on the line.

"Dorina Keane asked me to call you, Bishop. She explained to me your concerns, which I fully share. We'll issue a press release today to announce that we will consign Brother Semyon's papers provisionally to the sealed archives in the basement of Regenstein Library. We will also for a time increase the security guard at the library."

"Excellent. However, it will take some time to collect all the papers both from his apartment and his office and place them in some temporary order, will it not?"

"A few days . . ."

"Then I would suggest that you surround Swift Hall with outside security forces, sufficient to repel any invader."

"I am told that Reliable is very good. I believe I've met Mr. Casey, who presides over it and, as I remember, is an artist of some renown."

You're made a university president because you remember things like that. Or mayor.

"Tell them that you believe the offices of the dean and the safes therein are the most likely target for attack.

"You also advise in a low key the faculty of the Divinity School that the building will be closed at six until further notice."

"They won't like it, but I don't dare tell them exactly why."

"You might also point out to the dean that she is neither Queen Maeve nor Grace O'Malley and that the ban on being in the building applies to her."

"I'm told, Bishop, that Irishwomen don't like obeying orders. Nonetheless I will insist . . . There remains the problem of the secret file itself. What should we do with it? If it is something extremely sensitive, I would be reluctant, given the phone call I received when Brother Semyon first joined us, to put it in Regenstein."

If it were a file someone wanted to destroy, they might simply blow up Swift or Regenstein. Or the whole University. If it were one they wanted to possess and read, they might use other tactics.

"I think it would be wise to presume that under the circumstances you have Brother Semyon's consent and open the file."

"I suppose so. I would hope you would join me. Your advice would be very valuable."

"As a member of your faculty, I could hardly decline."

"We may have to double your salary."

"Let me suggest that you talk to Mike Casey about the whole problem and mention the secret file. If he agrees, then I'll be happy to be there."

Would Flambeau deny Father Brown access to such material!

"I will be back in touch with you."

"We'll need someone who can read Russian."

"Oh," he said lightly, "I think I can manage that."

Well, I bet he couldn't do Latin!

What kind of secrets would a man who was presumably a Cardinal Prince of the Holy Roman Church know? What possible material could he have compiled that others might kill for?

I did not like it, not at all, at all.

The secretary called to say that Captain White had left a clothes bag at the door for me. I went downstairs and retrieved it. Then I ascended to the Lord Cardinal's room, where he was reading his breviary.

"I have a present for you," I said. "However, it may be only temporary."

He looked up and frowned. "Brother Semyon's sacred crimson?"

As I have occasion to remark on many occasions, Sean Cronin is nobody's fool.

I unzipped the bag. He fingered the fabric.

"Authentic, Blackwood . . . What do I do with it? I don't need a second set."

"You keep it over here against the possible return of Cardinal Popov. No one will think it strange that you have such robes. If it were discovered in my closets, some might think that I had plans and aspirations."

"Also they might be lost permanently in the inner secrets of your closets . . . Well, I don't know, Blackwood. You never can tell when the Holy Spirit will tire of the bullshit and lay down orders that you must ascend to the sacred crimson. We could always alter this set."

"The Holy Spirit may be a comedienne, but She does not have to work that hard for laughs."

He took the clothes bag and hung it in the closet where his various crimson fashions were stored.

"Never say never, Blackwood. Never is a long time."

"Harry Truman," I said, escaping from his suite.

I had a phone call to make. To whom?

I couldn't quite remember.

The family would disown me if I ever paraded around in the sacred crimson.

Then I remembered. Another overseas call. France again.

"Jeanne-Chantal," the voice at the other end announced serenely.

"Call me Blackie."

"Ah, *M. l'Evêque.* You call again. There is trouble, *n'est-ce pas?*"

"And how fares *l'enfant?*"

"*Le petit* Jean-Claude grows up too quickly. His father and I are greatly consoled and amused by his presence with us."

Jean Claude was named after his uncle, her twin, a Dominican brother replaced by her at the time of his ordination. That, however, was another story.

"And Jean-Laurence flourishes in his practice of the law?"

"*Mais certainement!* However, he now loves his family more."

"Wise man."

"And *mes amis,* Marie-Bernadette and Jacques-Yves."

"They prosper. Their first record did very well and they receive many invitations to play. They also receive good grades at the Conservatory. As you doubtless know they are awaiting a child."

"*La petite* Marie-Bernadette promises me that if it is a girl she will be Chantal. When you see her, say that I will hold her to that promise . . . Now what information do you need?"

"Has there been any mention in Paris lately of a Russian monk called Brother Semyon Ivanivich Popov?"

"But of course! He was lecturing here at the Sorbonne on Russian mysticism to great acclaim. Jean-Laurence made me attend one of them. Not one word did I understand. However, Jean-Laurence said it was brilliant. Then, poof! It was announced that he was unable to continue the series. Some say he simply vanished. You have some familiarity with such matters if I remember correctly, do you not?"

"I do not think Brother Semyon has a twin sister."

"Never be sure of anything, *M. l'Evêque.*"

Even over the phone her charm radiated. That was why as *Frère* Jean-Claude she had taken France by storm. Like I say, that's another story.

"The cops are looking for him, are they not?"

"With the same diligence that they used to find *Frère* Jean-Claude."

"Which is to say they really don't want to find him?

"*C'est vrai.* Disappearing monks cause much embarrassment, no?"

The little witch was laughing at me.

"You, however, will find out where he is, if indeed he is?"

"I will listen very carefully. There are always rumors around the Sorbonne. I do not think that Brother Semyon is quite so clever as *Frère* Jean-Claude."

"And you are much more clever than the one who found out where the latter was?"

"Not quite, *M. l'Evêque*, not quite!"

So he had been lifted in Paris. By whom? Did the Vatican keep in contact with their in petto cardinals? Did they know that he had been lifted? Were they looking for him or were they protecting him? Not questions the people involved, the spook side of the Curia, would want to answer. Did they know about his secret file? If they had him, he could have told them where it was, unless he didn't want them to see it. Or denied its existence.

And why was it so important anyway.

Then Mike Casey was on the line. We used the safe line of public phones again.

"It looks like I'll have to start paying you commissions, Blackie."

"This one could be big, Mike."

"You mean your friends could ride into the quadrangle with a T-54 tank or a troop of Cossack cavalry?"

"They are very dangerous people, Mike. Bring your toughest cops and tell them all to wear their body armor."

"You really expect a serious assault?"

"We will know more when we read the file this afternoon. Let me rehearse the facts of the case as I know them at the moment."

So I went through the story. He whistled when I stopped.

"Did the Sicilian guys call you about the visit from the Russkie?"

"Not yet. I don't think they have a shadow on the Rectory or on Rodion Petrovich. Still, they probably know everything that happens. No reason to warn me . . ."

"There are a lot of players involved."

"There seem to be . . . You know about these Trans-Dniester folk?"

"Yes indeed. They are the craziest criminals in all the world. The president should have turned them loose on Al Qaeda. They move at two speeds—charge and faster."

"They might try to blow up the Divinity School."

"Oh yes, they might indeed. The major advantage we have in dealing with them is they're not very bright . . . Has Sean tried to pry any information out of the Vatican?"

"Without much success so far. I don't think he has used much clout yet, though in truth American cardinals have very little clout over there."

"Sean more than most of them, I assume."

"Arguably . . . Depending on what we learn this afternoon I may lean on him to pick up all the markers he has over there."

"Suppose that the imposter found the file for which he was searching and sent it on to his employers, what would he have done then?"

"Most likely he would have disappeared."

"Or would have been killed anyway?"

"Perhaps."

"Do you think the real Brother Semyon is still alive?"

"I'm not sure who the real Brother Semyon is or was. Just now I think he may not be alive, though perhaps some relatively benign group is holding him."

"Too many players." Mike sighed. "Well, I'll see you out there at the dean's office at four. I think I'll bring along some of my guys as well as whoever is watching you."

I had forgotten that there was a team of gumshoes following me around.

"Mike, that advice about the body armor applies to you too."

Silence for a moment.

"You really are serious, aren't you?"

"As we say in the mother tongue, *sicut grex, sicut rex*."

"You've got it backward, Blackie, but I'll do what you urge."

"Order," I said, as I wondered whether our opponents, whoever they might be, could be tapping the public phones too.

As soon as I had ended that conversation, Dean Keane was on the line.

"What's happening, Bishop Blackie? Why are we meeting in my office at four and why is the Div School locked down after six indefinitely and who are the cops that are lurking around here?"

"Don't ask."

"We're going to open that file, aren't we?"

"I said don't ask."

"Oh."

"And don't share your suspicions and hunches with any of the local silverbacks."

"Very heavy stuff, huh?"

"Arguably."

"Okay . . . Can we have lunch with you today at the Q-Club? I won't ask any bad questions."

"We?"

"Myself and the silverback. No big deal yet. Maybe there never will be."

"Finally, that will be up to you."

She didn't reply. Perhaps she understood now that closure belongs to the woman of the species.

I arranged for Mr. Woods to pick me up and deliver me to *The University*. Presumably Mike the Cop would see to my safe return to the Cathedral Rectory.

Then I paid court to Milord Cronin to report the unfolding

events. He was standing at his desk glancing through a file whose cheap paper said "Vatican." He was clad in his Chancery Office garb, black suit, clerical vest, barely discernible red edge around the collar.

"Idiots, Blackwood," he exploded. "You're right. We are a long way from Peter and his bunch, and all of it downhill."

"And if my memory of the scriptures serves, they were not all that swift a crowd either."

He laughed grimly.

"Have you wound up the Brother Semyon case yet?"

"We progress, but very slowly."

I filled him in on the more recent developments.

"You really think a bunch of commandos will try to raid *The* University for a secret file some Russian monk kept?"

"I think it not improbable . . . You will remember that the monk is also a brother Cardinal Prince of the Holy Roman Church?"

"Maybe . . . Maybe it's all a big hoax . . . Have you thought of that."

"A hoax in which people are murdered and this venerable Rectory is sprayed with automatic weapon fire, apparently on order of the Feds?"

"There's that . . . What do you think is in the file, Blackwood?"

I had not permitted myself the time to speculate.

"Arguably a secret history of covert dealings over the years between certain elements among your very good friends in the Vatican and certain elements of the Russian Orthodox Church, including the involvement of various spook agencies around the world in these dealings. And perhaps some information about still-obscure aspects of the Polish situation."

I sighed at the end of this exercise. For instant speculation it seemed very reasonable. Now I half believed it.

Milord Cronin put the curial file on the polished oak desk and stared out the window at the traffic on Superior Street.

"I wouldn't put it past them, Blackwood. They do some things not because it is in their interest to do them but because it is in their nature . . . I don't think we should be involved anymore."

"Arguably not. Nonetheless, I should at least learn what is in that file, should I not?"

"Yeah I suppose so."

"Moreover, if Cardinal Popov is still alive, we should try to protect him, should we not?"

"I'm not so sure about that. There's an upper limit to how many chances we should take to cover their tracks for them."

"I agree," I admitted.

"So we'll review this whole thing tomorrow morning, right?"

"Patently."

"It is," he said as he put the Vatican's file in his tooled-leather briefcase, "at least more interesting than this shit."

"And than most of my e-mail."

We rode down the elevator together, he to leave for the Chancery and I for *The* University.

"I don't want you to get shot, Blackwood," he remarked, as the elevator door opened on the first floor. "See to it."

Crystal was waiting for me with a teen schedule she insisted I must approve. It was quite impossible. The parish premises would swarm with sweaty kids.

"Fine," I said.

"Be careful, Bishop Blackie," she warned me as I opened the door to Wabash Avenue. "I don't know what we'd do without you."

"About the same as you're doing now," I replied, trying to sound casual.

Worries from both the Cardinal and the fair Crystal were enough to create a certain glacierlike chill in the pit of my stomach. The dark clouds and the pelting October rain did not enhance my confidence.

Because of Mr. Woods's great skill in navigating the construction on Lake Shore Drive, I arrived early at the Quadrangle Club and joined those loitering in the stone-floored lobby waiting their luncheon partners in monastic silence. One did not disturb the important thoughts of a colleague in such a situation.

I wandered into the billiard room, where men were actually playing billiards, odd behavior in a place dedicated to the winning of Nobel prizes.

I returned to the lobby. A short man, with blinking eyes behind thick glasses, little hair, and a red face approached me. He looked like a gnome or possibly a leprechaun, though a very unhappy one.

"You're Bishop Ryan, aren't you?"

"I'm afraid so," I admitted.

"I want to say to you that you and your kind have done a great disservice to the stability of the world by permitting the current chaos in the Catholic Church."

He waved a trembling finger at me and charged on.

"You and the rest of the bishops are not intelligent enough to know what's happening, but you're still responsible for dismantling one of the strongest institutions that has ever existed. You have done enormous harm to the whole world. We desperately need peace and order and you have created conflict and disorder."

"You're a Catholic, sir?"

"No, I'm not. But I have always valued the service of the Church in conserving the continuity and the traditions of the West. Now you are destroying them. I am outraged."

It was not the kind of assault I might have anticipated here at *The* University. I searched for a response while he continued the assault.

"You are obviously uneducated and do not even belong on the grounds of this University, which still stands for order and stability. We are under constant pressure here. You have made our task worse. I suggest you leave."

When you are at a loss for words (as well as when you are not) the best action is to follow the advice of the Founder and turn the other cheek.

So, filled with my own sense of virtue, I said, "I appreciate your sharing your opinion with me, sir."

Then I remembered where I had met him before.

"By the way, sir, haven't I met you in a novel somewhere?"

His face turned red and he stomped away.

The other cheek turned and the last word won, I felt inordinately proud of myself.

The local silverback appeared.

"That guy giving you a hard time?"

"As far as I could understand he believes that the changes in the Church for which I am responsible are destabilizing *The* University."

"That's his line on just about everything. *The* University is a fortress under attack from all sides. It's survival is in doubt. Enemies are everywhere . . . Did he order you to leave?"

"He did and I declined."

"Not so long ago he had enormous power around here. Now it's gone, but he doesn't seem to understand that . . . Did you tell him that you're a visiting professorial lecturer at the Div School?"

"Lacking documentation, I did not."

"Just as well. He would have put up a big fight against you. He would have lost of course. But it's not worth the fight."

Just then the Keen Dean appeared in a dark maroon knit dress, rushed and flushed, and we climbed the stairs to the dining room.

"Our old friend tried to order the good bishop out of here," her swain said to the dean.

"Oh, that awful man . . . I'm sorry, Bishop Blackie, he's just a little round the bend. We have a lot of characters around here. He's still fighting against the 1960s. Did you tell him that you were joining the Div School faculty?"

"As I remarked to the local silverback, I had no documentation to prove this."

"Oh, we'll get it to you soon. If he knew, he'd make trouble. He'd lose. No one but a few of the old-timers take him seriously. But we wouldn't want to get into a dogfight with him. I'll tell the president this afternoon . . ."

A dogfight might save me from further appearances in the Div School classrooms. I could retire a martyr. In our society nothing succeeds like failure with the possible exception of martyrdom.

We chatted amiably. About the Church. About *The* University. About the Chicago Bears. But not about Brother Semyon or about themselves. Yet they seemed relaxed with one another, Dave's outrageous wit setting the tone of the relationship and Dorie accepting the tone with pleased amusement.

The trouble with the custom of delayed marriages is that men and women become excessively cautious, observing as they have all the things that have gone wrong in the marriages of their friends and acquaintances. Yet a decision made at twenty-five or even twenty-two is not guaranteed to be less wise than one made at thirty-two. Clearly my two young friends were counting the risks and the costs.

As we walked over to Swift Hall, Dave began to kid about the secret meeting and the lockdown of the Div School. Dorie, to give her full credit, just shut her mouth.

"Come on now, Blackie, you don't really think, do you, that there's going to be some kind of bombing at Swift tonight?"

"I'll tell you what I think, Professor David Dolan. I think at six o'clock you take the good dean in your care and drive out to your mother's house for dinner and assign her to you sister's bedroom in the house."

"She'll lock the door!"

"Be that as it may."

"You're serious, aren't you?"

"Indeed!"

"Dorie?" He cocked one of his huge black eyebrows.

"I think I'd like one of your mom's home-cooked dinners."

"Then we'll do it."

"You'll phone us, Bishop, if anything happens?"

We paused at the entrance to Swift.

"Most likely," I said, "it will be a quiet evening of which the Northern Baptists Founders of this University would be proud. Yet I promise a call."

We left Dave Dolan at his office.

"I haven't locked the door the last several times I was there," Dorie said to me. "He doesn't show up."

"You've invited him to?"

"Of course not. His mother and father sleep just down the corridor."

"Indeed."

"You think I should have told him the door was unlocked?"

"Certainly not. There are more subtle ways of achieving the same result."

"I don't understand." She frowned at me.

She did, of course, understand.

I sighed.

"I put it to you that the current model for your relationship is both inadequate and inaccurate. It assumes that David is the one that wants to marry and that you are hesitant. In fact, the reverse is the case. He hesitates as men usually do and you have yet to push for the closure which is always the woman's privilege."

She lowered her head and bowed her eyes. Then she sighed almost as loudly as I did.

"We'd better go into the meeting now," she said, turning away towards the door to her office.

Then, as an afterthought, "You're right."

"Patently."

Two of Mike Casey's stalwarts lounged unobtrusively in the outer office, one of them my old friend Tina, a short Latina with the heart of a whole pride of lions. They studiously ignored us, which is part of the drill.

We were the first there. Reed Alan and Mike the Cop appeared. The president introduced Dorie to Mike.

"I think she'll be president of this University someday."

"Which serves you right for letting an Irishwoman in," I said. "There goes the neighborhood."

Another guffaw. I figured I had milked that line for all it was worth and better come up with another.

We gathered in a conference room outside the dean's office. Dorie went into her office and came back with a thin, crudely wrapped package covered with Scotch tape. She put it solemnly, like the gifts for the Eucharist, in the middle of a large table around which we had arranged ourselves.

The president picked it up and examined the Cyrillic script scrawled across the package.

"It says in effect 'personal and confidential. To be opened only in case of my death or disappearance.' "

"That seems to fit the situation," Mike observed.

"I trust we are all clear on how confidential this session is and must remain," the president said solemnly, even more solemnly than Sean Cronin would have said it. "Not to be shared even with our wives or"—glancing at Dorina—"our sweethearts . . . Bishop, we might let you share it with your Cardinal. In fact, Dorie, we may let you Xerox a copy for the Cardinal."

No one seemed to disagree with that.

12

Dorina laid a letter opener on the table next to the president. He lifted it and deftly began to cut through Brother Semyon's transparent tape mess. Everyone else watched quietly, almost reverently. It was a solemn high moment.

"I would suggest that we save the wrapping paper," I ventured. "Presumably it will bear the good dean's prints and arguably of someone who does not match the prints found in Brother Semyon's office or apartment. Moreover, we might dust a page or two of the manuscript before the evening is over."

"Good idea," Mike the Cop agreed.

"Mr. Dolan, whose father is a retired police captain," the dean said in an excessively neutral tone, "tells me that neither the prints nor the DNA from the dead man correspond to the same things on a glass out of which Brother Semyon had drunk."

"I don't imagine his former bosses are pleased with that," Mike said.

Gingerly, the president removed a thin stack of papers, fifty or sixty pages at the most, from the wrapping and slid the paper in Mike's direction. He began to read, cautiously picking up the pages by the corner so as not to leave his own prints on them.

He swallowed a couple of times as he went through the first three pages.

"This is most extraordinary," he said, rubbing his chin.

"Patently Brother Semyon was Polish," I said, indulging in a wild guess.

The president stared at me in astonishment.

"Quite right. He tells us that he was born in Lublin of a Polish Catholic father and a Russian Orthodox mother. He was named, after his father, Jan Sobieski Ostrowski. He was raised in both religions. His father and mother, who did not live to see him ordained a Catholic priest, loved each other very much and there was no religious conflict between them. Though he leaned in the Catholic direction, he himself found no great difficulty being both. He rarely spoke of this during his seminary training at the Anselmiano in Rome in 1965."

A man now in his early sixties, older than his colleagues had believed and older than the man who was killed.

"Benedictine college," I offered. "Perhaps already a Catholic monk."

My guess wasn't all that great because I knew that he was probably a Cardinal and hence more likely Polish than Russian.

"He spent a year in Rome after his ordination studying Russian mysticism. His teachers were astonished at his command of the language and even the thought patterns. He himself took it for granted that because of his background he could and should do that work for the rest of his life. Then one day in 1966 he was summoned to the offices of the Ecumenical Congregation.

"The men he spoke with praised his work for its subtle understanding of Russian language and culture. He was suspicious, but he assumed that he could trust them. He adds that now as he writes these words, he is not so sure.

"They told him that as a result of the Vatican Council there would be new openings by the Catholic Church to other Christian denominations, conversation, dialogue, eventual unity. He himself expressed some skepticism. Dialogue would be very difficult with the Russian Orthodox. The division between East and West had happened before the organization of Orthodoxy in Russia. The Russian Church had never been in union with Rome and was profoundly suspicious of heretical popes. They responded that yet on many things there was a similarity of belief and even of custom. Had not his own experience suggested that?

"He was surprised that they knew about his parents. He had told very few people. He replied that his parents were simple peasants who believed in God and the Virgin and the Saints and loved each other very much. They knew nothing of the *filioque* clause. They did not care about the ancient historical animosities."

He paused to permit me to explain the *"filioque."*

"A debate between us and them about the interrelationships of the Trinity," I said. "We say that the Spirit proceeds from the Father and the Son, they say only from the Father. The issue has been much mooted through the centuries, usually with acrimonious charges of dishonesty and stupidity. I am led to believe that with some goodwill it might be finessed in these days, but the goodwill is not yet there."

My own feeling is that the Members of the Most Holy Trinity might be just a little displeased—I used the word analogously of course—at the human stupidity that somehow had involved Them.

"Father Simon, for such was his name then, expressed doubt about how much willingness there was on either side to put aside the controversies of a millennium, though he says he also added that he personally believed that history was more of an obstacle to unity than theology, history, and different religious cultures.

"His interlocutors were much more optimistic. The Pope ardently desired that there be unity between Catholic and Orthodox in this century. He believed that his preliminary conversations with Russian Orthodox representatives who had come to Rome gave grounds for that hope . . .

"Father Simon says that he told them that such men were probably KGB agents and their words should be listened to with great suspicion. He said that much patience would be required to sweep away the rubble of history.

159

"They then asked him what he had considered himself to be when he was growing up. He said that he had thought of himself as both Catholic and Orthodox, though he had been baptized a Catholic. He found no conflict in celebrating the festivals of both religions, indeed he thought it gave him a great advantage to have two Christmases.

"Why had he chosen to become a Catholic priest instead of an Orthodox monk? He tells us that he hesitated and then answered it was probably because of his Polish name.

"Then he tells us that they asked him the question they had been saving through the whole conversation: could someone be a Catholic monk and an Orthodox monk at the same time?

"He reports that if he knew what they were planning he would have said that it would be quite impossible. In fact, he said that for someone who understood both religious cultures it would probably not be all that difficult. They told him that the Holy Father wanted him to attempt just such a life. He said that he thought they meant a Uniate monastery . . ."

"There's a small group of Russians who have been in union with Rome since the agreement at the Council of Florence in the fifteenth century," I explained. "They are stubborn people who lived in what was once Eastern Poland and now Beylorus, very proud of their own tradition. However, they are hated by the Orthodox and held in contempt by Latin Rite Poles. They would prefer to be called 'Byzantine' than 'Uniate,' which they take to be a slur. All very unfortunate."

"They told him that they meant an Orthodox monastery called the Monastery of St. Catherine and the Virgin in the foothills in the Urals near the city of Sverdlovsk, where the monks did serious scholarship on the mystical tradition of Orthodoxy. They were tolerated by the government because their historical work was respected by those outside Russia. He admitted that he had read some of the work of those monks. They told him that they had papers that would get into the Soviet Union as it was then and permission to enter the monastery. He asked them how they had arranged that and they did not respond to his question. They also said that the goal was not to spy on Orthodoxy but to understand it from the inside. The Pope was very eager to have someone advising him who could do that. Five years perhaps, at the most eight or nine years. Father Simon says that he reluctantly agreed. They assured him that they had channels that would sustain communication with him. He met with the Pope for ten minutes. He says the Pope praised his courage, wrung his own hands, promised prayers, and imparted an agonized blessing."

"Does all of this sound implausible, Blackie?" Mike asked me.

"Wildly so, Mike. That doesn't mean that in the optimism at the end of the Council, some group of people in ecumenical work might not have thought it up."

"He tells us," the president continued, "that it was the first of many lies. He never heard from the Council for Christian Unity again. He also says that he was afraid to keep notes for fear that one of the KGB monks would discover them. So he wrote down words on scraps of paper that would recall images and enable him to write about his experiences. He concludes this introduction by saying that he was happy during the early years at the monastery. The monastery was deeply spiritual as well as dedicated to serious scholarship. Later, during the Gorbachev era, the Church lied to him again and made his life difficult and dangerous."

"What a horrible story!" Dorina Keane exclaimed

"That's the end of the introduction?" I asked.

"Yes," the president said. "This was apparently written sometime ago. The rest, quite astonishingly in English, was written—typed out actually—much more recently. He refers to Sverdlovsk by its old name which is now used again—Yekaterinburg, Catherine's city."

"Where the czar and his family were killed," I remarked.

The president passed the manuscript around to us sheet by sheet. We read it in silence. The only sounds were the flipping of pages and an occasional gasp of astonishment, though not from me.

Andrew M. Greeley

EXCERPTS FROM THE JOURNAL OF
BROTHER SEMYON IVANIVICH POPOV
Sometime in the early nineteen seventies

I suspect that the Vatican has forgotten about me. My Benedictine memory is fading. Monastic life here in the pine forests is different in some ways yet similar in others. I have grown to accept the long liturgies and more frequent interruptions of my work for the chanting of prayers. The diet is sparse, more rigid than one would find even in the Trappist monasteries in the West, mostly bread made from the wheat we raise in our garden and potatoes also raised in our garden. Even by the standards of my native Poland the weather is unbearably hot in the summer and cold in the winter. There is little heat in the monastery. We stay warm by wearing thick clothes and big blankets and drinking vodka (but only in the winter). Sometimes I cannot write because my fingers are so cold. Most of my fellow monks are cheerful men. Life is simple, God is close, we do our work, we avoid the peering eyes of the monks who spy for the KGB.

Yet I have become a devotee of the "Jesus Prayer." I say it often every day and it banishes fear and misery from my bones. Perhaps it is kind of a drug. Yet it helps:

Lord Jesus Christ
Son of God
Have mercy on me a sinner.

The local religious affairs official comes by periodically to question all twenty of us about our political sympathies. Since we have no idea what is happening in the walls beyond our monastery, we have no political sympathies. He is professionally suspicious in these interviews, hinting that we are lying and that he knows the truth, and that if we are not more careful, he will close down the monastery. I learn very quickly that this is all a ritual, an act that enables him to submit a report to his superior. My colleagues do not take him seriously either. Since I am relatively new, he is stern with me. What do

I know about the new government in Moscow? I tell him that I know nothing and that I came to the Monastery of St. Catherine and the Virgin to escape such worries. He questions me about my work. He cannot understand my answers because he is uneducated, an ignorant peasant turned into a bureaucrat.

When he has left, I return to my work.

As the years passed I began to wonder how my entrance into the monastery was so smooth. At the border between Poland and Russia a young border guard glanced at my papers and waved me through with a happy smile. I was asked for my papers several times on the train to Moscow and then across the steppes to the Urals. Each time I encountered no skeptics, no one who doubted that I was an ethnic Russian, Semyon Ivanivich Popov, born in Lviv in what used to be Poland and now is part of the Ukraine SSR. Even at the monastery of Zagorsk outside Moscow no one seemed to doubt that I was destined by God for the monastic life here on this eastern edge of Europe.

Moscow was a drab, dull city. Its people poorly dressed and un-smiling. Russians, I had learned from my mother, were a wild, slightly crazy people—just like the Poles (she would nod with a smile towards my father), but crazy in different ways. I saw no sign of her wit and humor in either Moscow or Zagorsk. Warsaw was grim too, but the Poles were still Poles, cynical and bitter perhaps, but always laughing. The farms I saw outside the railroad car window were poor, but grain still grew in the fields. In Russia the farm homes were mostly hovels and the fields on the collective farms were often barren. Polish farm-ers own their land, Russian farmers do not. I read somewhere before I left that more food is produced on the small private gardens the farm-ers are now permitted than on the great fields of the collective farms.

Russia was depressing as the train to Yekatrinburg slowly moved across the endless plains between Moscow and the Urals. We cross the Dnieper, the Don, the Volga but the steppes seemed never to end. This should be some of the richest farmland in the world, I thought, yet it is almost sterile. Something is terribly wrong.

I was perhaps big and strong, but I was also young and inexperienced. I knew that Communism was evil, but I did not understand the link between that knowledge and the barren fields.

I also did not reflect on how easy it was for me to move physically from Rome to Yekatrinburg, from Benedictine monastery to Orthodox monastery. Later, when I would return intermittently to the world outside St. Catherine and the Virgin and encounter the obstacles to free movement across Eastern Europe, did I begin to wonder why it had been so easy. I attributed it to the Jesuits, who for many years had sustained a secret Russian mission. Now I realize that a foreign intelligence agency of one sort or another must have directed and guided my path to Urals.

Some of the people who live near the monastery make offerings of food from their private gardens for us, food of which they don't have enough for themselves. They also visit our chapel on great feast days. Most of them are elderly and very devout in the ways that old peasants in Poland were devout when I was growing up.

There are a few young people, including one pretty girl. I look for her eagerly each time there is a public liturgy. From a great and—safe—distance I love as I loved Sister Modesta at the Anselmiano. Yet I am happy here in my work and in my spiritual growth. I wonder sometimes whether if I should receive an order from the Vatican that I should return to Rome I might not ignore it. That is the world of whom the Holy Fathers of the early Church warn us.

Late nineteen seventies

My work is being published in France. It has taken several years for this word to reach me. I have been sending manuscripts in French off for some time. I did not know whether they ever reached the journal to which I sent them. They could have been swallowed up in the bureaucracy. I don't know which manuscripts might have been published. I do, however, receive letters occasionally that suggest that some of them have received a little notice. I find that I am enthused over this reaction. I worry about this happiness. One should work at all times as though no one will ever read what one has written. Yet one wants to know at least that one has not blundered too badly. I now write not only for the glory of God but also for my own glory. That is, I think, very sinful, though the abbot tells me that it is not.

Lord Jesus Christ

Son and Word of the Living God

By the prayer of your most pure Mother and all the Saints

Have mercy on us and save us.

The abbot is a happy man as are almost all the monks. He once said to me with what I now realize is a great deal of wisdom, "Semyon Ivanivich, you are a happy man here in the monastery because you would be happy outside the monastery. Someone who is not happy in the world would never be happy here. You are happy not because of where you are but because you had a happy Russian mother. You were fortunate. Russian women can no longer be happy the way they used to be."

I am still caught up in the blessed and holy routine of the monastery. I have slipped into the turn of the seasons, the changing length of the days, and am at peace most of the time. I don't know what the year is and hence I do not know how old I am. If I knew that Rome would abandon me, I would not have come here. Yet now I am content that I did. I no longer search for pretty young faces in the chapel. Well, sometimes I still do.

The young woman who was attractive when I first saw her, still comes here on the feast days with a husband and several children. She is still beautiful. She seems happy, like my own mother was. Perhaps she is an exception.

They say that there is a new pope, this time a Polish pope. I cannot believe that, but I hope it is true. Most of the other monks, for all their holiness, hate Catholicism and the pope. They think it is a joke that a Pole would be elected pope.

Andrew M. Greeley

Early nineteen eighties

I am to go to Paris to present a paper on the relationship between
the Mystical Prayers of the Old Believers and the Mysticism of the
Desert Fathers. I believe that in some respects the Old Believers have in
fact sustained the religious insights of the Fathers more than main-
stream Orthodoxy. I now receive enough journals from the West to
keep up with the newer developments in my field. I also learn that beyond a doubt there is now a Polish pope.

The bureaucrat tells me this when he informs me about my invitation, which the government has graciously approved. They will
even pay my fare on Aeroflot from Moscow to Paris. I will live with
the Dominicans at Mt. St. Jacques during the week I am there.

My emotions are mixed. I look forward to the intellectual stimu-
lation and, yes, to contact with the world again. What has happened
to the Church since I left? Has the excitement of the Council persisted? Does the Church grow and prosper and become more beautiful for its members and for the world, worthy and radiant bride of
Christ?

What has happened in Poland? What has happened here in Russia?
The bureaucracy seems less heavy than it used to be. When I hesitated
about accepting the invitation, the bureaucrat said that it was my solemn
duty as a loyal Soviet citizen to accept it because the invitation honored
the Soviet State.

Stalin is dead for a long time.

Yet I do not want to leave the cocoon of my monastic life. I have
found peace and joy here. Visiting Paris will be a grave temptation. It
will tear me away from the beauty I experience here all the time and
my occasional encounter with Beauty.

There will also be a temptation to return to my old world. If I tell
the Dominicans at St. Jacques who I am, they will find a way to get me
to Rome. Yet what will happen there? I'm sure that the men who sent
me as part of a crazy scheme will have forgotten about me. The pope
who blessed me is dead. The new pope is Polish. I could talk to him in

my native language, though I am not sure that I can still speak it intelligibly. I am certain that I will resist the temptation. I must now work on preparing my presentation in French, which no one will understand when I speak it, but at least they will have the paper.

We must see the hand of God in everything that happens in our life, the abbot tells me with a smile. This voyage of yours to Paris is very important or God would not have caused it to happen.

I wonder how my eyes, still and always hungry for the sight of a beautiful woman, will react to the women of Paris.

Paris, October 1983. Mt. St. Jacques

For the first time in seventeen years I am back in the world, not only the world, but the Western world and its most seductive city. I arrive in my monastic robes with my staff. I create the impression that I am an authentic Russian monk. I speak loudly, pound my staff against the floor, and drink vodka. Yet I attend Mass here in the chapel and receive Holy Communion. My hosts are surprised but tolerant.

Of the temptations of this city I will say only that my eyes are blinking all the time. Yet the most serious temptations are not the seductive women who are everywhere, but the beds here in the Dominican convent. Hard perhaps by Western standards, they are sinfully soft by the standards of St. Catherine and the Virgin.

There is much change in the Church. I cannot understand all of it or even much of it. However, it is clear that the leaders have lost contact with their people. You cannot begin a reform, then abort it. When you try to tighten the discipline after a period of reform, you risk a revolution. The men in the Curia cannot understand this.

I read in papers like *Le Monde* that Russia is suffering economically, that the "geriatric" regime cannot cope with the failings of the past. Yet it seemed to me in Moscow that men and women were clothed more fashionably—and more warmly—than they were seventeen years ago.

It is all so confusing.

I find it difficult to pray. I yearn to return to the peace and holiness of St. Catherine and the Virgin.

Lord Jesus Christ

Son of the Living God

Have mercy on me a sinner.

Yet I must admit part of me yearns never to go back. What does God want? He will tell you what to do eventually, the abbot says. I hope he is right.

The new liturgy in French churches is very beautiful. So much has changed. Yet among the Dominicans here at St. Jacques there is much anger and bitterness. Some even say that they wish that my Polish pope had not survived the assassin's bullet. They don't know, however, that I'm Polish. Something went wrong since I left Rome, something terrible.

I ponder my mission to Sverdlovsk. Is Orthodoxy ready for union with Rome? My answer has to be no. It will have to undergo a reform even more pervasive than Vatican II. It will be years, perhaps centuries before the men at Zagorsk would even consider the possibility of reform.

Can I say that and return to a Benedictine monastery in Rome? Or even Paris?

Whom could I ask? Who knows of my existence?

Later

My paper at the Sorbonne conference this afternoon went well. I am asked somewhat casually if I would return every year. I respond that it would depend on my abbot and the state. I am asked questions about the condition of Orthodoxy in Russia. I reply that it survives and that it is my impression that most people are still believers. This answer is greeted with skepticism. What do I know? Do not I live in a monastery in the Ural Mountains?

This evening three men come to see me, one of them was at my first meeting with the Council For Christian Unity. He apologizes that "because of circumstances" they were not able to maintain contact with me. They believe they will be able to correct that. I no longer trust them and tell them so.

I say that I can now easily answer their original question. Union between Orthodoxy and Rome is impossible at the present time and will be impossible until Orthodoxy has its own Trent and Vatican II combined. Moreover, the present state would not permit it.

A younger man, American I assume from the way he talks, says that there is now strong belief in Rome that the Vatican moved too quickly and that a certain restoration is necessary. He says that with the enthusiasm of an ambitious young man. I shrug my shoulders.

Then he speaks like he is a cowboy in an American film. The Holy Father knows of me. As a Pole he is very proud of my work. He now has a new assignment for me. I am to be ordained a bishop and return to Russia to organize an underground church. It may be a half century or more before Communism collapses. It will be a long, hard fight. There may be many martyrs . . .

His eyes shine brightly. He, however, will not be one of the martyrs.

I tell him that there are very few Catholics in the Soviet Union. They do not need and could not support an organized church.

He replies, speaking as though he knows more about it than I do, that there will be many more as Orthodoxy withers and people with no religion look for something to believe in. I insist, forcefully I thought, that most Russians are still in some sense Orthodox, many have been secretly baptized. They assume that Orthodoxy will last longer than Bolshevism. Catholicism is foreign and strange. They will not accept it.

The young man does not hear me. He says that the faith and courage of Catholic martyrs will impress them just as it did the ancient Romans. The blood of martyrs, he tells me as if I had never heard the cliché before, is the seed of the faith.

I try again. I say that there are no candidates in Russia for the priesthood or the bishopric, except for a few Uniates in the Western Ukraine, who already have their own bishops. And their own martyrs.

The cowboy assures me that many candidates will appear eventually. It will be important to have a bishop for the whole Soviet Union who will ordain them.

I tell them Sverdlovsk is on the eastern side of the Urals, with Asia spread out beneath it. No one comes there except state officials. It is a worn-out city, still suffering because of the death of the czar. I cannot leave the Monastery of St. Catherine and the Virgin and wander about the country in search of men who want to be bishops. Nor could they come to me without attracting notice of the KGB. I do not mind the danger of being the Bishop of the Soviet Union. I do mind its impossibility.

Archbishop, one of them says, as though that would make a difference.

The Soviet is changing, the cowboy argues. Its leaders are old, its bureaucrats sloppy. Our chances will improve in the years ahead. We will work out the details later. Now we merely want to ordain you and send you back to your monastery a Catholic archbishop.

He was wrong about the durability of the regime, though so was everyone else. He was wrong about the possibilities for Catholicism improving, though I think everyone did know better than that.

They show me the documents naming me as Archbishop of Yekatrinburg and of all Russia. The documents say nothing about the other Soviet republics, perhaps because those that wrote the documents were unaware of them. There is also a warm note from the pope addressed to "my brave son." It is clear to me that I have no choice.

I agree to be ordained in the cellar of St. Jacques that night. I tell them that I can take none of the documents with me. The police will search me carefully when my plane lands in Moscow. They try to make me take a Catholic ritual in the Russian language with me. I say that they would then have one martyr and no bishop. Should I ever have someone to ordain I would do it in the Orthodox rite.

They are concerned about whether that would be valid and

finally admit that it probably would. I also refuse a ring and a pectoral cross. For conspirators they are remarkably stupid. I wonder if the men who work for the various intelligence agencies like the KGB are equally stupid. Probably they are. However, to use a word I would learn much later, it is not proper for the Catholic Church to have its own spooks. Or to cooperate with someone else's spooks.

Lord Jesus Christ, Son and Word of the Living God

By the prayer of your most pure Mother and all the Saints

Have mercy on us and save us.

So now I return to my pine trees not just a Catholic monk in an Orthodox monastery but a Catholic Archbishop in an Orthodox monastery. It will make no difference because nothing will come of their foolish schemes.

1985

I have regained the peace that my visit to Paris destroyed. I have my work, my monastery, my fellow monks, the turn of the seasons, the sweetness of my contemplation. With God's holy help nothing will take that away from me ever again.

The monks who have some contact with the outside—KGB spies—whisper that there is a new leader in Moscow, a younger man who talks of openness and change. I cannot believe that anything will change as long as the Party is in control.

Of the cowboy's mad scheme to convert Russia to Catholicism, I hear nothing at all. They have forgotten me once again.

That makes me very happy. I wish to spend the rest of my life here in prayer and work.

1986 Paris

I am here to teach a brief course under the order not of my new abbot, who is suspicious of too much scholarship, but of the Patriarch himself. In the name of *glasnost*—openness—Orthodoxy must be ready to dialogue with other religions. He doesn't really mean it. Someone in the government has given him the words to say. I am here for three weeks, enough time to lose my mind as well as my soul.

The women are even more attractive than they were when I came here for the first time and the beds at St. Jacques even more comfortable. Also, despite the winter, it is warm in the Dominican monastery, though most of the friars say it is too cold.

I know enough French now to be intelligible to my students, who want to know more not about Russian mysticism, but about Russian politics. Can Socialism survive *glasnost* and *perestroika*? they ask. I reply that I am a monk and a scholar not a politician. But the country has changed greatly since my last trip to Paris. First Secretary Gorbachev is sympathetic to Orthodoxy. All persecution, save for petty annoyances, has stopped.

Surely, they tell me, secularization has eliminated the appeal of Orthodoxy to the ordinary people. Its ancient customs and superstitions and ceremonials will not have survived three-quarters of a century of socialism.

I respond with a shrug and say that more and more people come to our great feast days at the Monastery of St. Catherine and the Virgin.

In my heart I believe that Socialism is dying if not already dead and that Orthodoxy is about to rise from the grave. Or maybe come out of hiding. I almost say catacombs, which might give me away.

I am invited to supper often. I know that I should stay at St. Jacques and pray. Yet I accept the invitations. I want to know more about ordinary Parisians. Or so I tell myself.

I learn that those with whom I share the evening meal are not active Catholics and only barely believe in God. They have contempt for the bishops and clergy and think my Polish pope, for all his charisma, is a disaster for the Catholic Church. I forget for the moment that I am a part of the Catholic hierarchy.

I learn that these French intellectuals and aristocrats are intelligent, witty, sophisticated and empty. I learn that many of the women are beautiful, brittle, and bitter—words that I would not use if I were not writing these memories in English. They flirt with me because they have nothing else to do. Fortunately I am immune to them, most of the time.

At one of these dinners an American with silver hair and twinkling blue eyes takes me aside and proposes lunch the next day. I decline at first, saying I must prepare my class. He is insistent. I agree.

We meet at *les Deux Magots* across from St-Germain-des-Prés. He tells me that he is a Catholic, a graduate of the famous Notre Dame University of which I have never heard. He works for the American government, he says, and then that he knows who I really am.

I am terrified. I did not trust the men from Rome who insisted on ordaining me. I did not think, however, that they would tell the American government about me.

He explains that the Vatican and the American government have worked closely with the Solidarity movement in Poland and that they expect it will revive soon. The Polish pope, he argues, is pushing Socialism towards its inevitable end. Only a few more years.

He then says that I will shortly be transferred from Sverdlovsk to Zagorsk, the main center of Orthodoxy in Russia. There will be no trouble from the Soviet government. Periodically an American attaché from the embassy will call upon me with coded messages from the Vatican.

I listen carefully to what he says, but display no interest, as if I didn't believe most of it. Unfortunately, I do believe it. Can the Vatican, the CIA, as I have learned is the name of the American secret police, be cooperating with one another? Does that not make me some kind of a spy?

I am shivering when I return to St. Jacques and fall on my knees in the chapel. Have my friends in the Vatican now turned me into a spy for the American government?

Should I return to Rome and beg to see the pope himself and tell him this madness?

Would he believe me?

I yearn once again for the solitude of my pine forests with the clear blue sky above and even for the winter cold.

The Feast of the Resurrection 1989. Zagorsk

The Lord is Risen Alleluia!

He is risen indeed Alleluia!

Everything changed today in this country. Men and women and children swarmed into the streets and the churches to celebrate the Lord's resurrection! They exchanged the old greetings, they sang the old hymns, they carried lighted candles. The monks here at Zagorsk are ecstatic with joy. Not only is Jesus risen, so is Orthodoxy.

Some pretend that they knew all along this would happen. But they did not, none of us did. In the space of two or three years of *glasnost* and *perestroika*, Russians have come to understand that their government will not interfere with religious worship. It is all right to be religious. In a few years, we Russians being what we are, will require that everyone be religious. We will forbid the publication of antireligious literature.

"We Russians" I write many years after the great day. I still remember how I began to think that way. I also remember how frightened I was to discover that some of the monks are saying that the Church will have all the power it had in 1915, only more because now the government cannot control us. This is not the religion men and women are celebrating in our monastery today. It is the religion of the Vatican transferred here to the Russian Vatican. Must we make the same mistakes they made? Or will they make the same mistakes we made? This is a great opportunity, just like the Catholics had at the time of their Council. They missed it. Will we miss ours?

I should have written "we Catholics." However I no longer have the slightest understanding of who I am.

Some of the monks are saying that the churches will be reopened or rebuilt and that the gold leaf domes will appear all over Russia.

The Czar and his family will be reburied in St. Petersburg and canonized as Orthodox saints and martyrs. A shrine will be built on the site of their murder in Yekatrinburg. They are already using the old names.

I think they are greedy in their hopes. Socialism will not die that quickly. Yet the exuberance today is so powerful that one is willing to believe in almost anything. That which the cowboy thought would take a half century took less than half a decade.

There is no blue sky here in Zagorsk, only the smog from Moscow; and no pine trees, only deserted fields; no happy monks, only anxious bureaucrats. No one has a good word to say about Catholicism or my Polish pope.

I feel all the joy and hope of this marvelous resurrection, though just a few days ago, on the Feast of Holy Thursday as the Romans would call it, I exercised for the first time my office as Archbishop of Yekatrinburg and all Russia.

A young man from the American embassy came for a brief visit. He handed me a sealed envelope and quickly departed. The envelope gave me an address in Moscow, a basement apartment where four men would be waiting for me. Future bishops? I wondered. Can I do this? Can I do something that offends the Orthodox part of my soul?

When I arrived at the apartment I found that I could. They were good young men in their middle thirties. One Korean from Siberia, one Russian from Leningrad (or St. Petersburg as everyone is calling it now), one from Odessa, and one from Moldova. They were to be ordained priests and then bishops in the Latin Rite, not the Byzantine or Uniate. They are the first wave of Roman clergy to invade Russia. I quizzed them gently about their beliefs and goals. They did not consider themselves either missionaries or revolutionaries. Much less did they perceive that they were in competition with Orthodoxy. Their field was white with the harvest, one of them told me, of people who had no religious roots at all. They all agreed that they were willing to die, indeed expected to die.

How can one not be a missionary if one speaks of fields white

175

for the harvest? Were they unaware of the resiliency of Orthodoxy?

A couple of years ago I would have thought their expectations of martyrdom realistic. Now I was not so sure. The Soviet Union had changed so much that a few years in prison would be their worst punishment. Pain would come from the experience that they would find very few people who wanted to be Catholics. Failure, not martyrdom, would face them.

There was a small celebration afterwards, a bottle of vodka, some brown bread, some soft singing. Then I returned by bus to Zagorsk, profoundly uncertain about what I had done. Yet I could not find it in my heart to refuse them.

Now, after this glorious Russian Easter, I believed that they would not even be sent to jail but perhaps expelled from the country.

I went to the chapel to pray for them, to pray for new Catholic bishops in an Orthodox monastery. Zagorsk is a holy place because it stands for a holy tradition, but it is not a prayerful place. I yearn for the pines of Yekatrinburg, as now I will call it, and closeness to God. I will never see that again. The Monastery of St. Catherine and the Virgin will change like everything else.

October 1992 Paris

Since the last time I was in Paris the Soviet Union has ceased to exist. My Parisian friends congratulated me on our new world. I was in Moscow lecturing at the university when the coup was announced. Like many others I rushed to the White House, the headquarters of the Russian Federation of which Yeltsin is the president, a believer the monks told me but also a terrible drunk. I saw him climb on top of a tank and defy the leaders of the coup. It was a great moment in our Russian history, even if he were drunk. Holy Russia was breaking with Socialism and the Soviet Union. The red, white, and blue flag of Russia flew in the breeze. I cheered as loudly as anyone.

The crowd was euphoric. We knew that the coup forces would come and kill us all. Yet we would all gladly die for Holy Russia.

Fortunately for us the coup fell apart. Gorbachev came back from the Black Sea to a gutted empire. The coup benefited not the Communist Old Guard who tried to play by the old Bolshevist game of force and had in fact put Yeltsin in power, a man who had already appeared on TV in a church, holding a religious candle.

Thus did Socialism collapse in the Soviet Union. Within a few weeks the empire had spun apart into its constituent republics. In the Western Ukraine, the Uniate Catholics took back by force the church buildings that Stalin had given to the Ukrainian Orthodox.

As I returned to Zagorsk on the crowded bus, I was so caught up in the excitement of the day that I did not think what that might mean to my own Catholic underground church in a country where religion no longer had to go underground.

I went immediately to the chapel to thank God for the liberation of Russian religion and asked Him to protect them all.

I had ordained three more bishops and twenty-four priests in groups of six. They all seemed like the previous ordinands—young men with dedication and zeal. I wondered where they had been trained. Probably in Poland. The trainers had done a fine job. In the last group there were three young women who expected to be ordained. My pope would disapprove. In my heart I could not refuse them. If God wanted them to be priests, that was up to Him.

Or so I told Him in the monastery when I returned from our basement chapel. I encountered the abbot outside the chapel. We nodded politely to one another. I laughed inwardly at the thought of how his smooth, soothing exterior would crack wide open if he knew what I had done.

How had I become a rebel? I don't know. Maybe the terrible madness of my whole enterprise had driven me to it.

Then the first day in Paris, the smiling, silver-haired man visited me at St. Jacques. The Russian Catholic Church is not on anymore, he told me. The Vatican does not want to offend the Byzantine Catholics.

What about those whom I have ordained?

177

They will be supported and cared for.

That was all.

After he left, I sat in the parlor where we had spoken and realized that I had been the victim of a CIA plot devised with the help of the Vatican. Or some people in the Vatican who had managed to get the Pope's signature on some documents. Were the people I had ordained CIA agents? Or were they men—and women—with vocations whom the CIA planned to use as sources in what they thought would be a long contest with the Soviet Union?

Now that the Soviet Union no longer existed, they would not be needed.

Since it was not necessary for religion to be underground anymore, there was no need for an underground Catholic Church. Those who disapproved of the idea in the Vatican—and there must have been some that did—saw an advantage in promoting their careers to cite the offense among the easily offended Uniates as a reason to terminate it.

Reasonable decisions for all concerned, except the priests and bishops I had ordained. Would the Vatican really take care of them?

Had they taken care of me?

I walked down the corridor to the chapel of St. Jacques and fell wearily on my knees. What had I done! The new freedom for religion in Russia had destroyed the venture that I had started with such reluctance and would surely hurt those who looked to me as their archbishop, though I had never seen them after ordination. Innocent people had been hurt by schemers, both in Washington and in London.

Then I realized that they had no more use for me. Presumably they would leave me alone, both the cowboy priest and the man with the silver hair. Once again in Rome I would cease to exist.

For that I thanked God.

I hated the Vatican. I hated what they had done to me. I did not, however, hate my Polish pope. How could I? But I did realize that the bureaucrats had played games with my life. And wasted it.

St. Nicholas Day, 1995. Zagorsk

It has now been thirty years since I left Rome to learn whether one could be a Catholic priest and an Orthodox monk at the same time. I conclude that it is not so difficult though one identity will dominate over the other. I now think in Russian most of the time. Polish is one of the languages I happen to speak, along with Italian and English and French. I often talk of "we Russians."

For a time I had also been a Catholic archbishop and had foolishly ordained priests and bishops who were probably caught up in a plot of some sort. Innocents used by the Americans with Vatican help. I hoped that God had forgiven me for my folly.

From Rome I had heard nothing at all and expected not to. I was simply forgotten. If I were arrested and put on trial, they would rise to my defense because they liked to have martyrs. Otherwise, they hoped I would not embarrass them.

I wonder about the FSB, as the KGB is now called. How much had they known? Had they cared about it? Was there some kind of working relationship between certain elements within the FSB and parallel elements in the CIA? There was enough paranoia in my Russian soul to suspect that there was a grand conspiracy.

And enough hardheaded Polish realism to say to myself that what had happened was more stupidity and incompetence than malice.

Yet I treasured the image of stalking up to the Vatican and denouncing by name those who had exploited me and the Russians I had ordained.

I would not do that because it would not help and I could prove nothing.

Relationships between Moscow and Rome have deteriorated. The Patriarch feels more powerful. He does not need support from Rome. He conditions friendly contact with my Polish pope on the repression of the Uniates. The Pope cannot do that. Neither side will or can move.

We have come a long way from the time when we said to one

another in Rome that the Orthodox and the Catholic Churches believe mostly in the same things. That still may be true, but it is, alas, irrelevant.

There is too much history as I said long ago and too much culture. History has produced too many long memories. The Crusader sack of Constantinople happened only yesterday. The persecution of Orthodoxy in Catholic Poland happened only an hour ago. The atmosphere of Zagorsk, so much like that of the Vatican, is a huge barrier. The Pope has been a scapegoat for too long. Catholicism has given up some of its worst narrowness, but no one here will believe that. They don't like infallibility, which may still be a problem, but they don't like the *filioque* clause either and are not willing to negotiate over the clause. We Catholics (I say this putting on for the moment my Catholic identity) think they are rigid and narrow. We forget that only a few years ago the same thing was true of us.

I see no hope of an easy or early solution. However, I did not think that the Party could so easily fall from power.

My work progresses. I publish often. I am invited to lecture in England and in America. Perhaps I will visit Harvard University. If I were still living among the pines of the Urals, I would say no. However, I have been corrupted by the move to the vicinity of Moscow. I was curious about everything and read all the newspapers very carefully and even watch the BBC and CNN on television.

I have not escaped from the world and indeed no longer try. Yet I still struggle to live a monastic life and to stay close to God's love.

Sometimes I think that God intended all of these things to happen to me and loves me despite all my foolish mistakes. I hope that is true. If it is, my life has not been in vain.

I am, however, very tired.

1998 Harvard

I am well received here, though some Russian priests come to my lectures because they want to argue with me. They are poorly educated and cannot express exactly what is their disagreement. I try to be patient, but I fear I pound the stage with my staff and shout. Even though I refused to become an abbot, I now act like one much of the time. I'm afraid that I would be a stern and truculent abbot.

The Patriarch, who claims to read my work, wants to make me a metropolitan, an archbishop. So then I would be an archbishop in both churches. The old question arises again as to whether that would be possible. It is as foolish as the similar question was long ago.

It might, however, be fun. Thus does the hidden Pole inside me speak!

The Boston Catholic Archdiocese sends a priest to listen to me to determine whether I'm speaking heresy. He is not a complete fool like the Russian priests, but nonetheless he is a fool. He tries to trick me into an answer on the *filioque* clause. I evade him easily. I tell him that the union of Brest is a more serious problem. He doesn't know what I am talking about. Why should the Archdiocese worry about me? Perhaps because it has so much power it feels it has to use it some of the time. For this we had a Council thirty years ago!

I write this reflection out, the first time that I have ever dared to do it. Now there is no longer anyone who would search my luggage for it. There might be some use in writing the whole story of my life. I must consider seriously the activity Americans call "setting the record straight." The treachery of the Vatican and the CIA is a story that perhaps should be told.

On the way to America I visited the farm outside of Lublin where I was born. It has not changed much, it is still poor and seems smaller. I prayed to my parents and asked them to speak to God for me. I wept as I did later at the cemetery. I was their life. I hope they are not ashamed of me.

At the farm I can hear my mother's laughter, bright and clear and silver like it always was. I see my father's broad smile, a Polish smile at its best. I tell them that I still love them.

After that visit I often think that I was cruel to leave them for the seminary, then for Rome. What if I had not chosen to be a priest.

181

They would have known grandchildren before they died. I would have loved a woman. I would have been poor, though not as poor as my parents. I probably would have lived in Cracow and taught at the university. I would do much the same work as I do now. Did I become a priest to escape the farm and its deprivations? I never thought about such matters then. But perhaps I did, perhaps the priesthood was a way out. Would it have been so terrible merely to be farmers like they were? If my wife and I loved one another as they did, perhaps it would have been worth it.

God knows. Probably He does not like these second thoughts, though perhaps He does.

Despite the spy from Cardinal Law, I am impressed by the Catholic Church in this country, so impressed that I find I am thinking Catholic rather than Orthodox in my split personality. I read some of their theologians and find them excellent, especially this David Tracy. At my lectures their lay people ask intelligent questions. They challenge me to compare Russian mystics not only with John of the Cross, an obvious question, but also with Julianne of Norwich, a question which is not obvious. Do "our" mystics agree with her that "all things will be well, all manner of things will be well"?

I say that there is great similarity in the thought, somewhat less in the expression of the thought. We like more complex expressions. I also tell them if I were forced to choose but one mystic in the whole Christian tradition, I would choose her.

They also wonder why there is not unity between Rome and Moscow or even between Rome and Constantinople. I reply, as I usually do, that we have the same triune God, the same Jesus and Virgin and the saints and angels. The pope is not really the problem, much less married priests. The problem is culture and history. Then I say that Orthodoxy needs a Council of its own and Catholicism needs to continue the reforms of Vatican II, which have unfortunately stopped.

They applaud and cheer, not, however, the priest the cardinal has sent to spy on me.

America makes me feel very reckless. Perhaps I should tell the Patriarch that I would be happy to be a metropolitan. Thus I would be an archbishop in both traditions. I have the feeling that neither he nor my Polish pope would like it. Nor would the pope like to know that I ordained women.

So I won't tell him.

Later. I know what I will do. I will write a book about unity between Rome and Moscow under a nom de plume—Simon Sobieski. I already have two identities. I will create a third about whom no one will know. It is God's will. Only a comic God could think up such an idea. I will make use of all my experiences in both churches to point a way towards unity.

Neither, I am sure, will be interested in what this obscure theologian has to say about unity. They will disregard his advice completely. Yet someday, perhaps someone will listen to him.

Rome

I had not even left Boston to return to Paris and Moscow when I received a phone call from the Patriarch himself. He wants me to go to Rome as his personal though informal delegate. The Vatican has suggested informal consultation with the view of clarifying the possibilities for long-run dialogue between the two churches. The Patriarch was dubious. It is only one more of their tricks, he tells me. Yet we cannot risk being completely cut off. Therefore will you go to Rome and talk to them? A Msgr. Agostino.

What should I tell him?

No dialogue is possible now or ever unless you repudiate the Uniates?

Do you think that is possible for them?

Pause.

That is not our problem. If it is impossible, then we must demand the impossible.

I understand.

So I am here to be an obstructionist. I must be loyal to the Patriarch, yet I must also perhaps give some hints as to what the Vatican might do if it is serious about unity—about which I am not altogether sure. I must therefore be truculent and charming. I will pound my staff and I will smile.

Rome has not changed much in thirty-five years. The laity and the clergy and religious still ignore one another on the streets. No one smiles. The priests who work around the Vatican still try to create the impression that they are very important and know secrets that they cannot tell.

I went to the Anselmiano to find that it had not changed much either though the enthusiasm of the late sixties is gone. The young monks stared at me as though I were a visitor from another planet in my Orthodox robes and my staff, which I pound on the floor often just for my own amusement.

I wonder if this somber Orthodox monk with the flowing robes and the long beard could possibly have been a promising student here so long ago. Obviously he could not. I smile softly to myself and, utterly marginal person that I am, I leave.

I must admit, however, that when I wonder whether I miss this monastery more than I do St. Catherine and the Virgin, the sunny warmth of Rome more than the crisp blue sky and the pine trees of the eastern Urals, that the score in the match is almost a draw, but I am still a Pole and still a Benedictine.

Some of the time.

We meet in the same office of the Council on Christian Unity. However, Monsignor Agostino is from the Secretariat of State. This means that our consultation is informal enough, but still important.

I ask discretely about the three men who sent me to Russia. My hosts seem surprised. All three have died. And the cowboy? He has left the priesthood to marry and is now living with his wife in Boston. I wondered to myself if he had come to my lecture at Harvard.

Not likely.

Agostino is an interesting man—handsome with curly black hair and astonishingly crisp blue eyes. His smile is quick and generous and he is obviously both very intelligent and very powerful. However, he lacks the anxiety that marks Church bureaucrats—of either tradition—who are ambitious. I suspect that he does not care about such things.

I ask him whether perhaps he has a Polish or Russian mother. He laughs genially and says no, worse than that. Irish. Everyone laughs, the other two priests nervously.

I tell him that the Patriarch's informal message is the same as his formal message. The Pope must abandon the Byzantines if he wishes any further dialogue with the Russian Orthodox Church. We talk for some time, at least an hour, and cover most of the outstanding differences between the two traditions. We agree that most could be resolved, even the *filioque* clause, if there was a will to. I tell him the problem is history and culture and two different Vaticans. I say again that we need a Council of Trent and Vatican II combined, that they (meaning here Catholics) need to restart the Vatican renewal.

He shrugs, indicating that he agrees.

At the end, I say that while we personally may agree on most things, the Patriarch's answer is the same: no conversation until Rome disowns the Byzantines.

I did not say Uniates. His eyes flicker at my slip, but he does not try to press any advantage.

Is there no unofficial advice you can give us? he pleads.

I consider it, thinking of the book I'm now certainly going to write.

Embrace us in spite of ourselves, I tell him. Announce one day that all past excommunications have been lifted. Tell us that you recognize us as part of the indivisible Catholic Church, that you recognize the Patriarch as part of that Church and have no intention of interfering with that jurisdiction, that you have no objection to intermarriage or intercommunion, and that in a certain number of years you will summon another Ecumenical Council to which you will invite Russian Orthodox and all other Orthodox churches. You will even say that you hope the Patriarch will cosponsor the invitation.

There is complete silence in the room as they ponder my suggestions and the other two as they await Agostino's response.

It's a good idea, he admits with a sigh. I fear the time is not yet mature for such a gesture.

By which he means that he could not get it by my Polish pope and the men around him. I tell him I understand.

We all part amiably with much shaking of hands and promises of meeting again and of prayers for one another. As I walked back to the tiny Russian monastery in Rome where I had been staying, I wonder what the gifted and intelligent Father Agostino would say if I had told him about my previous conversation in that Rome. I asked myself why I had not done so.

I didn't know the answer. Perhaps I was afraid of the consequences to me if I told him my story. More likely, however, I had felt I could not betray the Patriarch's trust in me.

Back in Moscow I told him in detail about my conversation with Agostino. He was impatient with the details. He did not want to know about the similarities in the two traditions. He desired merely to be reassured that I had insisted emphatically on his position that there would never be dialogue between him and the Pope until the Pope repudiated the Uniates. When I told him, truthfully enough, that I had done that repeatedly, he relaxed and nodded his approval.

What if the Vatican actually followed my advice? How would this man react?

He would probably dismiss it as one more papal trick.

I began that night to work on my book on the problems and possibilities of reunion and the deep and powerful and not unjustified Orthodox suspicions about the papacy.

Simon Sobieski, as I became when I started to write, wondered how long it would take to produce Orthodox theologians like those who had shaped the Vatican Council. Without such men, even the preliminaries to reunion would be impossible.

I feared it would take generations for such men to appear.

2000 Paris

My book—or I should say Simon Sobieski's book—on reunion between Russian Orthodoxy and the Catholic Church has appeared in America. It is published by The Liturgical Press at St. John's Abbey in a place called Minnesota. There have been some positive reviews, and some negative. The negative ones accused me of being either too optimistic or too pessimistic. I think that is very good.

Ironically, St. John's is a Benedictine monastery. They do not realize that the author of the book is one of their own! They probably never will. The paradoxes of my life multiply one upon another. When the first copy of the book came, I was suddenly a Benedictine again.

It has now been settled. I will go to America for two years, a summer at Notre Dame, then two years at the University of Chicago. The abbot was happy to give his permission. He implies that he would not mind if I stayed in America. I am a disruptive force in the monastery. I ask too many questions about the direction of the Church. I talk about the need for reform. The Church has only now escaped seventy-five years of oppression, it is too early to speak of reform. To which I say, respectfully I hope, that now we must reform before it is too late. Our people are no longer ignorant and illiterate peasants. We must give them substance as well as ceremony. He does not understand. Neither does the Patriarch. We must acquire the power we used to have, then we can talk reform. We will never have that power again, I argue, and if we could, we shouldn't.

I like Americans. They are rich, perhaps too rich for their own good. But they are generous. And expansive. They are more like us

Russians than either are like the French or the Italians or the English. When I'm in America I feel that I am American. Yet another identity.

Also I feel more Catholic, perhaps because there are many more Catholics there. And few Russians.

I ask God whether I'm doing the right thing. How can I tell? Maybe I made a mistake long ago when I decided to become a priest, another mistake when I chose to be a scholar, a serious mistake when I agreed to go to Russia, and a tragic mistake when I let them make me an archbishop. I do not know, God only knows. In the years left to me I must try to follow God's grace. If I have made mistakes in the past—and I am often sure that I have—perhaps it is not too late to correct the direction of my path.

Yet often recently I have yearned for the pines and the blue sky and the frosty air and the hymns of St. Catherine and the Virgin.

I also weep often for my parents.

I have become a sentimental old man. I am Polish after all.

Notre Dame

This is a most Catholic and a most American place, filled with symbols of both traditions. The great gilt statue of the Virgin above the dome. The "touchdown Jesus" on the side of the library. The grotto where young people are married. The football team, the parades, the bands, the cheering students, all of them bright, some of them very bright. I do not understand the football, which seems to be a very brutal game. Much of the art is deplorably bad. Yet the students are vivacious and open and the faculty often intelligent. I am made welcome here and have become, I believe the words are, "a campus character." The young people shout greetings at me in Russian and I wave my staff at them and shout back. I revel in these exchanges. Here among so many young people I feel almost that I myself am young again. Was I ever as young as they are? I doubt it.

I have spoken in passing to some people about this "journal" I'm keeping. That is probably not a good idea. Those who remember my past might grow worried if they knew of its existence. Again I have been imprudent.

Before I left Moscow I encountered one of my priests on the street. He was dressed as a worker, but he did not seem poor. I tried to talk to him. At first he pretended not to recognize me. Then he refused to say a word. I do not know what to make of that. I worry about it and somehow I am also afraid.

2001 Chicago

This University is not as exuberant as Notre Dame, but much more serious. Too serious perhaps. The students are extremely intelligent and my colleagues are some of the best scholars I have ever worked with. Yet the university seems somehow dry, perhaps because it has no football team. Or perhaps because it is not, as a colleague at Notre Dame said of that school, a Catholic theme park. Or maybe that's only because I feel so dry. The life I live here makes it possible for me to recover some of my monastic solitude, though it is more difficult to pray when you are alone than when you are in a chapel filled with monks.

Once I have gone to a Polish church to participate in the liturgy in my first language. It is very beautiful and I weep. Often these days I weep. The young priest is not sure about giving the Eucharist to someone dressed like a Russian monk. However, he smiles and shrugs his shoulders.

I have reread this memoir and realize how dangerous it might be. Sometimes I feel that I'm being followed. Surely the FSB does not have agents here in Chicago. Perhaps it is the CIA. Or perhaps it is Russian paranoia.

Russian paranoia and Polish tears. I am true to both heritages.

I will stop writing now. Perhaps I will begin again sometime. I will wrap it up and give it to the beautiful and efficient dean—a tall, pale woman with red hair, who in Eastern Europe would be considered either a witch or a vampire or an archangel. I will tell her to

189

lock it in a safe. I will write on the wrapping that it should be opened if I die or disappear. I do not expect either to happen. Yet now I do not want my story to be forgotten.

I will put this attached document in at the bottom of my memoir.

The day before I left Notre Dame, a somewhat officious young priest came to visit me in my room in Sorin Hall. He carried a bag in which perhaps some vestments might hang. He tells me that he is from the Papal Nunciature in Washington and shows me his credentials. I must hold in confidence the documents he will give me.

The Most Holy Father, he announces solemnly, has graciously seen fit to elevate you to the sacred crimson. I laugh at him. Surely this is a joke. He is offended. The elevation, he says, is in petto, if I know what that means. I laugh again. You mean I am a secret cardinal? He nods gravely. When it is his pleasure, the Most Holy Father will reveal the appointment.

I glance at the document. I am described as Msgr. Jan Sobieski Ostrowski. However, that young man died long ago. They do not know about Simon Sobieski.

I continue to laugh. Who was the last Orthodox theologian to be named a cardinal? Bessarion, was it not?

After telling me that neither the "elevation" nor the secret is a laughing matter, the young man offers his congratulations and takes his solemn leave.

I continue to laugh. It is probably a joke but it is a very funny joke. And, if it is real, it is an even funnier joke.

One of my colleagues comes in. I slide a manuscript over the announcement. I hope you're not in trouble with the Vatican, Brother Semyon, he says.

I dismiss his fears. They do not read my work there, I'm sure. Besides I'm an Orthodox monk. They have no jurisdiction over me. Not yet anyway. I've seen that fat fop before, he replies. He's the second secretary of the Nunciature. He was looking for a document they think they need, I tell him.

So it is real. It means nothing. It changes nothing. It is a secret like everything else in my life is secret. Perhaps in heaven my poor parents are proud of me. Orthodox that she is, my mother is surely happy. Pole that my father is, he is probably cautious and cynical.

When my colleague has left I notice the carrying case the young priest has hung on the hook behind the door. I open the zipper cautiously. Inside are the watered silk choir robes of a cardinal. And the pallium of an archbishop.

I look again at the notice of elevation. I am described as Jan Sobieski Ostrowski of the Order of St. Benedict.

My compatriot in the white robes knows my story. Like all Polish intellectuals, myself included, he is a romantic.

And he also has a sense of humor. I continue to laugh.

If anyone should ever read my little memoir, I hope they will laugh too.

Lord Jesus Christ, Son and Word of the Living God

By the prayer of your most pure Mother and all the Saints

Have mercy on us and save us.

13

No one around the table in the dean's office laughed.

"Where are the robes, I wonder?" the president asked.

"I can answer that question. They're in Cardinal Cronin's closet alongside his own robes. They will be returned to Cardinal Ostrowski when he asks for them."

"Surely he is dead," President Alan said.

"I can't believe that," the valiant Dorina insisted.

"Blackie?" Mike Casey looked at me.

"Oh, he's alive all right. Whoever has him wants this document. Since we have it and they don't, he's still alive."

"Where?" Dorina asked.

"I propose to find out."

"Am I a witch or a vampire?" she asks with a laugh.

"Most likely an archangel," the president tells her.

"Or the Madonna," I venture.

We had read the little memoir page by page, passing the pages around the room. When we had finished with several pages, Dorie made one Xerox copy of each for Milord Cronin.

"If no one minds," I said, "let's put the copy of this somewhat elaborate papal document in with the rest of the copy for Cardinal

Cronin. I think the original papal announcement would be more effective with the cardinal robes."

No one protested. My head was twirling with plans to find Brother Semyon or Cardinal Jan and freeing him.

"An astonishing story," the dean said. "I suppose it is all true?"

"I argue from its improbability that it has to be true," I told them. "Can you imagine that little scene in Sorin Hall a year ago! High drama! This little booklet would be a great commercial success."

"Are you planning on publishing it?" Mike wondered.

"That decision is up to him," I said.

"The imposter," the president rubbed his forehead, "came here searching for this document."

"Almost certainly," I agreed.

"And someone killed him before he could get it?"

"Perhaps. Or perhaps the imposter was killed because he was thought to be Brother Semyon. The people behind the killing wanted to keep this document secret. Now we assume they'll try to find it."

"But who would want it?"

"Everyone who knew about him and heard about his writing a journal—the CIA, the Vatican, the FSB, assorted Catholic busybodies."

"It's a powerful document," the dean observed.

"Very powerful," I agreed, "and also very careful. No dates or names given. One could guess perhaps who the CIA man in Paris was and the priests from the Vatican. Brother Semyon—or Father Jan as one might call him—is sufficiently Slavic to distrust any reader. Some of those who are after the document would regret that there are no dates or times or names in it."

"I'll wrap it up again," Dorie said.

"And by your leave," the president said, "I will take this to a certain place, far from here, where it will be utterly safe."

"I will provide you with one of my cars," Mike Casey offered. "Less conspicuous than a university police car."

"Good idea, Mike," the president agreed.

"And the rest of us," I said, "had better vacate the building since six o'clock draws near."

"Do you really think they will try tonight?" Dorie asked.

"When the University announced that it was transporting all of Brother Semyon's papers to the bowels of Regenstein Library, it alerted the relevant people that the document may be available. If they move at all, they will move quickly."

She and I were the last to leave the building. We made sure that it was empty save for Dave Dolan, whom we collected in his office.

"Big deal!" he observed, as Dorie locked the front door.

"I was told explicitly that I could not discuss this with my sweetheart."

"Who's he?" Dave pretended to be confused. "Someone on the faculty?"

"I don't know, but I do know who the president thinks my sweetheart is."

"Off with the two of you," I said, "to the security of Evergreen Park."

"You will call us?" Dorie pleaded.

"I will indeed."

As they pulled away in his ancient Ford, I ambled to Mike Casey's command car.

"Do you think they'll try the front or the back door?"

"Back door almost certainly. They can drive up Fifty-eighth Street, park their vehicles, dash into the small quadrangle, blow the door, and storm into the building."

"So we set floodlights to illuminate the quadrangle, flip them on while they come rushing in, and tell them they're surrounded and that they should drop their guns."

"They'll start shooting blindly," I suggested.

"As soon as they do, we'll shoot back. What will happen then?"

"They will throw up their hands and surrender. They're not heroes seeking to die for a cause, only mercenaries working for hire."

"And what do we do to them?"

"Turn them over to the Chicago Police Department who will charge them with disorderly conduct and firing dangerous weapons. They will plea bargain and be forgotten. Or maybe be deported immediately."

"Sounds reasonable to me . . . I've brought along some body armor for you, Blackie, and a helmet."

"No," I protested weakly. "I've never worn either before."

"Put it on. My wife made me promise I'd force you to wear it."

Under such circumstances, what choice does a bishop have, even a bishop who has a constitutional aversion to accepting orders? Obediently I put on the Kevlar. I also tried on the blue Chicago Police Department helmet, which I was sure made me look even more absurd.

I took it off.

"Put that back on," Mike ordered. "I promised Annie that I'd make you wear it."

At nine o'clock it was as dark as anyplace in Chicago ever gets. The darkness comes too early in October thanks to a regrettable decision by the Almighty about arranging the seasons for our planet and the local resistance to acknowledge that we ought to be on Eastern rather than Central time. It was also raining, a soft day as they would call it in the mother country—a steady drizzle, rain acting like it was ashamed of itself.

"A fine misty evening, isn't it, Your Reverence?" Mike Casey remarked as we left the car. "And, Blackie, put on your helmet!"

"I will look like a visitor from outer space with a blue head."

"A live bishop from outer space, however."

I dutifully put on the blue CPD helmet. Was this not an inappropriate crossing of the line which separates Church and state?

"You wait here." Mike gestured to the passage linking Bond Chapel to Swift Hall. "Don't stick your head out when the shooting begins."

I had, characteristically, not thought of bringing an umbrella or a raincoat. So in my Kevlar armor and blue helmet I cowered against the gray stone of Swift, shoulders hunched against the rain—a most undignified position, I thought, for a successor to the apostles.

As I waited for something to happen I reflected on Brother Semyon's diary. It was actually a very mild, though fascinating, document. It would cause some minor embarrassment for the Vatican and the CIA, but nothing that would cause a second day of news coverage. The FSB would look foolish only because its predecessors had not caught Semyon's masquerade at the beginning. Why all the frenetic activity to capture or destroy the document?

The answer was that the various relevant parties did not know that the diary was a relatively harmless document. Spooks always expect the worst, perhaps because they themselves would, if they thought it necessary or expedient, do the worst. Like stranding an innocent priest in Russia. Twice.

A distraction interrupted by reflection. Brother Semyon, through no fault of his own, did not understand Celtic mythology. The good Dorina, tall, slender, pale, and with long red hair, was actually Kathleen ni Houlihan, ancient symbol of Ireland. I would have to tell her that if this purgatorial night ever ended.

Then I saw the solution to the whole mystery. How silly of me not to have recognized it from the beginning. All the materials were there even without Brother Semyon's helpful diary. Then the elevator door closed and the solution was lost.

Then, remarkably, the door opened again and remained open. This time the solution locked into my conscious memory. Of course! Unpardonable for me not to have seen it.

I inched around the corner to whisper the solution to Mike the Cop.

Just then he said to the darkness, "Black van stopping on Fifty-ninth Street . . . Six armed men emerging . . . condition red."

The men charged into the passage between Goodspeed and Wieboldt Halls, hesitated a moment, and began to run towards me. I should have redeployed.

"Lights!" Mike ordered

Instantly the whole quadrangle was illuminated. The commandos stopped, startled by their exposure to the glare.

I did not redeploy. However, unlike my father, the good Ned Ryan, I did not charge them as he had attacked Japanese battleships with destroyer escorts. Rather I remained as if moored in concrete at the edge of the quadrangle of light.

"Throw down your guns! You are surrounded!" Mike ordered on the public address system that had been set up.

Someone repeated that order in a foreign language, presumably Russian.

A couple of commandos fired their automatic weapons, knocking out one of the searchlights.

"Fire!" Mike ordered.

Our off-duty cops discharged a variety of weapons—revolvers, shotguns, automatic weapons, mostly into the air. One commando toppled over. The rest dropped their weapons and threw their hands into the air.

I noticed that I was sitting in the mud and leaning against Swift Hall. I remembered a bee buzzing by my ear and someone swatting the left side of my head. I felt my blue helmet. There was a dent in it.

"Blackie down!" Tina shouted.

There are many false reports about what I said in response to all of this.

I did not rush into the chapel and cry, "Sanctuary."

I did not shout, "Once more for England, Harry, and St. George!"

I did not cry "Medic!"

I merely said, "Blackie is up," and struggled to my feet. Astonishingly, I was able to remain on them, albeit precariously.

Some cops were cuffing the would-be raiders. Others carried the wounded man out. Still others were collecting the weapons.

"Are you wounded, Blackie?" Tina demanded in something like hysteria.

I heard sirens in the background. The Seventh Cavalry no doubt.

Then I delivered what I considered an appropriate response, all things considered.

I pointed at the dent in my helmet.

"Unnecessary roughness. Fifteen yards. Clipping."

I gave what I fear was a poor imitation of one of the zebras hitting his right thigh in the clipping signal, then produced the dented helmet as proof. Tina held my arm lest I collapse back into the mud from which I had been formed.

Mike rushed up.

"What happened?"

I showed him the helmet.

"A splinter of Swift Hall!" he said, leaning over to pick up a bit of stone. "A ricochet must have knocked it loose! Thank God you were wearing your helmet!"

"Divinity School kills bishop," I murmured.

"How many fingers?" He held up his hand.

"Four," I said promptly.

Tina giggled.

"Four?"

"Plus one thumb."

"Your sisters' names?"

"Mary Kate, Eileen, and Tracy."

"My wife's name?"

"Annie."

"I'm still going to take you over to the hospital to have you checked out."

"Northwestern," I insisted. "That's home."

"Tina, help Bishop Ryan over to my car."

To my surprise I was able to walk.

"Let me try it by myself for a couple of seconds."

She let go of my arm. I wobbled, but I could walk. She reasserted her support.

The local on-duty cops collected the commandos into a squadrol (née Paddy Wagon) and departed. Mike's people had picked up the guns and the lights and drove away. The only evidence of the brief if noisy firefight was my dented helmet.

"Let me look at you!" Mike peered at me in the backseat of his command car. "Bump, nothing more."

"No blood?"

"No blood."

I sighed.

"No Purple Heart."

The people in the Emergency Room at Northwestern treated me like I was a returning war hero.

Cheers and all.

The resident went through all the rituals of testing for a concussion and admitted, reluctantly I thought, that I probably did not have a concussion.

"We'll keep you here overnight," he said.

"Yes," I agreed, "but in my bedroom at the Cathedral."

He accepted that compromise and warned me that if I experienced any symptoms like nausea or difficulty in breathing, I should call immediately and they would come over. Apparently they considered the Rectory to be an annex of the hospital. They gave me some pills for any headaches that might develop and warned me against any liquor for twenty-four hours.

"Lent in October." I sighed.

Back in the car I sat on my briefcase and only then remembered that it contained the memoir of Brother Semyon Ivanivich Popov. The angels in charge had apparently protected it.

I found my cell phone, peeled off the mud, and dialed Dave Dolan's number out in Evergreen Park. One of the angels swarming around Swift Hall that night must have whispered it in my ear.

"David Dolan."

"Blackie reporting. Enemy troops repelled and captured. No casualties. Swift Hall is safe. Please inform Keen Dean. Tell her that poor Brother Semyon knew no Celtic mythology and overlooked the patent fact that she is Kathleen ni Houlihan."

He laughed

"Are you a little groggy, Bishop? You don't sound quite right."

"That charge has been made before. I was assaulted by splinter from Swift Hall. Tell Dean Houlihan she will hear from my lawyers in the morning."

We pulled up to the door of 730 North Wabash.

"I'll walk you to the elevator, then take Tina home," Mike said.

I remembered that as a Christian I should be concerned about my enemies.

"What's the condition of the wounded Russian?"

"Not serious. They'll be quietly deported."

I realized that the offending bullet could just as well have been fired by one of our own. *BISHOP RYAN VICTIM OF FRIENDLY FIRE!* the headline might have said.

I fumbled with my keys at the door. He took them from me and opened the lock.

"Even unwounded I have a hard time doing that."

"I can well believe it."

I assured him that I could ride up in the elevator by myself.

The light was on in my suite. I had not left it on. A good pastor never wastes electricity, right? Patently Milord Cronin was waiting up for his teenager.

"Blackwood!" he shouted, putting aside a stack of mail. "You look like hell! What happened?"

"Wounded in action!" I said, offering my dented helmet as proof, as I collapsed into my couch.

"You belong in the hospital."

"Been there, done that."

"No concussion?"

"Much to their disappointment. They warned me to let them know if I incur any nausea or difficult breathing and they gave me pills for a headache."

"Details!" he demanded.

"In the morning. For the present, the guys on the white horses won, I have solved the mystery, here is the precious diary which you should read before you go to bed and put in your safe. Also you should consider who is a secure, honest, intelligent, resource bureaucrat in the Curia to whom I should report this story."

He thumbed through the file and startled when he saw the papal document.

"He really was a cardinal!"

"Is . . . now I'm going to bed."

"Maybe you should take a shower. You're soaking wet and covered with mud."

"Tomorrow."

I have no recollection of making it to my bed.

14

"You're still breathing," said Milord Cronin as he shook me gently.

"Arguably." I sighed.

"Headache?"

"I no longer have a head to ache."

"They said over at the hospital to take two of these every three hours."

He proffered two capsules and a glass of water.

"Breakfast?"

"Never again."

"Crystal said you should drink this cup of tea. It will settle your nerves."

Crystal Lane was not only our youth minister, she was the guardian angel of the whole parish staff.

"Herbal tea," I said.

"She says caffeine would not be good for you just now . . . The doctors from Northwestern will be over in a half hour."

"I shall attempt a shower before then . . . Thank Ms. Lane for her tea."

"I read the memoir," he said, standing up from the side of my bed, where he had been sitting.

"Ah?"

Andrew M. Greeley

His bedside manner, I reflected, was smooth and polished. Naturally.

"Damnedest story I ever heard! Knowing those guys over there, I don't doubt a word of it. Idiots."

"Patently."

"You noted his appointment document?"

"Yeah! He's right about Polish romantics, but he deserves it more than most of my crimson-clad brothers . . . Is he still alive?"

"I believe so."

"You asked last night about someone over there you could trust. What are you up to?"

"Freeing Jan Sobieski Cardinal Ostrowski of the Order of Saint Benedict."

He nodded.

"Figures."

"Jan Sobieski was the king of Poland who saved Vienna from the Turks in 1681."

"I'm not a complete illiterate, Blackwood . . . You could trust that fellow he talked to in Rome—Archbishop Rick Agostino. Honest man. Stand-up guy as your friend Mike Casey would say."

"Depending on what intelligence reaches me today, I will be off to Paris and Rome tomorrow or the next day."

"I'll give him a ring and tell him you're coming and that he'd better be straight with you because you know too much and are too dangerous."

"*Moi?*"

"*Tu.*"

Nary a word to warn me to be careful, much less advice to drop the whole matter.

I did manage the shower, pajamas, and a clean robe before four people, a resident, a specialist in head injuries and two nurses arrived from Northwestern.

"Solemn high," I said as I turned away from my e-mail.

They marveled at the lump on my head, urged cold packs,

expressed delight that the medication helped my headache, and warned me to be careful for a couple of days. I saw no point in causing excessive worry, so I did not explain that I was planning a flight to Rome with perhaps a stop in Paris.

"How did you get that bump?" the head specialist (woman) asked me.

"Doing the Lord's work," I said, which was, strictly speaking, the truth though hardly the whole truth.

They were charmed by Milord Cronin, who stuck his head in my room, dressed in black suit and crimson-tinged Roman collar (and wearing his ruby cuff links). Then they departed, warning me again to take it easy for a few days. I agreed that I would. Fortunately they did not see Sean Cronin's expression of skepticism.

"Will you tell your friend Ms. Lane to send my messages?" I asked, when the medics had left.

He shrugged his broad shoulders.

"Sure . . . I'll call my good friend Archbishop Ricardo Agostino and warn him to be on his best behavior when you show up at the Secretariat of State."

"No hints . . . I want to take him by surprise."

"Patently," he said, sweeping out of my room like the express train from Roma to Milano.

"Bishop Blackie?" Crystal Lane on the house phone.

"How are you?"

"Surviving."

"You take too many chances," she said softly.

"You keep praying for me, Crystal," I said, "and I'll be fine."

"Well you have a lot of interesting friends. There's that man from the Mafia and that man from the CIA and that Russian person and that sweet dean from *The* University and Mr. Casey and that lovely Frenchwoman from Paris."

"*La Belle* Chantal."

"*Oui*. She asked for *M. l'Evêque* and I said did she mean Cardinal Cronin and she laughed and said, oh, no, not Sean. Just Blackie."

"She would say that."

"Whom should I get first?"

"Whom do you think?"

"Chantal."

"Good."

"Ah, *M. l'eveque Blackie* (pronounced Blocky as in blockhead), your assistant was so sweet. She is very holy, no?"

"Yes."

Happy giggle.

"See, I know such things . . . My husband Jean-Laurence, you know is a Breton, very much *le* straight arrow as you Americans would say."

"Not so straight that he would not marry a woman who was ordained a priest."

A gentle laugh.

"He found me irresistible and still does, *n'est-ce pas?*"

"Why am I not surprised?

"*Bien* . . . He is a very honest and upright lawyer. Yet sometimes it amuses him to maintain some contact with the police, no?"

"They can be very useful."

"*Oui . . . précisément.* So he learns that some very-right-wing Catholics have lifted, as you would say, *Frère* Semyon. *Les flics* know where he is but are doing nothing because they wish to avoid controversy with the Church."

"Just as they did not seriously wish to find *Frère* Jean-Claude."

She chuckled.

"That required someone who understood the secrets of human hearts . . . *Eh bien,* the good Jean-Laurence continues to work on it. In a day or two he will know more."

"Good. I will be in Paris in a day or two on my way to Rome."

They would pick me up at Charles DeGaulle. I would stay with them. They had an adorable little apartment, complete with private bath and television, just for visiting bishops. Better even than the

Ritz. The little Jean-Claude would be delirious with joy to see me. No excuses would be accepted.

So none were offered.

I would bring two sweatshirts which indicated membership in the North Wabash Avenue Irregulars. The French version which dated from my search for her elusive brother—*Les Irregulars d'Avenue Wabash du Nord.*

I sat at my desk and applied an ice pack to the lump on my head. As I made the phone calls I kept it in place.

"Let's try the CIA man," I said to Crystal.

I didn't tell her who these people were. She just knew.

"What happened there last night?" he began. "It wasn't us, that I can swear to."

"It was your good friends from FSB, using superannuated Trans-Dneister commandos. We captured them easily and are deporting them quietly. I must say they were equally inept as your friend out on Wabash Avenue with the automatic weapon."

"The FSB doesn't usually do that sort of thing, not in this country anyway."

"They did this time, reverting to their old ways because they wanted the fabled memoir of Brother Semyon, just as your folks did. Warn them off. We have seen the document and locked it where it can't be found. Moreover, despite the panic it seems to have stirred up, there's very little in it that would last more than one day's news cycle. Neither your leaders nor the Vatican would be greatly embarrassed. The FSB has even less to fear, unless they mess with us again."

"I'm glad to hear that. There's no reason why we should not trust you."

"It would be most imprudent for you not to trust us. I assume you will pass this on to your principals, indeed at the highest level."

"That will be done before the day is over."

Don't mess with Blackie Ryan or you'll live to regret it.

207

I really didn't believe that for a moment. However, it was important for them to think that it was true.

"You might mention to those who are interested in the case that the Notre Dame man with the blue eyes and the silver hair who approached Brother Semyon in Paris is not mentioned by name. I assume one could work it out, however."

He gulped.

"I'm sure one could. I'll pass that on."

"Again let me assure you that we have no desire to see that this document goes into the public domain at this time."

I sighed at the end of the conversation. I had made my point.

Actually we would not want the memoir in the present form made public. The material about ordaining women would guarantee that Jan Ostrowski's "elevation" to the sacred crimson would never get out of petto.

Our next stop was Mike Casey.

"I don't think we need to use secure phones anymore," he began.

"If anyone is bugging me, they've heard me say that the memoir is much ado about nothing."

"Yet the spooks hear about it and they have to hunt for it, even to the point of murder."

"Indeed."

"At our end everything goes well. Our mutual friends from last night will be on a plane to Moscow tonight. Let the relevant parties worry about getting them down to Ukraine. You're all right?"

"Prospering. Isn't the Lord Cardinal himself taking good care of me?"

"As well he should . . . I assume the issue is closed?"

"Not till we find Brother Semyon or whatever name he goes by now."

"Should I keep the guard on you and the rectory?"

"Only till tomorrow, when I leave for Paris and Rome."

"Fair enough . . . Herself says you should come over for your cinnamon tea and raisin cookies."

"Tomorrow morning," I promised.

"Lets try Dean Keane," I told Crystal.

"She's so wonderful."

Crystal likes people. She's also a realist. So Dean Keane was a woman approved.

"Are you all right?" the good dean asked breathlessly. "Some of the cops told Dave's dad that you had been hurt!"

"I was assaulted by a chip of stone from Swift Hall. I will sue!"

"If you're responsible for damaging the building, we'll sue!"

"How could a big Protestant university win a suit against a poor, inoffensive little bishop?"

"Dave's dad said that if you hadn't been wearing a police helmet, you would have been badly hurt."

"If I hadn't been wearing the helmet, I would have been hiding in the safety of Bond Chapel."

"There's rumors all around about a shoot-out last night. There's no trace of it, but some people who were in Harper Library claim they heard automatic weapons fire."

"You know how rumors spread, Dean Keane. I would suggest, however, that you propose that your quiet little quadrangle be renamed the OK Corral."

"And we could build a monument to you as Doc Holliday Ryan."

The young woman had a tongue in her mouth, didn't she? Poor Dave Dolan.

"The Doc died a Catholic," I said for the historical record, "because of the prayers of a Daughter of Charity who had been his childhood sweetheart."

"Is it all over, Bishop Blackie?" she asked, serious once again.

"We think so. All relevant parties have been told that there's nothing in the memoir that they should worry about and they can't get it anymore even if they still want it."

Not quite true. The Vatican didn't know that, but it would hear that truth in a couple of days.

"And Brother Semyon is *really* still alive?"

"It would appear so. We hope to free him soon."

"Will he come back here?"

"That remains to be seen," I said cautiously.

"You'll stay in touch with us?"

"Oh, yes. For the present your stance must be that the problem is over and that Brother Semyon must be presumed dead."

"Should I tell the president?"

"Superintendent Casey has told him already."

Someday, one of Jan Sobieski Ostrowski's personae would come in out of the cold. At some later day much of the truth could be revealed.

"And David's struggle for tenure?"

"I don't ask. But people tell me that it's certain."

"And then?"

Long pause.

"We'll just have to see, won't we, Bishop Blackie?"

I still had the Italian and Russian "outfits" to deal with.

Milord Cronin appeared on his way to the Chancery Office. He had on his brusque, businesslike mask, which hinted at the need to stir up some turbulence.

"I talked to Rick Agostino. Gave him the full dope on you and warned him that he had better be very careful as you were an extremely dangerous person and we were lucky you still were on our side."

"Excellent!" I said.

One must humor cardinals in their moods.

"He wanted to know what it was about and I told him that it was too secret to disclose on the phone . . . What's your strategy going to be?"

"Simple and respectful. I will tell him the whole story, well most of it, and demand that Jan Sobieski Cardinal Ostrowski be released by the end of business in two days or we'll go public with the whole thing."

I think that Sean Cronin gulped.

"And if he says the situation is not yet mature enough for that?"

"I'll show him this."

I held up the announcement of Jan's elevation to the sacred crimson, which I had not entrusted to him the night before.

"And I'll tell him about the robes we found in the Windemere."

Milord nodded solemnly.

"That will get their attention all right . . . Rick is a man utterly innocent of bullshit, Blackwood. He knows he might be pope some day, but he just doesn't give a damn. He can play the game with them all, but for him it's nothing more than a silly game."

"Must be his Irish mother."

"Patently . . . Well, see to it, Blackwood!"

He sailed out, quite satisfied with himself.

I chose my friend out on the West Side.

"You okay, Bishop? I heard something went down out on the South Side last night and you were hurt. The friends of my friends are upset to hear that."

In Chicago, you could keep no secrets.

"Slight bump. I'm fine."

"I'll tell my friends to tell their friends that. They'll be happy to hear about it."

"Thank you."

"They tell me their friends are also worried that someone might think they were involved in this thing that went down."

"I don't think anyone thinks that."

"I hear that they're wondering if it might have been some competitors of the friends of my friends."

"Ah."

"You know what I mean, some Eastern European competitors."

"You wouldn't be all that wrong if you passed on the word that the individuals involved were of Eastern European origins, but are from out of town."

"That's very interesting . . . Could I mention to them the name of the town?"

"Moscow."

That settled that.

"If you have any trouble, any trouble at all, Father, just let us know."

How come I had to hold the hands of organized criminals to reassure them that they were not in trouble with the Church? Not the proper task for an ineffectual little auxiliary bishop. Not at all, at all. I shifted the ice pack from one hand to another. I should be answering my e-mail instead of talking to these odd characters on the phone.

I was about to punch in the numbers for my old friend Rodion Petrovich, the "outfit"'s competition, when the parish secretary who had replaced Crystal Lane was at the phone.

"Your sister, Dr. Murphy, Bishop."

I could have written out the dialogue before the conversation.

"Punk, what the hell kind of trouble did you get yourself into last night? I hear on the street that you were shot in the head!"

"You know you can't believe everything you hear on the street."

"Where there's smoke there's fire, especially when it's your smoke."

"An insightful observation."

"There's nothing wrong with you?"

"Nothing more than usual."

"Were you out hunting for Sean?'

"In a manner of speaking."

"Did you get the bad guys?"

"Blackie Ryan always gets the bad guys!"

My sibs bring out the worst in me.

"Except when they get him . . . What should I tell the kids when they hear the rumors?"

"That I'll be out of town for a few days."

"A hospital somewhere?"

"Hardly."

"Where?"

"Paris, Rome."

"What are you going to do there?"

"Import a little bit more cosmos on chaos."

"Yeah, like you always do . . . Did they give you any medication for your headache?"

"I take Tylenol occasionally."

That was, strictly speaking, the truth. However, I was not taking it presently. If I had told her what I was taking, there would be a whole new catechism.

"Yeah, well do they know you're going to Europe?"

"Would I go without telling them?"

"I hope not . . . Well, anyway, be careful."

"I always am."

"You weren't the other night."

A telling last word. The sort that the senior matriarch in our family always claimed.

Before she could get to the doctors who had treated me and ask them about a trip to Europe, I called them. How did I feel? Pretty good. Medication controlling the pain? It seems to. Swelling down? I felt it. Considerably. Is this trip essential? Man's life may depend on it. Hesitation. All right, but call us if you experience any unusual symptoms. Certainly. And only one glass of wine a day. Only one? Well, two if you're in Paris. Thank you very much.

What I wanted to do actually was to go back to bed.

I had one more call to make. Who was it now? Ah yes, Rodion Petrovich.

"Ivanoff," he bellowed into the phone.

"Bishop Ryan."

"Bishop, I hope you are not seriously injured. I heard there was some trouble last night."

"Don't believe all you hear, Rodion Petrovich."

"Believe me, it wasn't us."

"Certainly it wasn't."

"Those Trans-Dneister thugs?"

I calculated.

"It would seem so."

"They should be sent back to Moldava, where they belong."

"I believe that's going to happen."

He murmured several words in his native tongue, curses unless my ear for such things was mistaken.

"Who were they working for?"

"It is my impression that they were on assignment for some individuals in Moscow."

"FSB?"

"It would seem so."

More unintelligible curses.

"Those individuals do not give up easily. They will try again."

"I take your point. However, there are solid grounds to believe that they will not. Some of their American counterparts are quite upset."

"Well then, God be praised, there will be no more trouble."

"I'm sure there won't be."

"If you have any trouble, any trouble at all, Father, just let us know."

Should anyone try to circle the Cathedral Rectory again, I would have reserves to summon—both the boys in the blue and the boys in the gray.

I called my travel agent. Business class seats (by reason of upgrade) tomorrow Chicago to Paris and then the next afternoon Paris to Rome. Four days at the *Atlante Star* in Rome—just off the Via Concilliazione. Tickets to be collected at the airport.

"You get into Rome at noon on Monday, Blackwood?" Milord Cronin, back from the Chancery for lunch, strolled into my office, while I was making the reservations.

"*Si, Eminenza* . . . You will make an appointment for me with your friend Rico that afternoon?"

"Rick, not Rico. And no I won't. You'll be so confused on

Monday that you won't even be able to find St. Peter's. I'll make it for Tuesday morning."

"I must hurry back."

"Why rush? I'll take over your work."

A day as the real pastor of his Cathedral would force Milord Cronin into an early retirement.

"You can't do my e-mail for me . . . What did the good archbishop have to say?"

I would of course bring along my portable computer to keep up with the e-mail.

"I've stirred up his curiosity."

"How did you do that?"

"I told him that the story you have to tell is the most astonishing and most shocking I've heard in my fifty years as a priest."

I pondered that.

"And he said?"

"He said that he knew some stories in which both he and I were involved, so he thought that this one must be a real shocker—or some Italian equivalent."

"I'd say crazy."

"That too . . . Are you taking anyone with you, a nephew or a niece or some nice minder like that?"

"Why should I need such?"

"So you don't lose your tickets and your passport and your carry-on baggage and your wallet and so you don't get on the wrong plane or take the wrong taxi—that sort of thing."

A point well taken. I am notoriously poor at finding my way when I am outside the boundaries of the Cathedral parish or the Beverly neighborhood where I grew up. Even the back streets of Grand Beach, Michigan. I could easily end up as a South Side Irish Flying Dutchman.

"If I do get lost, I'll call instantly."

He sniffed.

"Well, call me every day and let me know where you are, if you know . . . See to it, Blackwood."

And he ambled out.

Another call from the office.

"Ms. Mary Jane Mulhern of Channel Six on the phone for you, Bishop."

Ah, the fair Mary Jane had heard the stories.

"Tell her that Bishop Ryan has been summoned to Rome and buzz the Cardinal."

I thereupon hurried to the Cardinal's suite and found him engaged in a leisurely—and of course charming—conversation with Ms. Mulhern.

"Yes, he's been summoned to Rome . . . I think they've finally caught up with him . . . Or maybe we need a second cardinal here in Chicago . . . I think it's time we got another, don't you? . . . Sure you can quote me . . . No one will believe it . . . You want the TRUTH? . . . Well why didn't you say so? . . . Bishop Ryan will report to the Vatican about some very delicate matters on a subject about which he enjoys enormous respect over there . . ."

He turned and winked at me.

"Not only is he bright, Mary Jane, he is patently the brightest bishop in the United States and arguably in the whole world . . . Everyone knows that . . . He'd look adorable in cardinal red? . . . I quite agree."

He put the phone back in its cradle with a manic grin.

"Skillful obfuscation," I observed.

"Praise from a master . . . You're leaving tomorrow afternoon?"

"I must tie up some loose ends around here."

"And diminish the size of that bump on your skull."

I realized that I was still pressing the ice pack against my skull.

"Well, *bon voyage* and give my best to Chantal and Jean-Laurence."

I stumbled back to my room and collapsed into bed. I thought of the medieval statue of the Madonna in my office and could hear my mother's voice whisper, "Johnny, you're out of your mind."

Mary Kathleen Ryan Murphy, my pushy medical sib, is a pale cupcake compared to our mutual mother.

I tuned her out by falling asleep. In my dreams Mike Casey and I, occasionally helped by the good dean, defended the Wieboldt Arch against massive waves of Russian and Sicilian-American Mafiosi.

15

I knew I was in Charles DeGaulle Airport, but I had no idea where and which way to go to get out of it. I reflected on *le general* (as he was called and never more than a two-star general at that). It was said of him that he considered himself to be France—an embodiment like Jeanne d'Arc. On the record he was entitled to think that. Several times when the leaders of France were sniveling incompetents, he stood firm for *la gloire*. A man of solid republican loyalty and solid Catholic loyalty, he had also had mitigated the conflict between clericals and anticlericals.

Nonetheless he had failed to create a tradition in which La Belle France built intelligible airports.

There had been much ceremony to mark my departure. Crystal had assembled the Megans and some of their dorky boys to sing farewell to me.

Somehow I did not think that "Johnny, We Hardly Knew Ya!" was appropriate, though I was assured that they would all pray for me every day. Alas, their prayers did not extend so far as to getting me out of the airport. Moreover, Chantal and Jean-Laurence had not showed up to rescue me.

American Airlines had generously upgraded me to first class, which on a 767 was about as good as overnight trips across the

Atlantic will ever get until one can beam oneself over like the folks in *Star Trek*. I had even managed to make it to the plane before they definitively closed the doors.

My headache pills made it possible for me to sleep across the ocean. However, the flight attendant in the first-class cabin, who had only me to supervise, found it hard to wake me up when we touched down at DeGaulle.

She also found it necessary to remind me not to forget my carry-on bag, the only luggage I carried because no one at the cathedral had any confidence in my ability to recover checked luggage. I had stumbled and bumbled and staggered around the arrival lounge and finally by some mistake encountered an immigration line. The man who stared at me and my passport photo in disbelief, muttered to himself in French something to the effect that one could expect from the Catholic Church nothing more than a horse's ass as a priest. That stirred enough energy to cause me to reply—in excellent French if I do say so—that it took one to know one.

He stamped my passport and returned it to me.

I quit while I was ahead, though a number of additional retorts had sprung to my lips such as the suggestion that his mother might have been a donkey, not a nice thing for a bishop to say even to a Frenchman.

Then I found myself wandering. I knew I was in Paris, even that I was at Charles DeGaulle Airport. Only I did not know where I was or what I should do next. I could call someone on my cell phone—if I could find it. In fact I could call the virtuous Chantal. However, I did not have her number memorized or coded into the phone. Besides she and the stalwart Jean-Laurence were doubtless at the airport searching for me.

I could return to "Go" and start over, only "Go" was O'Hare International Airport, an inconvenient distance away.

"Blockie!" a familiar voice rang out.

I looked around. Chantal was peering around the corner of a green wall which was probably a "Nothing to Declare" exit. She was waving frantically. How clever of her! I waved back. She smiled at the customs inspector who had permitted her to peer in so that she might find *le pauvre petit prêtre.* I remembered to pick up my carry-on bag and trudged obediently towards the exit.

I had enough presence of mind to say to the customs man, *"Merci, monsieur."* He saluted.

Jeanne-Chantal, twin of and ordination substitute for her brother Jean Claude, was a slim little woman with long black hair, dancing brown eyes, and enormous enthusiasm, much of which I suspected was driven by sexual energy. Paradoxically, she also seemed like a waif, a fragile and vulnerable little girl child. She had left the Church as a young woman but, while pretending to be *Frère* Jean-Claude, she had acted her way back home. Part of the appeal of the man she chose to marry—the tall, broad-shouldered Jean-Laurence—was that he was a Breton and hence by definition a devout Catholic. He was holding in his arm a boy child of perhaps eighteen months who was grinning broadly.

She hugged me and kissed me on both cheeks. Jean-Laurence smiled proudly—as he seemed always to do when his wife did any-thing—shook hands vigorously.

"Pauvre petit evêque. A horrible trip, *n'est-ce pas?"*

The boy child reached out his arms to me. His father carefully handed him over.

"Bonjour, M. Jean-Claude," I said.

"Bonjour, M. l'Evêque," he said carefully making sure he had all the words right.

Such interaction with small children, even the very shy ones, is routine for me. Also dogs, even the most ferocious. My sibs suggest that both varieties of God's creation see in me one like themselves. Milord Cronin attributes it to what he labels as "Your phony gentle Irish smile."

Regardless.

Chantal retrieved her son. Jean-Laurence picked up my bag. The two of them led me to the parking lot.

"You have a very beautiful son," I said to Jean-Laurence.

"*Merci, M. l'Evêque.* He is beautiful because he looks like madame his mother."

Chantal sniffed dismissively.

They were still very much in love, more so than ever. How could one not be in love with a wife like Chantal.

I was put in the front seat of the Mercedes with Jean-Laurence. Jean-Claude was secured in the backseat with his mother. He promptly went to sleep. As best as I could remember it was Sunday morning. There ought not be traffic jams in Paris. But there were. The city of light was covered with gray foglike murk. It was, after all, autumn in those regions bathed by the Gulf Stream. It would be murky till March, till May in the Isles.

We spoke of their friends Marie-Bernadette and Jacques-Yves, who were beginning what looked like it would be a successful career playing Celtic music with violin and viola and of their upcoming daughter, who would be named Chantal.

"Did not *La Belle* Nuala Anne predict it would be a daughter? Is she ever wrong?"

Nuala Anne, who some think is the best detective in Chicago, is a bit of an Irish witch. She has unfailingly predicted the gender of children even before they are conceived.

We then spoke of Chantal's career with *La Comédie Français* at the Odeon. According to Jean-Laurence she was particularly success-ful at playing the adolescent ingénue. "Is that not, after all, who she really is?"

"I will graduate soon to being the sweet old grandmother." She laughed. "*Bon!* It is all great fun!"

We finally managed to slip across to the Left Bank and into the Latin Quarter and up the *rue* Napoléon to the Luxembourg Gardens, on the edge of which was their apartment building. It was a plain enough edifice from pre-Revolutionary times.

"It is close to the Sorbonne," Chantal explained breathlessly, "near the Odeon, and only two metro stops away from my husband's law office. I sold my apartment up on Montmartre."

"Too many memories," Jean-Laurence commented.

Their second-floor apartment (third floor in our more reasonable numbering system) was furnished in a manner appropriate for a duchess in the time of the *le roi sol*—in addition to all the comforts of air-conditioning, large-screen television, a couple of computers, disk players, and an impressive array of kitchen electronics, all of which the duchesses of the Sun King's era could not imagine.

Jean-Laurence was patently a successful attorney.

I was directed to my quarters at the end of a corridor and told that both *le petit Jean-Claude* and *le pauvre petit evêque* would take short naps.

I would certainly do that or else fall asleep on my feet, as I have done on other transoceanic occasions, once even standing upright in the men's room.

I noted with some relief that I was several doors down the corridor from what was patently the master bedroom and hence sounds of lovemaking would not keep me awake.

What else does one do on a murky October Sunday afternoon in Paris? Especially if one has a delectable little wife like Chantal.

For supper we consumed a cold soup, veal with a French sauce, and huge lettuce salad with an overpowering dressing. All, *mais naturellement*, prepared by *Madame*.

I deplore the abominable French custom of substituting salad for dessert. Remembering that, Chantal provided a hot fudge sundae, *pour l'americain*!

Then over dessert wine (sauterne) we turned to the reason for my visit, *le pauvre* Brother Semyon.

"Are you aware," Jean-Laurence said, in the didactic tone lawyers in whatever language adopt when they're about to explain something to you, "of a group which calls itself the Brotherhood of Gregory VII?"

"They have escaped my notice."

"Do you remember who Gregory VII was?"

223

"I was not alive in that time. However, it is my impression that he was a fairly tough Benedictine monk turned pope who, among other things, forced a German emperor, in fact a Sicilian, to crawl in the snow to a castle called Canossa at Christmastime, not that this was, as it turned out, sincere penance."

"The brotherhood," Jean-Laurence continued, "that takes his name is a group of young Frenchmen from the far right of the political spectrum who have dedicated themselves to reestablishing monasteries that follow the Rule of St. Benedict in all its rigor, even more rigorous, in fact, than that demanded by Abbot DeRance."

"From the monastery of *La Trappe*."

The good Chantal smiled impishly at this ponderous exchange between two men who amused her.

"They have not received any official recognition from the Vatican, which suspects them of, how should one say it, *le fanatisme*. For their part they have been highly critical of the current style and behavior of the Roman Curia, which they say is not nearly rigorous enough."

"Ah! Death to the heretics!"

"And infidels, Blackie; they don't like Muslims."

"Naturellement."

"Nonetheless," Jean-Laurence continued, "they are also most assiduous in their reverence for the present pope. They are confident that they will eventually win approval because God is with them."

" '*Gott mit uns,*' as another language puts it."

"*Précisément.* They are Fascists in Benedictine robes."

"They are the ones who have lifted Brother Semyon?"

"Without doubt. After an evening lecture at the Sorbonne. They took him to their monastery in the Alps, east of Aix-les-Bains on Mt. Coin, where there was once a monastery long ago. It is a crude, log place, as they say the earliest monasteries were. They are holding him there, in a cell and on bread and water, until he reveals to them some document they think is very important. They also say he is responsible for the death of one of their monks."

"A man who was sent to replace Brother Semyon in search for the document and was subsequently executed by the FSB."

"Incroyable!"

"I quite agree . . . How is it that one can learn all these things?"

"Les flics know all about it. *La Sûreté* has people down there watching the monastery. Indeed, they've had the monastery under surveillance even before *Frère* Semyon was kidnapped. That's how they knew where he was. Some of the tradesmen who bring things like newspapers to the monastery every morning have been spying for *La Sûreté.*"

"Newspapers! That doesn't sound like St. Benedict or St. Bernard!"

"D'accord! They reserve to themselves a right to a certain flexibility. Nonetheless, they themselves eat little more than they give their prisoner. He, *les flics* say, remains steadfast. Refuses to speak at all."

"That would be like Brother Semyon." I sighed. "But why don't the police release him?"

Jean-Laurence shrugged his elegant shoulders.

"In France everything is political, even the police, especially the police. It does not matter in fact if something is not political, they will make it political. They are fearful of conflict between the Church and the anticlericals, such as those that survive."

"But M. Chirac is not on the anticlericals' side!"

"All the more reason for not embarrassing him."

"I see," I said.

"No, you don't, *M. l'Evêque*," Chantal interrupted. "Only if you were French and that only some of the time. We have our own logic that we ourselves often don't understand."

"Nevertheless, it is always logical!"

"C'est vrai." She giggled.

"If *Frère* Semyon were to be murdered, they would of course intervene to save him," Jean-Laurence said with a wicked grin.

For a moment I pondered the possibility of mobilizing a posse, descending on Mt. Coin, and freeing Brother Semyon. Then I realized

225

that my recent experiences made me think like a cowboy instead of the harmless little parish priest that I really am.

"This is all very helpful, Jean-Laurence," I said. *"Merci."*

"Is there anything else we can do?" Chantal intervened to take over the conversation, something which she had been waiting to do for some minutes.

"I don't think so . . ." I continued to examine the situation as I noted in the distance the lights of the Eiffel Tower. Ugly structure, despite all its fame.

"Do you know why they want this document that *Frère* Semyon is supposed to have access to?"

"It is possible that it would be something that would embarrass the Roman Curia; they are eager to do that whenever they can."

"How would they know about it?"

"One hears that some of the monks were once members of the *Deuxième Bureau,* the French military intelligence agency."

Spooks spreading their stories all around.

"Why does that not surprise me?"

"What will you do, Blackie?" Jeanne Chantal asked.

"I will go to the place where all of this began thirty-five years ago."

"Vatican City?"

"Mais oui . . . Jean-Laurence, can you pass on little hints to your sources which will reach the important people in *la Sûreté.*

"But of course!"

"Tell them that one who has actually read the document testifies that it contains little information that will embarrass anyone for longer than a single day's news cycle."

"They will be very interested to hear that."

We were interrupted at this point by a very sleepy Jean-Claude, who wanted to sit on the *M. l'Evêque's* lap. His mother permitted this indulgence for a minute or two, then carried him back to his room. She did not note that I had already put him to sleep.

It is the only certifiably magical power I have.

The next morning after one of those deplorable continental breakfasts which would have pleased Abbot DeRance, Jean-Laurence went to his office, Jean-Claude taught me how to play with his trucks, the nanny came, and Chantal drove me to the airport. We must leave early so that I would make it through the security check in time to catch my Air France flight to Rome.

During the tedious and difficult drive, the sun stubbornly fought against the murk and finally routed it. Paris again was beautiful. Not as beautiful as Chicago, however.

Chantal occupied herself during the ride in extended praise of her husband.

"He is the most wonderful of men," she insisted as though I were about to question that truth.

"It appears to me that he has the same emotions towards you."

That was irrelevant.

"I did not realize when I was imitating my brother the priest for *tout le monde* that I was tearing myself apart. I had opened wide wounds that existed through all my life. My shrink and my husband helped me to put myself back together."

"You were very fortunate indeed," I agreed. "However, if I were to ask Jean-Laurence, he would argue that he was also very fortunate."

Silence for a moment.

"I am perhaps good for him in some small ways."

"Chantal!"

"You priests!" she exclaimed. "You will permit us none of our evasions."

"Précisément."

"Very well, *M. l'Evêque,*" she said with a proudly maternal laugh, "we both are very fortunate. I am not without certain assets as a wife."

"Good cook anyway."

Then we both laughed and went on to discuss the absolutely unique wonders of *le petit* Jean-Claude.

At the airport I realized that the three sweatshirts of *Les Irregulars d'Avenue Wabash du Nord* were still in my bag—one extra large, one medium, and one for an infant. With some difficulty I retrieved them and presented them to *Madame* with all the solemnity I could muster.

She responded with two kisses on both cheeks.

The Air France security was typical of the French government— incompetent, rude, and arrogant. I finally escaped to the Admirals' Club, where I phoned M. le Cardinal Cronin.

"Cathedral Rectory, Cronin."

"Ah, you're on call!"

"Someone has to do the work here while you're wandering around the world enjoying supper with a beautiful woman."

"And her mammoth husband . . . both of whom send their best."

"They're happy?"

"As God intends man and woman to be."

"Your head?"

"I fear that I have done that which the good Dr. Mary Kate Murphy suggests I would someday do. Like St. Denis, I have lost it."

"Very funny. Are you still taking the pills?"

"I don't need them anymore."

"Well, if it isn't completely better, keep taking them. We're not Christian Scientists."

"Patently."

"What did you find out about Brother Semyon?"

I recounted what I had learned *chez* Chantal.

"Why do the French have to be so weird?"

"A valid question."

"I'm surprised you didn't mobilize a small army and go down there."

"In this country one little man in a gray coat is enough for a millennium."

"Yeah . . . You're mellowing with age, Blackwood."

"You hear from our mutual friend over on Vatican hill?"

"As a matter of fact, I did. He was on the phone yesterday . . . Sunday of all days. Worried about whether it would be a major crisis."

"And you told him?"

"I told him in no uncertain terms that unless he listened closely to you, a tidal wave of shit would come rolling down the Tiber."

"In so many words?"

"Yeah, why not."

"And his reaction?"

"He kind of laughed nervously."

"Good enough for him."

My appointment with Archbishop Ricardo Agostino tomorrow morning would doubtless prove very interesting. The fate of Brother Semyon, aka Jan Sobieski Cardinal Ostrowski, would be decided not in the mountains east of Aix-les-Bains, but in the dicastery offices of Vatican City.

16

At 9:30 the following morning, I ambled up the Via Concilliazione towards the Dome of St. Peter, gleaming in the gentle autumn sunlight. Many people tell me they'll never forget the awe with which they viewed that edifice the first time they saw it. As one who is more impressed by people than by architecture, I reply that my first thought was that it had cost us Germany.

I had played over in my head before I fell asleep the night before how the discussion would flow. I had no intention of losing control of it, no matter how charming and powerful the Archbishop might prove. I had all the important cards in my briefcase, which I had to return to the *Atlante Star* to retrieve because I had left the first time without it. Fortunately, I had not entered Vatican Palace when I discovered its absence. Also fortunately, my headaches had disappeared. I did not have to face this fabled curialist with what M. Poirot calls the little gray cells blurred.

I presented myself at the appropriate gate off the Belvedere Courtyard at 9:50 and informed the Vatican cop in English that I was Bishop Ryan from Chicago and that I had an appointment with Archbishop Agostino at 10:00. He considered me with utter contempt. The two Swiss Guards moved their pikes so that they crossed one another, thus to prevent a possible assault on the Vatican Palace.

The cop punched a number in on his phone. The line was busy, I assumed, though he didn't explain that to me. I waited two minutes. Blackie Ryan is not late, I told myself, and demanded, "Again!"

The cop could not have been more shocked if I had accused the Pope of incest. But he did call again. This time someone answered. He muttered what sounded like curses into the phone, all the time glaring at me.

Then he hung up, as one dismayed by the poor taste of those who governed the Church, and waved me through. The Swiss Guards presented arms. I saluted back by touching my hand to my forehead.

All of this was not unlike whistling past the graveyard in the dark—building up my male hormone supply for conflict.

Blackie Ryan, middle linebacker.

An elderly usher, bent over from the waist like all Vatican ushers, conducted me to an antechamber. A youngish priest, patently of Celtic origins, was working a computer behind a small desk littered with papers.

"God and Mary be with this house," I said to him in Irish.

"God and Mary and Patrick," he replied with a grin, "be with all who visit this house."

"Ryan," I said, extending my hand.

"McCaffery," he said, rising from his chair and gripping my hand firmly. "I know who you are."

Another young man, with movie star good looks, emerged from the inner office.

"I thought I heard an Irish conspiracy out here . . . Agostino!"

He seized my hand.

"Ryan," I said diffidently.

"Liam"—he turned to the young fella—"would you ever put on the teapot for us? You do drink tea, don't you, Monsignor Ryan?"

"Until such time in the day, Monsignor Agostino, as a splasheen of Bushmills becomes more appropriate."

In American and Ireland, "Monsignor" is a form of address

reserved for prelates who can wear purple buttons but who are not bishops. In Rome it is usually used for prelates who generally don't wear purple buttons but who are bishops or, more likely, archbishops.

Ricardo Agostino was a man of upper medium height, which is to say several inches taller than I am. In Chicago, the Mayor would have wanted him as a high-ranking member of the Organization. His dancing blue eyes, tight curly hair with a hint of silver at the earlobes, quick easy smile that revealed perfectly even white teeth, narrow waist, sallow skin, intelligent forehead, and musical voice—all suggested a likable man who might cream you in an argument. Moreover, I had been trapped in a situation that seemed to combine Irish word mastery with Roman—probably Roman nobility—charm.

Okay, the playing field was only slighted tilted in my favor.

"Let me take your coat, Monsignor Ryan," he said as he ushered me into his office, a rather plain, smallish room with a computer, a cell phone, a real phone, a hot plate, and a neatly stacked pile of papers on an unexceptional wooden desk. There were no file cabinets and no pictures on the wall, save a color photo of the Pope and Msgr. Agostino. A window looked out over the courtyard to the left of his desk and the usual crucifix hung on the wall. Two chairs, mildly comfortable and a small table, filled most of the empty space in the room.

All very low-key. If you had power, the office said, you don't have to flaunt it.

The occupant was wearing a black clerical shirt without a Roman collar (which lay next to the cell phone on his desk), my usual uniform around the Cathedral Rectory.

"Lovely pectoral cross," he said. "I see a lot of them, but this is the first St. Brigid Cross."

"Made my by cousin Catherine Collins Curran, who also did the ring."

"New Grange," he said appreciatively.

233

We sat down and prepared to begin the sparing.

"Cardinal Cronin tells me that you're a very dangerous man, Monsignor Ryan."

"Patently he exaggerates," I replied.

"We shall see, Monsignor." His eyebrows lifted skeptically.

"Blackie," I said.

"Rick," he replied, gesturing with his right hand to sweep away needless formalities.

His facial expressions changed almost as rapidly as did those of my colleague Nuala Anne McGrail. Like all Italians he talked with expressive gestures, but only brief movements of fingers and occasionally hands.

At that point Liam entered to pour our tea.

"Milk is it, Bishop Ryan?"

" 'Tis not. I don't pollute me tea with that stuff."

Light laughter in the room.

The tea set was from Limoges.

"I'll keep it on the hot plate, Monsignor," Liam said as he left the room.

Now we would get down to serious business.

"Sean Cronin tells me that you have an interesting story for me, Blackie."

"Actually it is a story of three men. One is Brother Semyon Ivanivich Popov, a Russian Orthodox monk whom you met in recent years in an office over in the offices of the Council on Christian Unity, an informal delegate from the patriarchate, who proposed to you even more informally a plan to promote unity between Rome and Moscow by embracing them, willy-nilly."

"I remember the man very well, charming fellow, expert on the Old Believers, as I remember. I have heard that he died recently."

He shifted with slight unease as he sipped his tea. No comments, however, about crime in Chicago.

No scones. Mistake.

I sipped my tea too. I had caught him a little off guard by my allusion to Brother Semyon's suggestion.

"My second man wrote this book," I said, "on union between Moscow and Rome. His name you'll note is Father Simon Sobieski, O.S.B."

"I've read it," he said. "Good book . . . I'm afraid that I didn't realize that it presented the same thesis as Brother Semyon did."

"You'll note the letters after the author's name."

"Order of St. Basil?"

"Saint Benedict."

"Same man," he said, his face tightening in a worried frown.

"Arguably."

"The third man is a young Benedictine monk from Poland who was fluent in Russian and Polish and several other languages. Some of your colleagues or more likely your predecessors met with him in the fall of 1965 in the same office in the Council for Christian Unity. As to their names, I believe that Brother Semyon mentioned three names when he met with you more recently. You wondered why he asked, but it didn't seem important."

"It should have been?"

"Perhaps . . . In any event that young monk's name was Jan Sobieski Ostrowski. The men who spoke to him had a brilliant idea. They would send him to an Orthodox monastery in the Ural Mountains to live inside the Orthodox tradition so as to understand it better. At some unspecified point in time he would return to Rome to report on what he had learned."

"These three men are the same, I assume?"

He put his teacup on its saucer and rested his head on the edge of his fingertips.

"There is ample reason to believe so."

"I have no trouble"—he lifted his head to stare at me—"believing the 1965 story as bizarre as it is. Those were, I am told, heady times. Hamlet Chicognani was Secretary of State, a pleasant old man who worked only in the morning and spent most of the mornings at the Council. It surely would have been possible to devise such a scheme without his knowing it."

"Not, however, to have presented Father Semyon to Pope Paul VI for his blessing."

He gestured dismissively with his left hand.

"I fear that could have happened too. Hamlet wouldn't have known what was happening and the Pope perhaps only a little more. He had a lot on his plate in those days—birth control and such matters."

I avoided the invitation to turn to that subject.

"Yet this story is not impossible?"

"I wouldn't argue that it is. Like every bureaucracy in the world, the Vatican does have little cells of people with what they think are bright ideas. Sometimes the ideas are truly bright. Other times they are crazy. In that era forty years ago, perhaps there was more opportunity to activate the crazy ones. Or maybe it wasn't crazy, I don't know."

He raised both hands in a gesture that conveyed the same notion that a shrug would.

He filled my teacup again, then his own.

"What happened to Father Jan?"

"He journeyed to the monastery of St. Catherine and the Virgin in the Urals near the city of Sverdlovsk once and again properly called Yekatrinburg, where the czar and his family were liquidated. He had a monastic vocation and while the conditions were extreme in the monastery, especially in winter, it was a happy monastery and he adjusted to it easily and became happy as he continued to be a monk and to work on the mystical soteriology of the Old Believers."

"He heard not a word from those who had sent him?"

"For many years it seemed that they had forgotten him."

"Typical . . . How did they get him into Russia and up to the monastery?"

"When he went to Russia he was a young and inexperienced man to whom such a question did not occur. In later years as he traveled in and out of Russia with the government's permission, he wondered that himself."

"His conclusion?"

"That either the Jesuits who did have some kind of Russian mission or a foreign intelligence agency had arranged it."

"Fools!" he exclaimed impatiently.

"Arguably."

He recovered himself and leaned back in his chair.

"I mean no disrespect, Blackie," he said lightly. "I assume that you will be able to show me some proof of all of these stories."

"Oh yes."

He smiled wryly.

"I was afraid so. What happened next?"

"In 1983 he is invited to lecture at the Sorbonne. Both the Church and the state tell him to accept. Seventeen years later he finds that there is still some memory of him in this congregation. Three priests meet him after his lecture, one of those who had sent him off to Yekatrinburg and two others. They tell him he has been named an archbishop and will be sent back to Russia as the head of a Latin Rite Russian Church. He will ordain bishops and priests who will begin the conversion of Russia promised by Our Lady of Fatima. One of the priests, a young American, sad to say, tells him that since Orthodoxy is dead and since people need religion, they will turn to Catholicism in the long years of Communist rule that lie ahead. They will all be martyrs, this young man says with a zealot's glow in his eyes, but the blood of martyrs is the seed of the faith. You may remember the name of the fourth priest about whom he inquired when you met him, a man you told him had married, left the priesthood, and moved to Boston. Brother Semyon thought it was a mad scheme, but he was loyal to the Church and loyal to his Polish pope and agreed to the ordination. He believed that nothing would come of this mad scheme.

"However, in 1987, when he returned to Paris, an American layman who had attended Notre Dame told him at *les Deux Magots,* of all places, that he would on return be transferred from Yekatrinburg to Zagorsk and that periodically an attaché from the American embassy would provide him with a list of names of men to be ordained and the place of ordination—the latter usually the basement of an apartment in Moscow.

"He ordained them?"

"Of course he did; he believed it was the Pope's orders, which it may have been. The candidates all seemed well trained and dedicated. What would you have done?' "

He shoved the teacup aside with the first hint of anger he had shown in our conversation.

"The memory of the man who left the priesthood from this office was insanely ambitious, but unfortunately for him too clever by half. He stepped on too many toes around this building and was sent home. None of what you say is beyond him. It all fits together, damn it. I'm sure the files are somewhere in this building . . . You have ruined my day, Blackie, perhaps my week."

He flashes a wide and somewhat ironic grin.

"He is in Moscow on Easter 1989 when Orthodoxy rises from the dead. When he returns to Paris in 1992 the man with the silver hair tells him that plans for a Latin Rite Church in Russia have been abandoned because Orthodoxy is so enormously popular. He wonders what will happen to his bishops and priests, like any good archbishop would. The CIA man tells him that the Church will take care of them. He doubts the truth of that promise."

"With good reason," Rick says bitterly.

"He travels to America, which he likes. He visits with you in Rome. He begins to piece together his memories of the last thirty years of his life, using a code that he had devised. Unfortunately, he hints to some people that he's working on it. Then he comes to the University of Chicago for a two-year visiting term. He plays the role of the Orthodox monk to the hilt. He shouts, he bangs his staff, he stomps around. Some people love him, some can't stand him. Secretly he goes to the Eucharist at a nearby Polish church and weeps for his memories. Still very much a sentimental Pole, you see."

"The memoir could be dangerous," Rick says uneasily.

"Oh yes . . . He goes to Paris in the summer as he usually does and returns to the Divinity School in mid-September—two weeks before classes begin. He seems uneasy, not his usual flamboyant self. Then one stormy night at the beginning of October, a young assistant professor named David Dolan is working at his desk in Swift Hall where the school is located. He hears an explosion, he smells cordite, he rushes to Brother Semyon's office and finds the door locked. He is joined by three other faculty members. He calls the dean on his cell phone and she literally rushes over to the University to get the key that will open Brother Semyon's door . . ."

"She?"

"Oh yes. However, even when the regular office key is used, the door won't open because Brother Semyon has installed a dead-bolt lock that can be opened only from the inside. Professor Dolan, whose father is a retired police captain, calls the police. Then he breaks a chunk out of the window on the office door and opens the dead bolt. They open the door and observe that Brother Semyon's body lies across the desk with his head blown off and pieces of his brain and skull spread about the room."

Rick's face turned white.

"How terrible! The poor man!"

"The dean runs to the office to phone the president of the University. Professor Dolan rushes to the door to let in the police. They return to the dead man's office and realize they have a locked-room mystery.

"Unless the window to the outside was opened, how could the killer have escaped? Would the dead man have let him out of the office, then locked the door?"

"How did it happen, Blackie?" He smiled wanly. "I must know the solution."

"The killer fired his gun from outside the open window and escaped immediately. While the dean was calling the president and Professor Dolan is opening the door for the cops, one of the three at the door, a compulsively neat person, notices that papers are being blown all over the floor. She rushes over and closes and locks the windows. Her colleagues know she has done it, but don't report her."

"So Brother Semyon's killer escapes?"

"Not for long. His body, without its head, is found in a wooded area near the Holy Virgin Protection Cathedral in Chicago on the day of his funeral. He too is Russian."

"Who was he?"

"A commando from the Trans-Dniester on a contract from one of the many agencies who thought that his memoir might be very dangerous."

He shook his head sadly. It all made sense and he would have to do something about it.

"Which agencies?"

"CIA, FSB, you folks, for example."

He did not become angry at the suggestion.

"If all of your story is true, I can see why you suspect us. However, we stopped killing people a long time ago."

"Then a new element enters the picture. It turns out that the man who was shot in the Divinity School was not Brother Semyon. He was too short by several inches. We found traces of Semyon's DNA in his apartment. Someone had substituted for him and had been madly searching through his papers for a manuscript of some sort."

"You're sure?"

"Absolutely. The question became what was he looking for. The dean remembered that Semyon had given her a sealed packet of paper and she put it at his request in a special safe in her office. The dean, the president of the University, a police official, and I read it. The memoir was potentially a very dangerous document. We secreted it in a place where no one could have access to it under ordinary circumstances. No one but me."

A little twist at the end to protect Sean Cronin.

"That's how you know about the involvement of this office?"

I didn't bother to answer. What would I sell out for? That would emerge soon.

"The University announced in the press that it was placing Brother Semyon's papers in a secret and hidden archive. That night, as we suspected, a group of former Russian military commandos attempts to raid Swift Hall. They were repulsed and arrested and deported."

"That's where you received the bump on the side of your head?"

Nice save.

"The headaches are gone and the bump is diminishing."

"His Eminence must have been deeply disturbed."

"I'd rather say, 'concerned.' "

"Of course."

A brief wave of his fingers.

"That's the end of the story?"

"No. At least one more puzzle."

He frowned thoughtfully.

"Oh, yes, who was the substitute and why was he looking for the memoir. CIA?"

"Not exactly . . . One of your groups, named happily as the Brotherhood of St. Gregory VII."

He clapped his head.

"Of course those fools would do anything! They killed the poor man!"

"No, they lifted him after one of his lectures in Paris and kidnapped him to their fortress on Mt. Coin. He is still there. They are slowly starving him to death on a diet of bread and water. The *Sûreté* knows about it and has its people in Aix-les-Bains watching. They won't move in to save Brother Semyon or Father Simon or Brother Jan Sobieski Ostrowski of the Order of St. Benedict."

Andrew M. Greeley

"Why not?"

"Some obscure cavil about creating political problems for the French government."

He sighed, doubtless in imitation of his Irish mother, rose from his chair and walked to the window.

Finally, he turned to face me.

"I will check all these matters of course. It will take days, perhaps even weeks. I'm sure we'll find documentation to support your story . . ."

Now was the time to use my knockout punch.

"Rick, I'm afraid that won't do."

"Won't do?"

"This is Tuesday. Unless Father Simon Sobieski, as I prefer to think of him, is released by the end of business on Thursday, this whole matter will become public. My only goal now is to save his life. That should be the only goal of his Church, which has treated him so badly."

He sank into the chair behind his desk.

"You can't threaten us, Blackie," he said firmly. "That just isn't done."

"I'm sorry, Rick. It is done and I've just done it."

"It won't work. We'll free him eventually. It will take time. The Vatican moves slowly."

"This time it will have to move very quickly."

"Why? Because you say so?"

He was becoming angry with me.

Good. That was part of the design.

"There's one or two details I left out."

"What are they?" he snapped irritably.

"Tools for you to speed the process with your superiors."

I removed the document telling Father Jan Sobieski Ostrowski of the Order of St. Benedict that he had been elevated to the Sacred College of Cardinals.

He rushed towards me and reached for it. I pulled it back.

"I don't want to take it from you," he retreated in embarrassment. "I just wanted to look at it . . . Summer before last."

"He was at Notre Dame. According to the memoir some rotund functionary of the American Nunciature showed up with it—and the robes of a cardinal. Will this color photocopy do?"

He glanced at it.

"I'm sure it will."

"One final point. When the police searched Brother Semyon's apartment after the killing they found a clothes bag in his closet that contained the sacred crimson itself. The garments were given him by the man from the Nunciature. It was the size that would fit a tall man, Cardinal Cronin for example. Not the man from the Brotherhood of Gregory VII."

"The Pope was involved?"

"He appoints cardinals, does he not? And no one else?"

Rick nodded glumly.

"Moreover, not only does he know Brother Semyon's real name, he knows that he's a Benedictine."

"The man deserves the crimson," he admitted. "That's the least we can do for him. It was good of you to bring us this story . . . We have how long, two and a half days?"

"I do not want the poor man to starve to death."

"I understand."

We both rose from our chairs.

"We'll do it," he said flatly

"See to it then," I said, imagining for a moment that I was Sean Cronin.

As I left the door to his office, he shouted after me.

"You were the one that solved the locked-room problem?"

I nodded.

"Cardinal Cronin told me that you never lost a case."

"Not yet."

The papal gendarme ignored me when I emerged into the courtyard. The Swiss Guards snapped their salute. I winked at them.

Back in the hotel I called Chicago, even if it was five o'clock in the morning.

"It had to be you, Blackwood." He sighed. "Did you stick it to him?"

"I did."

"Good . . . What did you tell him?"

"Brother Semyon is released by the end of business on Thursday or we go public."

"And he said?"

"He'd do it."

"Cardinal thing tipped the balance?"

"Patently."

"You didn't give him the original, did you?"

"Not hardly. He was content with the color copy."

"Wind it up and come home, Blackwood. See to it. Friday."

He hung up before I could answer.

17

I devoted most of the rest of the day to sleep and to spaghetti Bolognese at a *trattoria* just off the Concilliazione. Much of Wednesday I spent in prayer at a little church off the Borgo Pio. I prayed for my family, especially the good Mary Kate who would doubtless hear that I was overseas and hassle Milord Cronin about this most recent exploiting of her poor little brother.

Le pauvre Punk!

And for the Cardinal and the Cathedral staff and the parish and the Archdiocese and for the Pope and the whole Church, especially Monsignor Agostino on whose plate I had dumped a large load of very hot potatoes.

I asked the Lord to arrange as quickly as he could a reunion between the two traditions. I prayed for Jean-Laurence and Jeanne-Chantal and their admirable little urchin. I also asked God to take care of the young lovers at the Divinity School and observed that it was most unlikely that either would ever find a more appropriate life partner. Finally, I expressed my gratitude for the aid of the Holy Spirit thus far in this most unusual case. I also commended to His attention any remaining phenomena for which I should be praying but which I had forgotten.

Then I remembered Brother Semyon.

He is, I told the Lord, as You well know, a remarkable man. He has been true to his vocation under extraordinarily difficult circumstances. Protect him and guide him in the freedom I hope he attains by the end of business on Thursday.

No one disturbed my solitude, save for a couple of American tourists. Romans are not much given to praying in church. October sunlight continued to bathe the Eternal City in a pastel haze.

In the evening, *Madame* phoned me from Paris. *Le bon* Jean-Laurence reported that there was considerable agitation in police circles about the situation near Aix-les-Bains and that there was some possibility that the Mobile Guard (equivalent to our state police) might be dispatched to deal with the matter. I asked to speak to Jean-Laurence and inquired whether Cardinal Cronin could hire him to accompany the Guard as a legal representative concerned about the rights of Brother Semyon. He agreed enthusiastically.

Had Msgr. Agostino himself flown to Paris?

I would not have bet against it.

On Thursday I stayed near the phone save for meals. When I returned to my room, *Madame* was on the phone again. The good Jean-Laurence had reported from Aix-les-Bains that after some resistance the Brotherhood had released Brother Semyon, who seemed in good spirits, if a bit thinner than he had been in Paris in the summer. A young priest in a black turtleneck seemed to be in charge.

I called the Cathedral Rectory and asked Crystal, who was at the phone, to tell the Cardinal, when it was convenient, that the eagle seemed to be out of the cage.

Finally at six-thirty, Msgr. Agostino was on the phone. He sounded weary. From the background noise it suggested he was at Fumicino, the airport for Rome. The work had been successful. Could he take me to supper? He would pick me up. My choice of restaurants.

"*Ristorante Sabbatini* in Trastevere."

He chuckled.

"Appropriate for a celebration."

"Blackie," he said, when I boarded his chauffer–driven Mercedes, "do you have representatives all over the world?"

"We try to be prepared . . . Patently you encountered *M. l'avo-cat.*"

"One could hardly miss him. He is a very good man. Very proud of his wife and son."

Msgr. Agostino, I noted, was still tense. Doubtless his day had been long and difficult.

"Not without some reason."

"He claims that they are all Celts."

"Breton that he is he can make a valid claim. However, Rick, in France today everyone is a Celt."

We chatted about Curial gossip on the way down the Tiber to the wondrous Piazza Santa Maria in Trastevere, the place where the beautiful people had moved when American tourists who had seen too many Fellini films took over the Via Veneto. The *piazza,* even in the early-evening hours was filled with people. The shops along the side streets were open. The floodlights on the very old mosaic on the front of the very old church were hardly necessary because an autumn full moon had deigned to make an appearance.

The arrival of Monsignor Agostino and the hardly visible little auxiliary from the shores of Lake Michigan created a bit of a stir at the *Ristorante Sabbatini.* Only when the wine steward opened a bottle of Frascati and Monsignor had tasted it with a satisfied smile, did he begin to relax.

"This wine does not travel well," he confided to me (unnecessarily), "but in Rome it remains delicious."

I agreed after taking my own solemn sip.

"Where is Brother Semyon?" I asked.

"Father Simon Sobieski, as we are now calling him for the moment, is at St. Anselm's Monastery here in Rome, whence he departed in 1965. He is resting comfortably in the infirmary but seems in good condition . . . He even has his staff, without which he would not leave Mt. Coin. Do you want to visit him?"

Clean sweep. Off Mt. Coin and into St. Anselm's.

"That won't be necessary," I said. "It will be enough for me to quote you to *Signor Cardinale* for him to be reassured . . . Father Simon is happy to be home?"

"He tells me that it is as though he never left."

"And what does the future hold for him?"

"Whatever he wishes. He wants to continue to be a monk and a scholar. He plans to write on the historical and cultural forces that have shaped the relationship between Rome and Moscow."

Although the fish in the *Sabbattini* logo indicated its *specialita* was pasta with seafood, I ordered my usual spaghetti Bolognese.

"He remembered you from your previous encounter?"

"Immediately. He expressed some surprise that a person of my rank would be involved in a prison break. I told him I was there only because we were not able to send the Secretary of State, as Cardinal Cronin and Monsignor Ryan seemed to want. That's when your *avocat* friend introduced himself."

"I have never met Father Simon."

"Well, he knows about you now."

"I trust he does not know about his memoir."

"I told him that the University had placed all his papers in a hidden archive. If he wants anything, presumably he could get it. I admitted that I knew about the memoir from you, but denied that I'd ever seen it. He seemed reassured."

"And the Brotherhood of Gregory VII?"

"It is safe to say that they will disband."

"How did Brother Semyon get the red hat?"

"Polish Benedictines . . . That's a fascinating part of the story. Apparently he told some of his young confreres where he was going when he disappeared. Perhaps he merely hinted. Or perhaps they guessed. Anyway, they have been watching for years, especially since he reappeared in his publications. They recognized the themes and the style. The Abbot President appealed to the Pope that Simon, his name in religion by the way, should be honored for his years of very difficult work. After checking the records and learning that Paul VI had approved his mission, the Pope was happy to elevate him in petto until it became possible to acknowledge him publicly."

"Did the Pope know about his being named an archbishop?"

Rico smiled as he tested the red wine—Barolo from the Po Valley.

"He was horrified, as you might imagine. However, he understood why Msgr. Ostrowski, as he called him, would accept what he thought was a mission authorized by the Holy See."

"I didn't mention the other day that the Patriarch wanted to make him a metropolitan. He would have been an archbishop in both churches."

Rico raised his hands in the gesture that meant a shrug.

"It is just as well that we didn't have to account for that . . . Interesting question: how could a man who was already an archbishop be made an archbishop again? . . . Ah, well, we don't have to worry about that, thanks be to God."

"I assume that you had some difficulty persuading the relevant parties that my story was true."

"Until I presented your copy of the document announcing that Jan Sobieski Ostrowski of the Order of St. Benedict had been elevated to the rank of cardinal. None of the people above me in the Secretariat were prepared to argue about that or to resist immediate action to free Cardinal Ostrowski."

"There was no need then to repeat my threat."

He grinned broadly and waved the fingers of both hands.

"I assure you that I took it seriously. It was perfectly correct for you to make it. I said merely that you felt it was necessary to act both to save the life of Father Simon and to restore control of his memoir to him. No one argued."

I dug into my spaghetti Bolognese with my accustomed gusto.

He gestured with his wineglass.

"Everyone was quite impressed with your skill in dealing with the matter. They'll be even more impressed when I tell them tomorrow about your *avocat* in Aix-les-Bains."

"That will not be necessary," I said. The invisible little auxiliary bishop should be especially invisible in Rome.

"The Holy Father says, 'Who is this Monsignor Ryan?' We tell him that he's an auxiliary to Cardinal Cronin. He holds out his hand to indicate a certain height and says, 'Ah, little man with kind blue eyes and a mischievous smile. He is very smart. Perhaps he should write *romans policers*—mystery novels.'"

Papal infallibility, fortunately for all of us, does not extend to judgments about almost invisible auxiliary bishops.

Mischievous smile, indeed!

I waved away the suggestion. Better not to be known in Rome at all.

"It is true then, is it not," Rick pursued the case, "that if the team of Gregory VII had not replaced Brother Semyon, he would have been killed that rainy night at your university?"

"Not exactly mine, not yet anyway . . . What you say is true. They replaced him so that the replacement could find the papers. Then the FSB, or more likely a rogue group within them, killed him, thinking he was the real Brother Semyon and might release the papers."

"It could not have been easy to replace a man that way."

"I assume they're very clever people?"

"Oh, yes, very learned men, two members of *L'Académie française*. They want the repeal of the Vatican Council and a return to monastic simplicity here in the Vatican."

He lifted his hands again as if they were asking for the squaring of a circle or some other impossibility.

"It might not have been so difficult. M. le Cardinal Ostrowski had lectured in Paris, the unfortunate one who replaced him, perhaps a trained actor, had ample opportunity to study and imitate him. Moreover, he was to be present only for a short period of time at *The*

University and that at the beginning of the term when the faculty was in the usual beginning-of-the-term disorder and more involved in preparing the quarter than observing their colleagues."

"Yet he must have had a colleague there to direct and advise him."

"Oh, yes. Someone who was in Paris at the time of the kidnapping and who hated the American government intensely. Doubtless that person was delighted that embarrassment would come upon the CIA."

"That person is known?"

"Yes."

To me, at any rate. Eventually certain representations would be made to her about leaving the University.

"And that person will be suitably punished?"

"Indeed."

With a demotion to a less distinguished appointment somewhere else.

We both sighed.

"It is mostly our fault." Rick refilled my wineglass. "We have not always behaved well since the end of the Vatican Council."

"A general loss of nerve," I suggested.

"That is true. We have missed many opportunities. We have done many foolish things . . ."

"Arguably."

I sipped my wine very slowly, but continuously enough to prevent the leprechaun who steals wine from my glass to find an opportunity for theft.

"I was too young to be there, but in retrospect it seems a remarkable and indeed quite improbable event."

"Relatively modest reforms," I said, "that completely destabilized the structures of a church organized to resist the impact of the French Revolution on the premise that the Church could not and would not ever change."

"We are busy trying to restore that premise," he said sadly.

"Such a reaction," I assured him, "is understandable as men of a certain age, with most liberal instincts, suddenly see the only world they know collapsing. Surely you know their names as well as I do."

"*Revera.*"

"Yet we must not lose faith. Nor our confidence in the Holy Spirit. It should be patent that She was sweeping through the Aula of St. Peter's with much enthusiasm in those days. One can delay the fruition of Her work, but not reverse."

"Or restore the old order."

"As my young grandnieces would say, 'Aw gone!' ''

"*Revera* . . . So there are exciting times ahead."

"Patently."

Rick was a man to watch. Power had not, as Milord Cronin had insisted, corrupted him, not yet.

Yet all manner of things were well, as Julianne of Norwich might have said.

As we polished off the wine and the tiramisu and I became sleepy, I reviewed the situation. Matters had arranged themselves, as M. Poirot would have said. Two men were dead, but there was nothing that could be done about that, alas. I requested that the One in Charge take care of them too.

Eventually matters could be explained at *The* University, perhaps sooner rather than later. Those on the faculty who leaned in the postmodern direction would have no trouble coping with the notion that one could be at the same time an Orthodox monk and a Catholic monk.

"Simon is a remarkable man," Rick told me as we drove back to the *Atlante Star.* "Does the memoir convey the picture of a big, strong, affable Polish peasant with great wit?"

"The affability and wit," I said after thinking about the question, "appear only indirectly. He would have needed those characteristics to survive as well as he had on the margins of two traditions . . . What will he do next?"

"As far as the Vatican is concerned whatever he wants."

Back in my hotel room, I called the Cathedral Rectory.

"Cathedral of the Holy Name, Megan speaking."

"Father Ryan, Megan."

"Bishop Ryan is out of town and will be home tomorrow!"

"No, Megan, I'm Father Ryan."

"Oh, hi, Bishop Blackie. Are you still in Rome?"

"I believe so."

"Your sister has called every day looking for you."

"Why does this not surprise me . . . May I talk to the Cardinal?"

"Oh, he's over at Northwestern on a hospital call!"

"Admirable . . . Would you write down this message for him from me?"

"Sure."

"Do you have pencil and paper?"

"Just a moment . . . Okay, I'm ready."

"Bishop Blackie says the Polish eagle has landed safely in Rome." She repeated it carefully.

"Good, Megan. Make sure he gets it as soon as he comes in."

There is little more to be told. Upon my arrival at the Cathedral, Milord Cronin, allegedly exhausted from his week of ministerial work (which he had enjoyed enormously, truth to tell), required a detailed report.

He listened silently.

"You scared Rick Agostino?"

"It would seem so."

"Don't mess with Blackie Ryan, huh?"

"Patently."

"I've had a few calls from over there about you. They were all scared."

"Good enough for them."

"They also praised my wisdom for choosing such a wise and courageous auxiliary."

"You have appointed yet another?"

He dismissed that with an impatient wave.

"I didn't remind them that they appointed you because someone had created the illusion that we had fallen out."

253

Andrew M. Greeley

"The Pope, in one of his noninfallible modes, characterized me as small, with kind eyes, and a mischievous smile."

Milord Cronin nodded sagely.

"He likes you, Blackie. Of course, he doesn't really know you."

"He is an old man and forgetful."

"Not that forgetful."

On Halloween, while I was dispensing candies to the children of the parish, the resident Megan told me that Professor Dolan was on the phone.

"Associate professor, I hope," I said, beginning the conversation.

"Oh, that, yeah, I guess so. I'm told there were no negative votes."

"They were all afraid of the dean presumably."

"I don't doubt it . . . I'm calling about her."

"Indeed."

"We had a big argument last night. She said if we should marry there would never be any neatness or order or peace in the house and that I would take away her modesty and consume her on every possible occasion."

"Valid observations, doubtless."

"I guess so . . . Then she said that we had to be married at Thanksgiving so the consuming could begin on our honeymoon in December when the University kind of closes down."

"What could you say to that?"

"Nothing much I guess. Well, I told her it was high time she called for closure."

"And she said?"

"She kind of sniffed, like she was proud of herself."

"Ah."

"So I told her that she should call you to see if you could do a

254

wedding Mass in Bond Chapel on the Thanksgiving weekend. She insisted that it was my fault and that I ought to call you. I guess I have to get used to doing what she wants."

"Like all Irish males . . . Might I say that I'm happy for both of you. As I explained to God recently, neither of you would be likely ever to find a better life partner."

He laughed.

"Thanks, Bishop. I think I'm a very lucky guy."

"Find out from the dean when Bond is free on the weekend and I'll be there for the great event."

"Yeah, it sure will. I can't quite get used to it yet."

"Dave Dolan, I don't think you ever will."

I thereupon called the dean to find her weeping tears of joy.

"I finally worked up enough nerve to demand marriage, Blackie. He's such a wonderful man. I can't believe how fortunate I am to have found him."

I figured their respective comments were good omens for the beginning of their union.

At the wedding liturgy I told my strawberry story.[2]

One quiet winter afternoon with a hint of snow in the gray sky, the Megan buzzed me.

"Bishop Blackie, there's a real nice priest down here named Father Simon who wants to see you."

"Send him up."

"He says he's afraid to intrude."

"Put him in the parlor."

I gathered his notification of elevation and his red robes from the Lord Cardinal's room, himself, alas, absent at the Chancery, and went downstairs.

"Eminenza," I said as I dashed into the room. "Welcome home to Chicago!"

He looked like a burly Polish auto mechanic—broad solid frame,

---

[2] *See* The Bishop and the Beggar Girl of St. Germain

snow-white hair, jeans, and a dark blue down jacket, and a smile as wide as Michigan Avenue.

"Blackie!" he said, embracing me in a bear hug. "I owe you everything."

"On the contrary, I owe you one glass of Irish whiskey."

He laughed and clapped me on the back.

"Today no time. I will be back often, however. I now go to St. John's in Minnesota."

"Not as cold as the Urals in the winter," I said, "but cold enough."

"I begin my new life."

"It is one of the great places in the American Church."

"Young woman says Cardinal not here."

"Working at Chancery."

"Too bad. I see him next time. I warn you before."

"Here are your clothes and your notification. If you ever want a copy of your memoir, we can find one for you."

His frosty eyes, so like those of the Pope, twinkled.

"Not now. Too soon. Maybe someday."

"We'll look forward to a longer visit."

"You bet . . . Young couple at Divinity School?"

"I officiated at their marriage at Bond Chapel a week ago. They're on their honeymoon. You won't be surprised to know that both are tenured faculty now."

"Good deal!" He gave me a thumbs-up. "Give congratulations. Cab wait. Merry Christmas."

As he rushed out to the waiting Yellow, the clothes bag over one arm, the papal document in the other hand, I thought to myself, there goes one heck of a fine priest.

"*Wesolych Swiat Bozego Narodzenia!*" I yelled after him in Polish. "Merry Christmas!"

Chicago
October 2002